PRAISE FOR *A LIGHT ON ALTERED LAND*

"For those who love Patricia Highsmith's novel *The Price of Salt* and the movie *Carol* that followed...*A Light on Altered Land* offers up the same tenderness and lesbian desire.... The [new lovers' road trip] takes the relationship to another level and the lovemaking that ensues is scintillating, satisfying, and sharp.... For those of us who may think we are too old [or] too spent...to revisit passion and lust ever again, this story offers up a different ending. Along with being a sexy love story, *A Light on Altered Land* is a fun adventure with twists and turns and familiar lesbian humor. It is also the tenderhearted expression of love that flickers through the novel with gusto and brilliance that is most captivating..."

—Sinister Wisdom

"A very well-written, well-edited, lovely romance [with] a lot of spirituality at its heart [and] good insights from both characters into what it means to get older, and to still want to live a full life. The way they thrived with each other was a joy to read [with] wonderful moments of humor."

—Curve Magazine

"[A] story of second chances and newfound intimacy...[the] prose is refined and psychologically nuanced...[as Bohan] explores the wounds and wisdom that accrue to women of a certain age...."

—Kirkus Reviews

"Intelligent romance for intelligent lesbians! ᵃ ᵖage-turning read with surprising plot tv᷿ ᵗce that speaks to the authentic heat ᵗls. Genuinely sizzling."

*is

*isappearing L

and *Sappho's Bar & Grill*

OTHER BOOKS BY BECKY BOHAN

FICTION

Sinister Paradise (1993)

Fertile Betrayal (1995)

NONFICTION

Living Consciously, Dying Gracefully:
A Journey with Cancer and Beyond
(co-author Nancy Manahan, 2007)

A
LIGHT
ON
ALTERED
LAND

A Novel

BECKY BOHAN

This is a work of fiction. All characters, names, and incidences
are the work of the author's imagination. Any resemblance to
actual people, living or dead, is completely incidental.
Several locations in the book are real; others are fictional.

Cover & book design: Sara Yager
Author photo: Nancy Manahan

ISBN: 9781654110871

nanbec
BOOKS

nanbec.com
E-book available on Amazon.com

For Nancy

TABLE OF CONTENTS

PART THREE

PART FOUR

*Ah, the knowledge of impermanence
that haunts our days is their very fragrance.*

—Rainer Maria Rilke

PART ONE

CHAPTER 1

The mid-morning crowd at Starbucks was spread neatly throughout the room, each person spaced equidistantly as though governed by the Law of Elevator Courtesy. Everyone was consulting a phone or laptop, except Ellie Belmont, whose head was bent to the opinion page of Minneapolis's *Star Tribune*. As Ellie looked up and took a sip of her iced drink, she noticed an attractive woman of mature years examining the human layout, as if trying to decide whose territory to invade.

When their eyes met, Ellie realized she had been staring. She quickly smiled and nodded at a seat across from her. The woman returned the smile and gracefully swooped toward the chair.

"Happy Spring Equinox," Ellie said.

"Thank you." The woman settled at the table with her steaming cup. She extracted a phone from her purse and put on reading glasses.

Ellie picked up the *Tribune* again but couldn't help glancing across the table. The woman, a few pounds over slender, had well-proportioned features and skin softened with age. Her hair, champagne laced with silver, curved in a soft below-ear cut.

The woman looked up, catching Ellie's gaze.

"I can't help but admire your scarf," Ellie said. "It's lovely."

"Thank you." The woman hesitated, fingering the cashmere. Its azure whorls on gold perfectly matched her felted wool jacket—and her eyes. "It was a present. From an old, dear friend."

"The best kind," Ellie said. She turned back to her paper.

"The news is so depressing. I can't bring myself to read it anymore."

"I want to know what's happening in the world," Ellie said, regarding the woman once again, "but I seldom read closely anymore. I don't think I have the spiritual capacity to handle the details." She picked up her drink and took a sip.

The woman cocked her head as though hearing an unfamiliar yet engaging tune. She half smiled and turned her gaze to Ellie's steel cup and straw. "Iced coffee on such a chilly day? You're brave."

"Actually, it's a dirty chai latte." The ice cubes clinked as Ellie returned the drink to the highly varnished table.

"What makes it dirty?"

"A shot of espresso."

"Oh. That sounds more interesting than my green tea." There was the half smile again.

The woman's phone chirped. She turned to it and read the message. "Oh," she said and tapped to place a call. "What happened?"

Ellie turned back to her paper but strained to listen.

"Well, let's reschedule." The woman listened for a moment. "Wednesday works, same place, same time. Gotcha." She went quiet for a few moments. "Not at all, Amy. Let's just say that you've given me the gift of a free morning." She set down the phone, took off her glasses, and turned to Ellie. "Well, that clears my day."

"What happened?"

"My realtor's car had a flat on the way here. We were supposed to meet and go look at a few places downtown."

"What are you looking for?"

"A condo. I'm downsizing."

"Really? I'm doing the same. But I don't want to own property anymore, so I'm looking at senior housing. I'm on the wait list at Highland Meadows and a couple of other retirement communities."

The woman's appraising gaze scanned Ellie's face. "Aren't you a little young?"

"No, I'm sixty-five." Ellie ran her fingers through her black hair marbled with gray and white.

"Well, that's young." The woman smiled. "To me."

"Maybe, but I'm so done with house maintenance, mowing and shoveling, especially now that I'm alone."

"Divorced?"

"Widowed. Three years ago."

"Oh, I'm sorry. How long were you married?"

"One year. But we were together twenty-four years."

Once again the piercing blue gaze probed beneath the surface. The woman raised her head slightly, the light in her eyes shifting quickly in calculation, then comprehension. "I'm glad you could be married before she died."

"Me, too."

"What was her name?"

"Mary."

"And yours?"

"Ellie."

"Nice to meet you Ellie," the woman said, reaching her hand across the table for a shake. "I'm Kathryn." The hand was strong and warm, like her face.

"My pleasure." Ellie caught an ethereal scent of perfume.

"Now, if you're willing, could you tell me more about these places where you're on a list?"

Ellie slipped the newspaper into her bag and took off her black-rimmed reading glasses. The clatter and barista cries at the coffee bar fell away as she described various living options for active seniors. She was happy to share her research and could answer most of Kathryn's questions. Behind her eloquence, though, a track in her mind was saying *What an attractive woman!* It was more than her physical appearance and expensive clothing and jewelry. There was a poise, a confidence in her presentation, the easy modulation of a pleasant voice, the unflinching gaze full of wisdom and life experience.

"Well, I can see the attraction," Kathryn said. "But, wouldn't it be easier and cheaper in a regular apartment? You'd still avoid all the maintenance issues."

"But what happens if I have a stroke or heart attack in, say, five years? I'd have to find a nursing facility in a crisis situation. I'm a single person without children or close relatives to help me, so I'd have to rely on friends. That's asking a lot of them, and who knows what condition *they* would be in." Ellie shook her head. "It's easy for elderly women who live alone to become isolated. I want to be in a continuous care community able to accommodate my needs as I age."

"You're very smart," Kathryn said. Her smile was infectious, and Ellie could not help returning it. "You've given me something to think about."

Ellie almost blushed. "Why are you downsizing?"

Kathryn paused as though weighing the prudence of disclosure. "Well, briefly, I've been divorced a little over a year. My husband left me for a younger woman—one of his nurses. He's a heart surgeon."

"He fixes other people's hearts but broke yours?" Ellie kicked herself. How many times had Katheryn heard that line?

"In a nutshell, yes," Kathryn said politely, lifting her perfect eyebrows in acknowledgement. "Anyway, I received the house with everything in it as part of the settlement. It's way too big for me, though, and truthfully, it feels lonely. Now that spring is here—literally," she took in and let out a deep breath, "it's a good time to move on."

"Are you retired?"

"I'm not sure," she said and pressed her lips together. "I retired at the end of December, as I had always planned, but I'm keeping the door open for another position. I thought Joe and I would spend our last years traveling and enjoying life. He had other plans, obviously, so now I'm thinking of returning after a nice long break." Kathryn stared at her nearly empty cup. "The irony is I've heard the same sad tale a thousand times from clients. I'm a psychotherapist."

"Where does a therapist with a broken heart go for support?"

Kathryn's laugh was quick, a low, rich sound, like a lush melody with a major lift. "It's not exactly a 'physician heal thyself' situation, is it? Luckily, I have friends. I try to be accepting about the whole thing, and wish him well, but sometimes I just want to kick him to kingdom come."

"Totally understandable." Ellie nodded. "What's your biggest challenge in downsizing?"

Kathryn tasted the last of her tea. "I think it'll be the pictures. I have so many albums. Some I can give to the kids, but others . . . I don't know. It's the sorting and choosing, and all the memories that will come up. I'm afraid it'll be a depressing task." Kathryn pursed her mouth and tapped the rim of her cup with long fingers, several of which bore rings. The nails were manicured, buffed but without polish. "What I save, I'll have digitized." The blue eyes caught Ellie again. "And you? What's your biggest challenge?"

"Books. I have hundreds. I feel sentimental toward some only because I have margin notes scribbled in them. When I read them I think, *Wow, how insightful.*" Ellie gave a crooked smile. "Then again, there are underlined passages where I wonder, *Now why did I think that was important?*"

"Glimpses of your younger mind and emotions?"

"Exactly—a different type of photograph." Ellie found herself grinning. "Can I get you another tea, Kathryn?"

"How nice, but no. I'll be on my way and let you get back to your paper."

No, Ellie wanted to say, *I don't care about the news anymore. I'd rather talk with you. Stay and let's have lunch.* Instead she said, "It was nice meeting you, Kathryn. Good luck with your condo hunting."

"Likewise with your housing."

Ellie sensed Kathryn's reluctance to leave. Her smile had a tinge of sadness, perhaps a hesitancy to return to a big house empty of love.

"You know," Ellie said, "I go out to Highland Meadows three times a week to use their workout room and pool—it's one of the perks of being on their wait list. If you'd like, I could take you as a guest sometime and give you an informal tour—you'd avoid the sales pitch of the marketing rep."

The corners of Kathryn's mouth lifted slightly with a calm, amused smile that reached her eyes. "That's an interesting offer."

Ellie wondered if she meant *that's a new pick up line.* Embarrassed, she said nothing and slid her gaze down to her drink.

"Well, why not. I'm curious about these places. Give me your number and I'll text you sometime. How would that be?"

"Excellent!" Ellie recited her number, watching Kathryn's fingers tapping on the phone, an electronic Pandora's box. Hope fluttered around looking for a place to alight, and its presence suddenly made the day even brighter.

"Now, I really should go," Kathryn said as she slipped the phone into her jacket pocket.

Ellie watched her walk toward the exit. She knows I'm looking, Ellie thought, but she couldn't turn away. Kathryn opened the door, turned back to Ellie, and with a waggle of her fingers, disappeared.

———————⟨∞⟩———————

Was I just propositioned? Kathryn smiled to herself as she walked toward her car. *By a woman? That would be a first.* Ellie's admiring gaze had warmed her and, yes, she had enjoyed feeling attractive even if it was to another woman.

The sun was higher now, and the south wind brought the tease of summer into the chill of late March. Kathryn drew her jacket closer and breathed in the aroma of roasting coffee beans wafting into the street. "This is too funny," she blurted aloud. *But flattering . . . I think.*

She started her BMW and checked for traffic before pulling out. At the intersection, she turned left, heading south to Edina, an upscale first ring suburb of Minneapolis.

Ellie had lost her life partner. She hadn't said how. An accident? Disease? It was not funny at all, and now Kathryn regretted her amusement at the supposed come-on. How egotistical, how banal, to make such an assumption.

A heart could be broken in so many ways. Ellie and every single person sitting in that coffee shop was nursing a wound of some sort. All Ellie had done was recognize a fellow traveler, another older woman who hadn't had a face-to-face conversation with anyone in a while.

No, it wasn't funny to be alone against one's will.

It still came as a shock that she was no longer married. After almost forty years together, how did things fall apart so irredeemably? Their marriage had worked for so many years.

But then things had changed, one cog at a time, without her even noticing, until the marriage had downshifted. She had been content to coast along. Joe had, too, until he fell in love with someone else. Her communication skills, so central to her self-image as well as her livelihood, had failed her miserably.

She had sought—and fought—to turn her anger into grief, to mourn for what she had lost and not turn her husband into an ogre. He was a good man and did not deserve to be demonized.

All the snow had melted in the warming weather, leaving the lawns and boulevards with a blanket of dry, golden grass anxious to be green again. Early spring was a dreary time for Kathryn, and it seemed especially dreary this year. Her job and the turmoil of the divorce were over, leaving her with long stretches of time alone. She should slip away to some place lush and warm. Take a direct flight to Orlando, where the grandkids could join her at The Wizarding World of Harry Potter. But the kids already had their spring vacations planned. Nate was taking his two to Chicago, and Jenn had something cooking, a sci-fi convention, as she recalled.

The dashboard screen suddenly sprang to life, as did the car speakers with the fanfare from *Star Trek*, announcing an incoming call from Jenn. *Of course. I think of my daughter, and she calls.* But this was early, too early.

"Hey, honey, good morning!"

"Likewise," Jenn said in her sullen I'm-being-inconvenienced tone.

"What's up?"

"Maddie got her period."

Kathryn hooted. "At last! She must be thrilled!"

"Yes and no. She's glad to join the ranks of womanhood, but she wasn't prepared for cramps . . . and don't give me any suggestions about herbal remedies."

"I hope it wasn't an awkward beginning."

"She woke up this morning with blood on the sheet."

"Well, bless her heart."

"Are you going to make a big deal out of this like you did with Gena? You know your coming-of-age ritual was too much."

"Lucky for Maddie I'm not in California." *And lucky for Gena she was in Minnesota with me when menses hit.* Kathryn shook her head at how their memories differed. Gena had been thrilled and touched by the overnight at William O'Brien State Park. Just the two of them in a borrowed tent—Jenn had wanted no part of it, and little Maddie couldn't understand why she had been left behind. The campfire, the stories of ancient mothers passing down the secrets of womanhood, the silver bracelet—which Gena still wore. Kathryn had loved the bonding with her oldest granddaughter and hoped to arrange a similar just-we-two occasion with Maddie. "I'll send her a card." *For now.* "A real hold-in-your-hands card."

"Another item for recycling."

"I don't know about that," Kathryn said. She knew Maddie to be more sentimental than her daughter. "Listen, Jenn, I'm in the car. I'll call you when I get home."

"No need. I just wanted to let you know about Maddie per your instructions. Talk to you later."

The call ended without a good-bye. So typical of Jenn whose social skills seldom included friendliness. But where would the logic of that be? Jenn would argue. Social pleasantries waste time.

But Maddie. A bubble of sadness bobbed in Kathryn's chest, like a lone balloon left behind at a party. Her youngest grandchild had officially entered puberty. It was a rite of passage and Kathryn rued Jenn's lack of celebration, but that was Jenn. Well, a handwritten note on the joys and power of womanhood would provide some ballast. And maybe the next time they got together . . . .

Oh! She could have checked with Jenn about their plans for spring break. Well, later. As Kathryn gained the freeway, the thought of Ellie and their conversation broke through her reflections on Maddie. Had she really asked Ellie for her phone number? What on earth had possessed her! She couldn't imagine using it now that she was out of range of those dark intelligent eyes. And those dimples and tousled hair! Ellie was kind of cute, Kathryn conceded. She had been dressed rather plainly in a U of M maroon-and-gold sweatshirt with fraying cuffs, but somehow her unadorned, casual look enhanced her features. Can a sixty-five-year-old woman be cute? Yes, of course. But handsome was probably a better fit.

She, herself, hadn't been drop-dead attractive since her mid-fifties—the age when she became aware—mortified would be a better word—that men had stopped noticing her. If Joe had left her twenty years earlier, she would have had a better chance at another marriage. Now many men her age considered her too old. Ageism and sexism: what a vicious brew.

What isms did Ellie have to contend with?

Kathryn became aware she was speeding. She let up on the pedal and moved to the right. Her exit was approaching. As she pulled onto the ramp, she realized she had not given lesbianism any thought in her own life. She had obliviously glided along on the hetero end of the sexuality continuum.

No, she needn't let her thoughts drift in that direction. Besides, Ellie probably wasn't being suggestive with her. She seemed to be a sincere person who had thought an invitation to a senior residence would be welcome. Maybe it had been an invitation out of pity. What did she know?

She had Ellie's phone number, but Ellie had shrewdly not asked for hers, saving them the embarrassment of a refusal. She had a habit from her years as a therapist of keeping her private life private, especially her phone number. Yet she had told Ellie about her marriage, or rather, her divorce, and her disappointment of a husband.

To whom does a therapist with a broken heart turn? Apparently, a stranger at Starbucks.

CHAPTER 2

"*Y*ou asked her out to a retirement home? Geez, Ellie, have you ever lost your touch!" Sandy Adams laughed as she stuffed the last of the yellow pickleballs into her bag.

"I wasn't asking for a date. I was being helpful."

"Are you sure? You're happier than I've seen you in . . . well, ages."

"You know how it is when you connect with someone. It feels good." Ellie zipped her paddle into its bag with a little more force than necessary.

The women slipped into sweatpants and jackets before heading toward the door of the Southside YMCA. The plinks of sharply hit balls and cries of triumph and frustration followed them past the steel doors.

"Doing anything for dinner?" Sandy ran her fingers through her short blond hair moist with sweat. She was five-six, the same as Ellie. Although built like a cube of muscle, she was amazingly quick and smooth on the court.

"Nothing special. I have some romaine lettuce that's getting a little tired. I was planning to make a Caesar salad."

"Why don't you come over for dinner? Kris has a pork roast in the cooker. Fix your salad and bring it."

"Is there any birthday cake left?"

Sandy had turned fifty-five over the weekend with a Double Nickels party. "Of course, we have a piece just for you." She thumped Ellie on the back.

Later that evening, Ellie took the salad and a bottle of wine to Sandy and Kris's home.

"Sandy tells me you met someone at Starbucks," Kris said. They were sitting at the oak dining room table laden with steaming serving dishes.

A sideboard held a vase with store-bought tulips. Candles burned to celebrate the equinox.

"I didn't meet-meet someone. I just talked to a nice woman who sat at my table." Ellie leaned over to pet one of the resident dachshunds snuffling around for dropped food.

"And you asked her out." On the young side of sixty, Kris had freckles and brown hair with a few strands of copper and gray.

Elle frowned at Sandy for putting a suggestive spin on the situation and shook her head. "No, I just told her I'd show her Highland Meadows, if she's interested."

"Pretty romantic, El," Kris said. She exchanged a smirk with Sandy.

"Laugh all you want." Ellie sank her fork into a roasted potato. "You know, I'm not interested in dating."

Kris narrowed her eyes but said nothing.

A silence filled the room like a ghostly vapor, and its name was Mary.

"Are you still wearing Mary's ring around your neck?" Kris asked.

Ellie pulled a gold chain from under her shirt. Mary's wedding band hung from it. The shiny metal caught the light of the candles, making the ring seem alive and flickering with power.

"I wonder if your rings aren't like cloves of garlic fending off potential suitors," Kris said. "Have you considered putting them away?"

"No." Ellie tucked the necklace out of sight.

"Well, it's something to think about . . . once you get back into the dating scene." Kris eyed the ring on Ellie's finger. "You know, there's nothing magical about a wedding band." She wiggled her ring finger at Ellie. "I had to take mine off before my rheumatoid arthritis made it impossible to do so. A ring is a symbol of love, not love itself."

"Ellie's situation is different," Sandy said, giving her wife a dark look. "Just saying."

"I know, I know," Ellie said softly. "I'll think about it."

Later as she walked the single block to her home carrying her salad bowl which now held two generous slices of chocolate cake and a baggie with pork and vegetables, Ellie reflected on the conversation. The three years since Mary's death could just as well have been three months. Or three weeks. Ellie had long ago made peace with her loss. Still the loneliness came in flashes that held the vastness of eternity, especially when she walked through the door alone after spending an evening with coupled friends. And yet today she had felt more alive than she had in years, all from talking with a lovely woman. Maybe it was time to think about dating.

In her bedroom, she picked up a photo of Mary, one of the last taken before her health had deteriorated. Mary was sitting by Lake Harriet, a pair of green-headed mallards floating behind her and sailboats in the distance. Her short blond hair was like a halo, her emerald eyes welcoming.

"Mary, I miss you." Ellie slid her thumb over Mary's body, clad in a white tee-shirt and yellow shorts. The room's silence was resounding, frightening in its intensity. She fingered Mary's wedding ring under her shirt, a tangible artifact saying yes, Mary had walked this earth, had walked on these very floors, the ones they had so laboriously refinished together. Was that project ten years ago already?

What would Kathryn the Therapist make of it? Would she see this wedding band as Mary's ring of fire lassoing her into an emotional rigor mortis?

Slowly, deliberately, she slid the chain with the ring over her head. She slept with it clasped in her hand and in the morning put it in the top drawer of her bureau, placing it carefully in a pair of her panties where, she thought with a smile, Mary had liked to be. The gold band stayed on her finger.

CHAPTER 3

*W*ednesday morning found Ellie back at Starbucks with the paper, sitting in a big stuffed faux-leather chair directly across from the door. She hoped Kathryn would show up for her rescheduled appointment with the realtor. She had dug out one of her nicer sweaters, a black Irish wool flecked with strands of gray.

Ellie did not see Kathryn enter or go to the counter to order. But when she heard her name spoken, she looked up to see those amazing blue eyes.

"Good morning! May I join you?"

"Of course."

Kathryn settled into the matching chair next to Ellie. "Anything interesting?" she said, nodding at the paper.

Ellie shook her head and gave a sad smile, "Lots of interesting things, none of them pleasant."

"Current events still exceeding your spiritual capacity?" Kathryn's smile was warm, her eyes playful.

"I'm afraid so." Ellie returned the smile. *She remembers our last conversation.*

"I wonder what it would take to contain the aggravation."

"Hmmm. Maybe to avoid it in the first place," Ellie said as she folded the paper and tucked it into her bag along with her glasses. "There!"

Kathryn set her take-out cup on the side table and unbuttoned her jacket. Her bracelets jangled as she lifted the drink to her lips. Six metal hoops danced on her wrist, some gold, some silver, and of various widths. One bore the Greek meander pattern.

"Those are lovely bracelets, Kathryn. You wore them the other day, I believe."

Kathryn gave Ellie a sharp look. "Very observant."

"Do they have special meaning?"

"Oh, not particularly. I've picked them up on my travels." She sipped her drink. "Why do you ask?"

"I'm curious. Jewelry is kind of a foreign territory to me. I appreciate it on other people, but I don't think it looks right on me."

"Except for your wedding ring." Kathryn nodded at the gold band with a setting of small diamonds and amethysts. "It's lovely."

"Thanks. Mary gets all the credit." Ellie hesitated. "A friend suggested that I take it off—it would psychologically free me to start dating. What do you think about that?"

Kathryn's face softened. "A wedding band holds a big emotional charge. Taking it off can mean letting go. Some people do it after a month, others never. You'll know when the time is right."

"Thanks." Ellie twirled the ring and brightened. "Condo hunting today?"

"Yes." Kathryn glanced at the door and back to Ellie. "My realtor should be here any minute. In fact, I think I see her coming through the door." Kathryn held up a hand and stood.

A woman in her early forties breezed toward them. When she took in the presence of Ellie, she slowed, confusion showing on her round, ruddy face. "Dr. Belmont? Is that you?"

"It is," Ellie said, eyeing the younger woman, trying to place her. She caught Kathryn's head swiveling quickly toward her, her expression now one of curiosity.

"You probably don't remember me. I'm Amy Gunderson. I took a writing class from you, oh, it must be twenty years ago. It changed my life."

"For the better, I hope." Ellie smiled as she stood to shake Amy's hand.

"Absolutely. I am where I am now because of you." Amy looked from Ellie to Kathryn. "Gosh, you two know each other?"

"We don't really," said Ellie. "We just met here the other day."

Amy laughed. "Small world, eh? Though I suppose you run into old students occasionally."

"It happens. After thirty-five years of teaching, a lot of a people have gone through my classrooms." Ellie considered her former student. "So, you're a realtor now."

"A very successful one," Kathryn chimed in. "She came highly recommended."

"It's a seller's market right now so business is a bit crazy." Amy plucked a business card from a small leather holder and handed it to Ellie. "In case you're ever looking to sell or buy."

"Thanks." Ellie inserted the card in the back pocket of her jeans. "I might need you in the near future."

"Well," Kathryn said, reaching for her drink, "shall we?"

"Let's." Amy turned to Ellie. "It was nice seeing you again."

"Likewise, Amy. Good luck to both of you." Ellie nodded and resumed her seat.

As she watched the two women pass through the outer door of Starbucks, she let out a deep sigh. She had hoped Kathryn would come early so they would have time for a nice long chat. But clearly she had come just to meet Amy. What did she expect? That Kathryn was looking for a new friend? Ellie's disappointment circled back to herself as she questioned why she had allowed expectations in the first place. She took a sip of her latte. It tasted thin now, exacerbating the ache in her chest where her hopes—for what?—had just withered.

The *Tribune* stayed wedged in her bag. Ellie pulled a pen and Moleskine notebook from the canvas tote and began to journal as customers came and went and the ice melted in her cup. She wrote in a small, clear hand about coffee and comfort, blue eyes and golden bracelets, hammered, perhaps, in a white-washed shop on a small Cycladic island.

As Amy drove Kathryn into the downtown commercial district toward riverfront condos, they passed the community college campus. "There's where I took a class from Dr. Belmont," she said, pointing at the glass edifice on Hennepin Avenue. "She was a great teacher. Did she say if she's still teaching?"

"She told me she's retired."

"Well, I feel lucky to have had her."

"You mentioned she changed your life. How did that happen?"

Amy rolled to a stop at an intersection. As she waited for the light to turn, she said, "I was never very reflective when I was young, but in her class, we had to really think about stuff. One of her assignments was to write an essay on what we felt passionate about and why. I found myself writing about houses, of all things, how I like walking in different neighborhoods looking at architecture and seeing the insides of people's homes at night when their lights are on. It was a great paper—I got a B plus. I still have it somewhere. Dr. Belmont wrote an encouraging note on it and asked if I was thinking of going into real estate or home design. The light bulbs just exploded. I got my Associate Degree in business and went on to realtor training. Maybe most important of all, though, Dr. Belmont gave me confidence in myself, in my ability to analyze and problem-solve."

"That's high praise."

The light changed and Amy's Mercedes shot forward. "She's my favorite teacher of all time. Everyone was a nervous wreck at the beginning of the semester because she had a reputation for being tough. It's the only college course I took, though, where I got to know the other students and where the teacher got a standing ovation on the last day of class. I think half the class fell in love with her."

Kathryn smiled to herself. *I bet I know which half.* She pictured Ellie with her plumb posture, the lightning in the black eyes, the infectious smile, and her piercing intelligence. In one word, charisma. The low-keyed kind, unconscious of its power. What student wouldn't be dazzled?

Amy took Kathryn to two units, one close to the Guthrie Theatre and the other a few blocks west. As they stood at the window of the second condo, surveying the Mississippi River and the Stone Arch Bridge in the distance, a sudden unease tugged at Kathryn like a shift of gravity. She imagined her new home through Ellie's eyes: will this suit me in five years? Ten? Twenty?

"I like this condo, Amy, more than the other. It's better suited for aging in place."

"Is that a concern, Kathryn? Are you looking for something more handicapped accessible?"

"I'm thinking I really need to take that into consideration, as well as maintenance issues. You know, I'm sixty-eight. People my age often start to have health issues. What happens if three years down the road I have a stroke? Or break a hip as my neighbor did?"

"Well, there's no predicting the future, that's for sure."

Kathryn turned from the window, from the river rolling through the heart of America. The decisions were so big and she so small.

"I don't know," she said, taking in the high ceilings, the stark white walls, and the modern artwork. Standing there, in someone's former space—her life seemed unreal, as if the last year had been a dream, and she should go home, pour herself a glass of chardonnay, and laugh about her real estate adventures with Joe when he came in late from the hospital.

"Should we go to the next place? It's in a building directly across from us on the other side of the river—in the old Pillsbury plant."

"Amy, what do you know about retirement communities?"

"They're not my specialty, but I know they're going great guns all over. Fifty-five plus for active adults. You have to look carefully at the terms and fees—each place is different. Some are condos, some apartments. There are cooperatives, for-profit, not-for-profit, no care, some care, lots of care. Of course, none would have the views you'd get here."

"No," Kathryn conceded, "they wouldn't."

"You could spend twenty years in a place like this before you'd need any assistance. Even then, you can have in-home care."

"True, but as you said, we can't predict the future."

Amy checked her buzzing phone for a message. "Okay! Are you up for more?"

"I think maybe that's enough for today, Amy. Let me do some research on senior housing before we look any more."

As Amy closed the door and checked the lock, Kathryn wondered if Ellie Belmont, even in her retirement, was still changing lives.

That evening, Ellie was curled up in front of a fire leafing through a catalog when a text came in displaying only the phone number. The area code was from a western suburb.

"Oh!" A thrill bolted through Ellie as she read the message: *Kathryn from Starbucks here. May I call you?*

Ellie quickly typed: *Of course.*

Immediately the phone rang. "Am I interrupting anything?" Kathryn asked. Her voice had the same, easy cadence as in the coffee shop.

"No, I was just looking through the 300-page film festival guide marking all the movies I want to see. I think I'll have to clone myself five times over. How did the condo hunting go?"

"I'm feeling overwhelmed, Ellie. I went to see a couple of places downtown. They were lovely in a generic sort of way, river views to stop the heart, but now I'm not sure they're right for me. You got me thinking about retirement communities. I checked online . . . there are so many . . . I just don't know . . . ."

"There are a lot of choices and so much information to wade through. Every place has its pros and cons. It is overwhelming."

"I brought up the idea with Amy, and she mentioned in-home care as an option."

"Definitely it's possible. What gives me pause about it is first, I'd have to find a reliable provider and that's not easy. And second, if I needed round-the-clock care, the best place for me would be a skilled nursing center. People can get shifts of home care-givers, but holy smokes, it's expensive and the quality of the providers can vary greatly. Also, who would coordinate everything?"

"Part of me just wants to give up and stay where I am. Let what happens, happen. But it seems unfair to the kids to leave them with all the decisions."

Was something deeper transpiring within Kathryn? This uncertainty seemed uncharacteristic in a woman of her bearing. "I'm wondering," Ellie said carefully, "is this the biggest decision you've had to make on your own—since your divorce?"

The line was silent for a few moments.

"Yes, it is. Maybe that's what's really going on. I don't have a spouse anymore to share the burden . . . and the excitement. Right now, I'm angry with Joe for putting me into this fix. Don't you feel terribly alone, Ellie, when you have decisions to make?"

"Yes, I do, at times."

"What do you do about it?"

"Just see it through. I remember after Mary died, I felt immobilized. I couldn't make a decision about anything, and yet I had to make so many. Like what to do when our dog got sick. Try to save her or let her go? I tried to talk my way through it with Mary in absentia, and, you know, it really helped to chat with her a bit. It's often clarified the path for me."

"I refuse to use that method with Joe."

"I totally understand." Ellie laughed. "That's what friends and family are for—to step in when there's no partner to help."

Friends. The word hung in the air. Was that what they were now? How do strangers who meet in a coffee shop become friends?

"But it's not the same, is it?"

"No," Ellie said, "you don't have the history together, the immediacy of communication when thoughts spring up—talking over the kitchen table, or when you wake up in the morning or are folding laundry . . . No, it's never the same. I always thought I appreciated the life I shared with Mary, the day-to-day business of getting on, but it wasn't until she died—or got really sick—that I realized how much of the load she picked up and how much easier it is to make decisions when there are two heads co-noodling."

"Co-noodling. I like that." Kathryn's smile came through the phone.

"Even with something as mundane as clothes. I miss Mary's help there. I was born without the style gene, as you've probably noticed." Ellie gestured at her plain, uninspired outfit as though Kathryn were sitting in front of her. "I marvel at people like you who are so put together. You always look so lovely, Kathryn, like a work of art."

"Why, thank you." Kathryn paused. "Ellie, I want to ask you what happened with Mary, but that's a face-to-face discussion, isn't it? Would you be willing to share?"

"Of course." She was pleasantly surprised by Kathryn's large step toward friendship. "Well, how about meeting at Highland Meadows on Friday? You can see a senior community in its concrete form."

"Exactly what I was thinking. But will you be swimming?"

"I don't have to swim. There's an on-site restaurant. We could just have lunch."

"I'd prefer that. Are you sure it would work for you?"

"Absolutely. I have a key card to the door of the fitness center. If we went in the back way we could avoid the hassle of signing in at the front desk, but it's a little tricky to find. I could pick you up at your place, or we could meet somewhere and I'll drive us."

After a pause, Kathryn said, "You live around the Starbucks on Lyndale don't you?"

"Yes."

"My place would be on your way to Highland Meadows, so why don't you pick me up here at home. I'll text you the address."

"Great. We've got a plan. How about eleven o'clock—that way I can give you a little tour before lunch."

Ellie double checked the phone to make sure it was off before letting out a whoop.

CHAPTER 4

*E*llie peered curiously at the façade of gray stone and banks of windows. This was the house where Kathryn had lived with Joe and raised a family. The neat yard was lined with dormant flowerbeds, and the grass needed a good spring raking. Before Ellie could pop out of the car, Kathryn appeared from the side door and slid into the passenger seat. Small talk filled the ten-minute drive to Highland Meadows, focusing on condos and the weather.

By noon, many of the tables in the Highland Meadows restaurant were full. Natural light poured in from the windows lining the south end, bathing the sandstone walls and room dividers with a golden glow. Large pots of flowering plants and lush foliage edged the space. Every table had a small vase with a live red tulip.

"I must say," Kathryn said, "this is a lovely place. Thank you for the tour." She was wearing a light camel turtleneck. A Southwest-patterned wool jacket hung on the back of her chair. "The building has good energy, doesn't it? But everyone here seems quite a bit older than we are—in their late seventies and eighties."

"True. What we're not seeing are the people who are still working or who are off doing volunteer work. That crowd is a bit younger."

"Where are you on the wait list?"

"I'm about two years from the top, assuming not everyone ahead of me accepts a unit."

"You said you were on two other lists."

"Yes. Those are both in Saint Paul. The one next to Saint Catherine's University I like a lot—especially the academic atmosphere—but the wait is at least eight years, and they don't have all the amenities of this place. The third isn't my favorite but would do in a pinch."

A waitress poured water into their glasses. They studied the menu and ordered.

The murmur of background conversation and the clinking of silverware and glasses filled the momentary lull in conversation. The two women regarded each other across the linen tablecloth and colorful crockery, took in the circle of activity around them, and then locked eyes once again.

"I like your sweater," Kathryn said. "Is it from Australia? It reminds me of Aboriginal art."

"Very good! Yes, Mary and I were there about eight years ago. I find it's the perfect weight in this type of weather."

Ellie watched Kathryn move her gaze up, her alert eyes now returning Ellie's own gaze. It was a searching look as though Kathryn were peering in, looking for the storybook that would explain just who Ellie was.

"If you feel comfortable, Ellie, could you tell me about Mary?" Kathryn asked.

Ellie knew the question was coming. She took a sip of water. "Mary was a nurse, which says a lot about her right there. Anyone who goes into that profession gets an automatic ticket to heaven in my book. They are angels walking this earth."

Kathryn raised her eyebrows and gave a closed, pensive smile.

"And Mary was the kindest, sweetest, most competent person you could imagine. And cute. And playful. She was an HIV nurse back when AIDS was a death sentence. The stories she could tell . . . ."

Kathryn nodded sadly. "How did you meet?"

"At the college. The English and Nursing programs were on the same floor. Mary worked at a nearby hospital and stopped by occasionally to meet an old colleague who taught there. I ran into her outside my office one day while she was waiting for her friend to finish with a student. We started chatting and really hit it off. We were a good fit."

"What happened to her?"

"Aggressive breast cancer. She did everything the medical-industrial complex could torture her with: double mastectomy, chemo, radiation. She went through hell."

"As did you."

"I witnessed hell. Mary lived it, and with amazingly good spirits. She was determined to live until she died. Only she died sooner than we expected. Her immune system was wrecked, so when she got pneumonia, she couldn't stay ahead of it."

"Were you with her at the end?"

"Yes and no." Ellie shook her head, tears threatening to form. "After all the days and nights I had been tending to her, I wasn't with her the moment she died."

"What happened?"

"It was a late morning in February and Mary wanted some lemon sorbet. She'd get these cravings and she was down to skin and bones by that time, so . . . I would have gone to the North Pole to get it. Anyway, I wanted some fresh air, so I walked to the grocery store, leaving her alone for maybe thirty minutes max. She didn't seem to be near death at all, but when I got home, she was gone. Just like that, it was all over. I didn't get to be with her as she passed. But she did die at home as she wanted."

"I'm sorry. It must have been difficult."

"It was." Ellie took a deep breath, grateful Kathryn had not said, as so many had, that maybe Mary needed her to be gone so she could die. "And beautiful, too. I felt her loving presence in the room for several hours. It was weird and wonderful—I experienced a sort of transcendent sense of eternity."

The light in Kathryn's eyes shifted as she nodded softly.

"We had arranged for a three-day home vigil, so after I recovered from the initial shock, I called my support team, and everyone jumped into action. It was awesome, Kathryn. We had her body on dry ice in the living room. People came at all hours to sit and sing and talk. There were lots of stories and tears and laughter. It was just the way she wanted it to be."

"You two must have done a lot a planning to make it happen according to your wishes."

"It was mostly Mary. She did tons of research and consulted with a local end-of-life group. She was very definite—she knew how things can get screwed up in the end-game chaos, so she had three pages of instructions, including contact numbers."

Both women laughed softly.

"Was it legal to keep her body at home for so long?"

"Totally. She was in hospice so there was no problem with getting the death certificate signed. And it's legal in Minnesota to have an unembalmed body at home—with certain restrictions, of course."

"What happened after three days?"

"Well, after three days, the reality of her death was palpable. You just knew her spirit was gone, and her body was . . . just the garment she wore in this lifetime. I was—everyone was—ready to let her go. A friend had a van and we transported her body to a green cemetery—the only one in the state at the time—and laid her in the ground wrapped in a shroud." Ellie smiled. "Actually, it was a beautiful linen tablecloth from her grandmother."

"A shroud, not a casket?"

"No. Mary wanted the earth to hold her body and give its nutrients back to support new life."

"Interesting. Is that what you want for yourself, Ellie?"

"I'm not sure. Cremation appeals to me more, even though it consumes fossil fuel."

The waitress approached their table with their salmon with rice and vegetables.

"*Buen provecho*," Ellie said.

"What a beautiful presentation." Kathryn reached for her fork.

The women ate silently for several moments.

"How was it for you taking care of Mary?"

"It was a privilege," Ellie said.

"And?"

"A challenge. I feel guilty that I wasn't a better caregiver."

Kathryn wore a neutral expression.

"I got impatient sometimes. I got tired of her being sick and having to clean it up and of the swirl of doctor appointments, the cascade of bad news, the sleepless nights. But I also felt it was the greatest honor in the world to look after such a precious soul."

Kathryn smiled kindly. "I think most caregivers feel the same way, Ellie. It's hard to be up day after day. Impossible, I'd say. I suspect Mary felt she was lucky to have you."

"She told me so repeatedly," Ellie said. "But I always felt I could be doing more."

"It wasn't within your power to take the disease away."

"No, no, it wasn't."

"And that's what we all want with our loved ones. Just to take the hurt away."

"To put everything back to normal, to the way it was." Ellie looked out the window to the bare trees in the enclosed courtyard. "You don't really think of how things will change when you're young and in love and have your whole lives ahead of you. But a chronic or terminal disease really changes a relationship. I'm sure you've heard plenty of stories in your practice, but it's shocking when it happens . . . when an independent person goes into decline and becomes dependent. I saw it happen with my parents, and I admired my dad taking care of my mom when she became cognitively impaired. He always showed great patience."

"You may be idealizing, Ellie. You can bet your dad had flashes of anger and resentment. No one is an angel, not even Mother Teresa."

"I suppose." Ellie was caught in Kathryn's gaze, as though it were a laser demanding truth. "Sometimes I felt my life wasn't my own. Everything had to be on Mary's terms. Really, on the cancer's terms. We'd watch movies and play music Mary felt she could enjoy. I played cribbage with her until I thought I could never bear another game." A memory pulled at Ellie's mouth. "In fact, I laid the board in her grave thinking she would enjoy it more than I ever would again. But now I miss it. Or maybe I just miss playing with her."

Kathryn nodded.

"I'm not a codependent person by nature, Kathryn, but I felt at times I had become one. It was the compassionate thing to do, the right thing . . . but I lost a bit of myself. I just wish I could have been better both with Mary and with myself."

"It gets complicated. Life endings are really challenging, partly because we never know how they'll unfold. People do the best they can. You have to believe that of yourself and let it go. Do you feel you've retrieved that lost bit?"

"Yes. Her death allowed me to breathe again. Painfully at first, but freely now." Ellie smiled. "I eventually stepped back into the cycle of life. I know how precious life and health are, and really, how little time we have to walk this earth."

"And how does that look for you, being back in 'the cycle of life?'"

"The main thing is being present, being attentive and compassionate. Bringing my whole self to an experience. I still experience loss and grief, but it feels integrated now into who I am." Ellie searched Kathryn's face. "Am I making any sense?"

"A lot." Kathryn's smile reached her eyes. "I feel myself toeing the Great Wheel these days, too. Maybe it's spring. Maybe it's just that a year is enough time for me to get over the shock of the divorce."

"You're bursting for change . . . like a new home."

"Yes, exactly. And I feel I have enough energy to tackle the job." Kathryn paused. "Is there anything else you want to say about Mary?"

Ellie shook her head. "No. Thanks for listening to me. It feels good to talk about it with you."

"It's my privilege. Thank you for sharing, Ellie."

"Well, you're very easy to talk to."

The women ate in silence for a while.

"The salmon was cooked perfectly," Kathryn said as she finished her last bite. "Meals are included in the monthly fee, right?"

While they were in the midst of discussing meal plans and costs, a bit of discontent rumbled in Ellie's mind. When it finally surfaced, Ellie put down her fork. "Oh, my god," she said, her cheeks starting to warm. "I forgot."

"What?"

"What I said about nurses being angels. Your husband left you for a nurse."

"Yes," Kathryn said, a sly smile emerging.

Ellie thought it the loveliest smile she had ever seen. Her heated cheeks took on a new dimension.

"But what you don't know," Kathryn said, "is that I'm a nurse, too."

"You are? I thought you were a therapist."

"I am. Officially, I'm a Clinical Nurse Practitioner with a specialty in Psychiatric Nursing. I can see patients as a therapist and prescribe drugs."

"I've never heard of it."

"Many people haven't."

"How did you get into that field?"

"I found I enjoyed talking to patients more than jabbing them with needles."

"You must be an extrovert. I think I'd choose the jabs."

Kathryn's laugh was low and rich.

"Is your specialty in demand?"

"Very much so. There's a nationwide shortage of nurse practitioners. Hardly a week goes by without someone, somewhere contacting me with a job offer even though I'm past retirement age."

"What's been your most tempting offer?"

"Good question." Kathryn thought for a moment. "Any clinic I would join would have to offer Complementary and Alternative Medicine—Western medicine is too limited—so that eliminates about eighty percent of the offers. The most alluring offer was a clinic on Long Island. I'd love to be in New York."

"I can appreciate that," Ellie said. "I love New York, too."

"But it's just a fantasy. Starting over alone, without family and friends nearby . . . ." Kathryn shook her head. "No."

A flush of relief passed through Ellie.

"I'm not in any hurry to get back to work. I'm enjoying free days like this one, where I can go to lunch practically on the spur of the moment."

"I'm glad I could take advantage of it," Ellie said with unabashed warmth.

The women strolled down a different corridor on their way to the parking lot. The grooved crown molding of the doors and the brass ring knockers suggested a New England theme. The art on the walls, much of it done by the residents, was colorful and tasteful, ranging from landscapes to still lifes. The hallway was silent, the thick beige carpeting absorbing their footfalls.

"You know, Ellie," Kathryn said, "I had a dear, dear friend—Anna— who had a goal to make a mistake every day—to slip up or do something outrageous. It was a way to remind herself that everyone is human."

"Huh. Interesting objective."

"I think your little faux pas about nurses could fall into that category."

"You mean I've accomplished something beyond making a fool of myself?"

"Yes."

"Well, that's putting a positive spin on it." Ellie gave a quick grin and turned serious. "Although mistakes can have serious consequences. You said she was a friend of yours, past tense. What happened?"

They reached a junction with a sitting area, a mini conservatory with bamboo trees two stories high, a burbling marble fountain, and benches along walkways lined with a variety of blooming peace lilies, philodendrons, and crotons.

"What a lovely spot," Kathryn said. "Let's sit here for a few moments."

After they had settled in, she continued. "Like your Mary, Anna died of metastatic breast cancer. Sixteen years ago."

"I'm sorry."

"Thank you. She taught psychiatric nursing. I took several classes from her. After I got my degree, she became my mentor, my confidant, my deepest friend. She was fifteen years older than I, but it often seemed like we were twins. In fact, sometimes we were mistaken for sisters. She was always the wiser one, though." Kathryn added with a light laugh, "In some ways I think we were closer to each other than to our husbands."

"Emotionally more intimate?"

Kathryn looked away. "Yes, you could put it that way."

Ellie stayed silent, watching Kathryn's shifting expression.

"She wasn't perfect. Nobody is. And she always reminded me that flubbing up is human and not to punish myself for mistakes . . . and often something that seems a mistake is leading us down the very path we need to be on."

"Good advice."

"It is, and one I take to heart." Kathryn's gaze rested on the nearby bamboo for a few moments. "Your telling me of Mary's death brings back Anna's end-of-life experience. She continued teaching right through all the chemo and radiation and shared her 'journey' as she called it, with her students. What an education they received! She didn't sugar coat what she was going through, either physically or mentally. Or spiritually."

"How could she continue to teach?"

"Teaching was her passion. She couldn't think of anything she'd rather be doing with her last days. And thanks to the alternative therapies she used, she stayed relatively healthy until the end. She didn't even lose her beautiful hair, although she stopped coloring it and let it go gray. She came to believe her cancer was caused by environmental toxins, including household cleaning products and the chemicals of the cosmetic industry."

"You don't wear makeup!" Ellie said, realizing it for the first time. "Is that why you don't?"

"It is. I gave it up to support her . . . and continued because I learned that makeup is unhealthy . . . and unnecessary. Natural is beautiful in my view."

"In mine, too. Cosmetics are not part of my tribe's ethos."

Kathryn laughed. "I'm afraid it is in mine. I'm an outlier there."

The women sat in a companionable silence, relishing the warm, moist air of the verdant lounge.

"Cancer sucks, doesn't it?" Kathryn said.

"Big time. Death, too. Whoever thought that was a good idea?"

"Ha! I suppose it was a way for the Designer in Chief to make life precious for us."

"I think I'd find it precious no matter what. How did you handle Anna's death?"

"I felt lost at first even though I was expecting it. I wondered how I could be on this earth without her. But we get through it, don't we?"

"Yes. I don't know that I'm a better person for it, though."

Kathryn smiled gently. "I'm sure you are, Ellie. Mary gave you a parting gift—a moment of transcendence when you felt surrounded by her love and had a glimpse of eternity. You can't help but be changed."

"You're right. Whatever fear of death I had vanished." Ellie's dark eyes bored into Kathryn. "Have you had any sort of experience like that?"

She was met with silence.

"Kathryn?"

"Not like yours. I wasn't with Anna when she died. But a couple of nights after her death . . ." Kathryn hesitated, her fingers twisting together. "I haven't shared this with anyone, Ellie, not even Joe. It's too . . . I don't know . . . too personal . . . too woo-woo. But . . . a couple of nights after her death, she came to me in a dream. It was more than a dream, though. I was standing in a forest clearing—in a very ancient land—and Anna walked toward me out of a fog. We sat on a huge log, as you and I are here, and I said, 'Anna, you're alive!'

"She said, 'No, my dear, I've left your plane.' I asked her where she was, what it was like. 'It's like a rainbow,' she said. 'You're alive now on the red end of the spectrum. I've moved to the orange. Soon I'll be moving on to the yellow. I'm just on a different wavelength than you.'"

Kathryn paused momentarily, as if lost in thought. "I said to Anna, 'I miss you so much.' She replied, 'Kathryn, dear, my time had come. All things unfold as they must. Trust your path.' Then I woke up, tears streaming down my face, but I knew everything would be all right. I could grieve. I could miss her. And I would get through it. Her spirit colors my life to this day." Kathryn's eyes were bright with tears. "Amazing, isn't it. I can still get emotional after all these years."

Ellie placed a hand on Kathryn's forearm. The women sat quietly for several minutes amid the lush greenery letting life nourish their souls.

"Kathryn," Ellie said at last. "Thank you."

They rose and made their way down the long, bright corridor.

CHAPTER 5

"*K*epler," Ellie said as she eased her car onto the frontage road behind Highland Meadows. "Is that your birth name or married name?"

"Birth name. I never changed it when I married."

"Good for you. That simplified things, I imagine."

"Yes and no." No further explanation.

"Kepler," Ellie repeated, tasting the name on her lips. "I like it. It's very scientific."

Kathryn sensed the tasting and the warmth it stirred.

"Does anyone ever call you 'Kate?' Or 'Kath'?"

"No."

Ellie noted the curt reply and said impishly, "How about 'Ryn'?"

Kathryn's laugh spilled out, a lovely sound. "No, not that either. Just Kathryn."

"Were you named after someone?"

"My grandmother on my mom's side. She's an old blue blood from out East. How about you? Is Ellie a nickname?"

"Short for Eleanor. My parents were big on the Roosevelts."

"I like Ellie. Though 'Nor' could grow on me."

"I deserve that." Ellie laughed softly. Shyly.

As Ellie navigated through the neighborhood streets, Kathryn's quick, practiced eye took in Ellie's finely sculpted lips, long black lashes, and the mouth that pulled to the side when teasing. She was a mystery, this Ellie Belmont; a good one, a cozy one. Kathryn felt caught in the plot and wanted answers. Like: How could this relative stranger get her to be so open, so vulnerable? To go so deep? "Have you dated anyone since Mary's death?"

"No, nothing serious. My friends are encouraging me to try Match. com, but I'm not there yet."

"My friends are doing the same."

Wouldn't it be funny if . . . no, impossible. Ellie tapped the top of the steering wheel. A solid reminder of the real world. "Have you checked it out?"

"No."

"What's stopping you?"

"I don't know. Starting a new relationship feels daunting."

"Tell me about it."

"And dating sounds so . . . high-schoolish."

Ellie smiled. "Yeah, all those old insecurities waiting to spring out like some Jack-in-the-box."

"Insecurities I can deal with. But two people trying on each other for compatibility when both have decades of baggage and ingrained habits? I don't know."

"Staying single seems the easiest . . . but having a partner, a true partner, is a wonderful thing, isn't it?"

"Well, 'true' is the operative word. I don't want to be in a relationship just to be in one, because I'm afraid of being alone." Kathryn paused. "Which I'm not."

"I don't want to settle either."

"So many people go through life in a bad relationship because they don't want to be single, as though there's some sort of shame in it. But I also understand having to make compromises. Children complicate things. As does money."

"And sex."

"Oh, God, don't go there." Kathryn grimaced. "You know, I've gone on precisely two dates, two different men. Both managed during the course of dinner conversation to mention the little blue pill."

"You. Are. Kidding."

"Sadly, no. As though popping a Viagra would impress me."

"Luckily that dating misstep isn't possible in my world."

The women were still laughing as Ellie steered into the long driveway and stopped at the side door. "You have a lovely home, Kathryn," she said.

"Thanks, but as you can see, it's quite large."

They were quiet for a moment, both women aware that something had deepened between them at Highland Meadows. They would not name it or define it. Neither one wanted their time together to end.

"Would you like to come in for a cup of tea before you're on your way?"

"I'd like to. Thanks." Ellie turned off the car.

They entered through the side door into a mud room where Ellie shed her lightweight down jacket. The kitchen was large with a rectangular island covered with gray Cambria stone. The long counters abutting two walls had matching stone and a back splash of blue tiles. The high-end stainless-steel appliances glowed with reflected light.

"Awesome kitchen, Kathryn."

"Thanks. I supervised the remodel myself. This is the one room I'll really miss when I move. Let me put some water on and we can go into the sunroom where it's more comfortable."

Heading toward the light-filled nook at the back of the kitchen, Kathryn said abruptly, "Wait, let's go into the den. I want you to see it." She put her arm over Ellie's shoulder and steered her to the other side of the room. "This way," she said, guiding Ellie ahead of her through the doorway and dropping her arm.

As they walked side-by-side down the hallway past the formal dining room and living room, she wondered why it had seemed so natural to have gathered Ellie under her arm like that. Was it because Ellie was shorter by a couple of inches and fit so well? Men had always thrown a protective arm around her. She liked it, and now, she had just done the same to Ellie, and she liked that as well. In fact, maybe better. It was not a matter of feeling dominant, though; it was a feeling of tenderness and of having the power to protect. She had been—they both had been—so vulnerable at the senior residence. Ellie's hand on her arm then and this brief touch now were comforting.

The den had solid cherry wood bookshelves on two walls, a large comfortable leather sofa, and a matching chair. A large globe took up one corner and an antique library table sat in front of the far bookshelf.

"An English major's dream," Ellie said, taking a three-sixty spin. "Even a beamed ceiling. It's as though I've been transported to Stratford-upon-Avon."

"I thought you'd like it," Kathryn said.

"It's odd, a room like this in such a modern home."

"It is, isn't it. The story, as told to me by a neighbor, was that the original owner was an architect who specialized in mid-century modern. His partner was a Shakespearean scholar at the U of M. He had completely different tastes apparently. This room was their compromise."

"A gay couple?"

"Uh-huh."

"Cool."

"Joe pretty much claimed this room as his own, but now that he's gone, I've come to love it. It's the second thing I'll miss most from this house when I sell."

"What a huge TV," Ellie said, pointing at the black rectangle affixed to the wall across from the sofa.

"It is. I was surprised Joe didn't take it with him, but I guess it's considered a fixture. He watched sports mostly, but I use it mainly for movies."

"Do you have cable?"

"No, I cancelled it soon after Joe moved out. There's so little I want to watch. I tuned into some 'comedies' right after he left, thinking they would cheer me up, but they were terrible. It seems as though the premise of every show is based on someone lying or withholding the truth. I don't consider that funny."

Ellie ran a finger along a row of DVDs noting their titles. "You must be a Jane Austen fan."

"I am. And of almost anything the BBC does."

"Me, too. I sometimes binge watch their shows on Netflix. Do you ever do that?"

"Occasionally."

Invite me for a movie night, Ellie wanted to say.

Back in the kitchen, Kathryn pulled out a drawer. "Here are your choices for tea," she said. "Unfortunately, a dirty chai latte is unavailable at the moment."

"Well, then, let me peruse the options." Ellie fingered several boxes and chose a lemon ginger tea.

"I like that one, too," Kathryn said, taking the kettle from the stove. "Pull one out for me, please."

They sat in wicker chairs overlooking the patio and backyard where shrubs were still covered in burlap to protect them from winter's cold. They sipped the hot tea as though the world did not exist beyond this yard where the lawn was barely starting to green.

"Look," Ellie said, pointing through the window. "Robins! What a day. Lunch with you and now the first robins I've seen this year."

Kathryn considered the birds cocking their heads close to the ground and the implication of Ellie's statement. She would not pursue it for now.

"Imagine having to hear your meal," Ellie said. "Really, how much sound can a worm make?"

"Enough, apparently," Kathryn said as a robin dipped its head and snagged a worm.

"They're lovely birds, aren't they, with their orange chests and spotted throats, but they're so common they tend to be overlooked."

Kathryn took in the profile of Ellie staring through the window. "I like how your mind works."

Ellie smiled at the compliment and sipped her tea slowly before asking, "Kathryn, what makes you come alive?"

Kathryn caught the sparkle in Ellie's curious, dark eyes. *You do,* she thought immediately. "That's an interesting question. Let me think a moment." She raised the cup to her lips and let the tea roll over her tongue.

"New experiences make me come alive," Kathryn continued. "Those often come when traveling. I find my senses heightened—new food, new smells, different clothes and customs. Astonishing sights. Being out of my element, feeling a little off-balance, a little danger in the unfamiliar. But it doesn't have to be as exotic as that. It can be in my everyday life, too, getting to know an interesting person. Like you."

"What a kind thing to say," Ellie said, smiling. "I'm feeling quite alive myself."

"To the start of a beautiful friendship," Kathryn said, raising her cup in a toast.

The women laughed, their pleasure reinforced by its reflection in the other.

"How would you answer your question—what makes you come alive?"

"I agree that travel makes me feel alive. I'd also say playing."

"Playing? Playing what?"

"Anything. When you're playing, you're immersed in the moment. It could be playing a sport like pickleball or tennis, say, or playing a musical instrument . . . engaging in any form of art, really, whether painting, sculpting, acting, whatever. It includes intellectual play—talking about books and ideas. I thrive on good discussions, when my heart and my head are fully engrossed. It's one of the reasons I loved teaching so much. Being in front of a classroom was performance art, an improv that required every cell in my brain to be awake."

"That's what made you such a great teacher, I imagine. You weren't going through the motions as some do."

"Well, the subject helps. Literature and writing engage the emotions, so if I could connect students with their feelings, they could experience something deep, something life-changing."

"As with my realtor, Amy."

"Precisely."

"Intellectual passion can stand on its own, though, don't you think? I remember back in my college days, being thrilled with anatomy and physiology. We didn't have the great passions of Heathcliff or Mr. Darcy in that subject."

"Oh, of course." Ellie smiled. "Mathematicians salivate over equations. When you can't name a passion, it's time to re-evaluate your life . . . or let it go." Ellie's face suddenly fell, her eyes thoughtful. "Mary and I talked about when it would be time for her to let go, and she said when she no longer showed any interest in cribbage or the Minnesota Vikings. Well, she lost her appetite for playing any card game by her tenth round of chemo.. . and when she got pneumonia, she didn't even bother to look at a Vikings calendar a friend gave her. I should have known . . . ."

"It can be hard, Ellie, to distinguish the fatigue that comes with pneumonia from the disengagement of the dying. If she had recovered, do you think she would have put on her Grendel braids and horns again?"

Ellie's face softened. "Yes. Along with her purple shirt."

"There you go." Kathryn's expression was kind, but serious. "But I'm not sure passion should be the arbiter of a life worth living, Ellie. It's wonderful to feel passionate, but it's also wonderful to feel contentment. A lot of people lead quiet lives, have simple joys and simple loves, and just bear witness to the world."

"'They also serve who only stand and wait.' John Milton."

"Precisely," Kathryn said with a nod. "I bet quite a few folks at Highland Meadows fall into that category. Everyone's life has meaning, Ellie, even Mary as she lay dying. Her experience gave you a chance to grow."

Ellie stared for a moment, wordless. "You're good, Kathryn the Therapist."

"Thank you. And to you, it's Ryn the Friend."

CHAPTER 6

*H*onesty was as core to Kathryn as the spine running up her back. It was one reason her husband's infidelity had been such a blow: he had been dishonest for many years. There was no going back after that type of betrayal. And when Ellie had asked what made her come alive, Kathryn had told the truth: Ellie made her feel alive.

The follow up question, which Ellie thankfully did not ask, was: What does that mean?

Now Kathryn sat in the leather chair in the den, a glass of Malbec on the inlaid mother-of-pearl side table, a sketchbook in hand. She was drawing from memory scenes of the day: the tulip in a vase on the table at Highland Meadows, the robins in the yard, Ellie's face. Kathryn would be the first to admit her artistic skills were limited, but that was never the point. She had discovered an affinity for pencil and paper when she was a nursing student and would draw various parts of the human anatomy— the bones, the nerves, the internal organs—as a way to memorize. In her adult life, drawing was often a way of doing something physical while the mind was processing in the background. Or in the foreground.

A bottom shelf held sketchbooks filled after Joe's shocking departure. They were bursting with drawings and furious prose, maudlin poems and solitary curse words mixed with phrases of Zen detachment. Ellie had asked who a therapist with a broken heart turns to. Kathryn had turned right here, in this Shakespearean fold of comfort, to her journals. Here, she could pour out her anger and humiliation at being dumped for another woman. Here she could face her disappointment in friends from whom she sought support but instead received silence and avoidance, and their sour fear the same fate could await them. Better to not be contaminated by her divorce disease.

And here she had turned to Anna. Anna had been her solace, her spiritual balm. She had wept out her grief to Anna's imagined—or was it real? —presence, sitting across from her, Buddha-like. What would Anna say? What would be her comfort? How Kathryn had wanted her wisdom, her embrace, her comforting pats on the arm.

Kathryn's field of friends had diminished significantly with the breakup. The foursomes could not devolve into threesomes, or perhaps the foursomes had just rearranged themselves with Joe and his new wife. Her handful of remaining, loyal friends was her bedrock now.

This new friendship with Ellie was different. Ellie was a lesbian, and Kathryn was unfamiliar with the rules of this territory. She could go deep with her old friend Judith, for instance, as well as tease her. Had she led Ellie on today by sharing so intimately? By teasing her?

The sensation of throwing her arm around Ellie's shoulder and steering her toward the hallway was vivid in her mind. She made the same gesture with many friends, but why, this time, did it evoke tenderness and not just unselfconscious affection?

To be honest, hadn't that touch and Ellie's hand on her arm given her a pleasing jolt? Was it because she sensed Ellie's interest? Or was there something on her end, too? Didn't she look forward to hearing Ellie's voice and seeing those coal-black eyes harboring diamonds?

"Anna, old friend," she said aloud, "what's happening?"

She pictured her dear mentor, her white pixie-cut hair, the chocolate eyes filled with amusement. Anna would say: *My dear, you know what's happening.*

But I feel unsure.

Every step of your life has brought you to this moment, Kathryn. Every path that lies before you is good. The more rewarding ones always carry more risk.

I know that.

Of course, you do, dear friend. And you know what to do.

Yes. Kathryn smirked to herself. Be myself. Be open to the path unfolding. Every experience is a gift. Trust the process. Yaddah, yaddah, yaddah. The counsel she gave others now seemed unpleasantly vague and unhelpful.

As the memory of Anna's hearty laughter played in her mind, tears came, gentle as an Irish mist.

"Did you see the weather forecast for next week?" Sandy asked as she slid into the booth of a brew house at Lake and Lyndale, a revitalized south-side neighborhood dotted with apartment complexes and eateries catering to millennials. "It's going to be sixty on Tuesday. We should gather the gang and hit the outdoor courts at Pearl Park."

"I'm in," Ellie said. She bent her arm a few times. "If my elbow calms down."

"What happened?"

"I hit a backhand the other day that aggravated my old injury. Time to see the chiropractor."

They both ordered small stouts and a basket of chicken wings to share.

"Any news of Kathryn?"

"We had lunch yesterday at Highland Meadows."

"You spry old thing!" Sandy teased. "Look at you go!"

"I'm going nowhere," Ellie said, "but I'm enjoying it. That's worth something."

"You bet. Get the old blood flowing. You don't think she's interested?"

"She looks at women as friend material, not as romantic partners."

"Are you sure? Things have changed a lot since you were on the dating scene—not that you're dating, of course."

"No."

A waiter delivered the beers. The dark stout had a nice layer of creamy foam on top. The women saluted each other and took a sip. A basketball game was playing on the half dozen TVs scattered throughout the bistro, and the running commentary murmured in the background.

"Older straight women who are divorced or widowed are opening to the possibility of other women," Sandy said, wiping suds from her upper lip. "But you do have to be careful. Kathryn may be dinking a few pickleballs into your court, but she might decide to stay on her side of the net."

"Right you are. I'm naturally cautious. I had my heart broken by more than one straight woman when I was young." And by your Kris, she thought, but did not say it. "Besides, I'm not dating."

"Yeah, yeah, but even so, Kathryn's really picked up your spirits, hasn't she? Put some excitement in your life?"

Ellie nodded.

"So, she may not be right for you, but you know what she's done? She's gotten the sap moving again. I think you're ready to start dating."

"It's been three years . . . ."

"The calendar doesn't mean a thing. It's when a person is ready. If you're feeling the old pitter-patter, it's a sign. Go ahead and try Match. com. It's the way people meet these days."

"I'll think about it."

The wings came, a hot, greasy pile in a paper-lined basket.

"When do you take off for California?" Sandy asked, picking up a piece glistening with barbeque sauce.

"Two weeks from Sunday."

"How do you feel about going?"

"Excited. I love road trips, as you know, but I'm kind of sorry to leave Kathryn. I'll miss her."

"See?" Sandy narrowed her eyes and tipped a wing in Ellie's direction.

"I know, I know."

Sandy studied her friend a moment. "You're downplaying again. You know this road trip—your visiting Mary's niece—is a big deal. Any time you want to stop . . . ."

Ellie looked around furtively. "I do what I can, old friend."

"You're making such a huge difference in Kris's quality of life. And mine. You're the best. Really you are."

"It's a privilege." Ellie stirred a wing in a dark pool of sauce. "Now, let's say no more about it."

"Okay. On a more pleasant topic, when will you see Kathryn again? Before you go, I hope."

"Me, too. If I don't hear from her this weekend, I'll call to line up something for next week. And, don't worry, our pickleball times are sacrosanct."

CHAPTER 7

*E*llie invited Kathryn to her home the following Wednesday for a quick lunch before shopping. Kathryn arrived with a bouquet of tulips in a vase.

"Keep the vase," she said. "I'm down-sizing."

"Thanks a lot," Ellie said with a touch of playful sarcasm at the vase she'd now have to downsize herself. "The flowers are lovely," she added with sincerity as she placed them on the dining room table.

The two women paused for a moment, taking each other in. Kathryn was wearing a rust-colored cashmere sweater and black pants with the same scarf of their first meeting tied loosely at her throat. Ellie was in blue jeans with a black turtleneck sweater.

Kathryn paused in the archway between the living room and dining room admiring all she could see. "A Dutch colonial. I've always liked these houses. And look at your woodwork! I bet it's old growth oak. You don't get this type of construction in the suburbs." She ran her hand along the gleaming trim. "And a real wood-burning fireplace. You have a very nice home, Ellie. How long have you lived here?"

"Almost thirty years."

"You bought it before you and Mary got together?"

"I had another partner then. Luckily it wasn't a joint purchase so when she moved out, it wasn't complicated."

"What happened to her?"

Ellie laughed. "She moved a block away. She's living with Sandy who is now my pickleball partner and former softball teammate. We're all a family."

"Your family of choice."

"Exactly. Come on, let's eat." Ellie led the way into a kitchen half the size of Kathryn's with a gleaming maple floor and sparkling white appliances. A slow cooker on the marble countertop bubbled with chicken wild rice soup, filling the room with a rich, creamy aroma.

"Oh, look at this!" Kathryn said, fingering a cotton dishtowel embroidered with a picture of a rooster. "Is this from your mother?"

"How did you know?"

"I still have a few of them from my mom with pictures of musical instruments mainly. When I cleaned out her apartment after she died, I found a whole stack of towels. My sister didn't want them, but I couldn't bear to throw them away."

"Same here—but as an only child, I didn't have to share either. I'm down to my last few," Ellie said as she retrieved a baking dish with cornbread from the oven. "I hope you don't mind the meal being a little heavy on the starches. There is a green salad."

"Perfect."

Ellie pointed to the small table by the windows. "I thought we could eat in here. It's cozier—and sunnier than the dining room." She fetched glasses from the cupboard and filled them with water while Kathryn set the cornbread on the trivet on the table.

"Okay," Ellie said, holding a soup bowl, "how much would you like?"

"Half full."

Ellie ladled the soup into their bowls.

As the women ate, Kathryn updated Ellie on her latest condo-hunting foray. She admitted her quest was more research at this point, rather than a serious venture into purchasing. But if the right unit appeared, one that really felt like home, she would take it.

"What makes a place feel like home?" Ellie asked.

"Warmth, light, space, good Feng Shui. Having some of my favorite items around."

"Like what?"

"Artwork. Books. A few favorite pieces of furniture. What about you, Ellie? What makes a place feel like home?"

"A few years ago, I would have said 'wherever Mary is.' Now I have to find a new definition."

Kathryn sat silently, her eyes steady and alert, never leaving Ellie.

"I think what makes a home is where I feel I can nest," Ellie said, "where I can be silent or turn up the music and dance."

"Where you can be yourself?"

"Yes . . . although I try to be authentic no matter where I am. Still, there are times when I feel I need to be 'up.' Who wants a moper at a party? And when I was teaching, of course there were tough days when the last place I wanted to be was in front of a classroom, but that was my job."

"Were you still teaching when Mary was ill?"

Ellie nodded. "I took phased retirement the last year she was alive, which left me with a two-year commitment after her death. I did take a little time off—my colleagues were wonderful about filling in, but I got back to work pretty quickly. I found the structure helpful, and I needed to keep busy."

"What about now? What are your days like?"

"I've taken advice from my elders regarding retirement. I don't have much planned this first year. I've traveled a bit—a couple of cruises— and I play pickleball regularly with friends. I work out at the gym. I occasionally read manuscripts for a small local publishing house. I don't have a set schedule."

"Other than Starbucks reading the paper?"

"Yes." Ellie drank in Kathryn's smile. "What about your days?"

"I'm still adjusting to retirement . . . or this hiatus. With the divorce finalized, I don't have that hanging over me and syphoning energy. I'm not much of a joiner, but I do belong to a monthly book group. I go to movies occasionally. I don't mind going by myself."

"Movies are one of my passions. I taught film studies for a semester at the college when a teacher had to take a sudden medical leave. I loved it, but it raised a few hackles with the film faculty. They didn't like someone from the English Department moving in on their territory, so I had to relinquish that role fairly quickly."

"You mentioned the film festival the other night. You'll be going?"

"Yes. I'll only be able to catch the last week or so of it. Even then, there'll be lots of good films. Maybe we could go to some of them together."

"I'd like that. Why will you miss the first part of the festival?"

"I'll be in California."

"California? What takes you there?" Kathryn broke off a piece of cornbread and buttered it slowly.

Ellie hesitated, wondering how much to reveal. "I'm visiting Mary's niece. It's becoming an annual trip."

"Whereabouts?"

"Northern part. Nevada City area, northeast of Sacramento."

"When do you leave?"

"In a week and a half. April 9th or 10th."

"You don't have your tickets yet?"

"Oh, no. I'm driving." *I have to drive.*

"By yourself?"

"Sure. I enjoy it—seeing the wide open spaces, listening to music and books. I take my time. If I don't feel like putting in a full day of driving, I don't."

"Well, aren't you full of marvels!"

"Not really." Ellie paused. "A friend gave me some great advice after Mary died. She told me to go away at least once a month—get out of town even if it's only for a weekend or overnight."

"The purpose being . . . ?"

"It's a way to keep connected with the world. You have to decide where to go, then you have to plan for the trip, make the trip, take pictures and organize them when you get home."

"Where are some of the places you've gone?"

"Oh, lots of short trips up north—I love the state parks along Lake Superior. A couple of cruises, as I mentioned—one to Alaska and one to the western Caribbean. I drove to the Black Hills last fall. Twice I've flown to Orlando to visit The Wizarding World of Harry Potter."

"Harry Potter?" Kathryn smiled.

"I'm a fan," Ellie said without apology. "Once I took the train to Chicago for the Art Museum. Oh, I checked out the Cahokia Mounds outside of St. Louis. And some filming sites in Cincinnati of a movie I love."

"You did all these trips by yourself?"

"Yes. It can be hard to find a travel companion in a coupled world . . . ."

"I know."

"Sometimes it's easier to go out of town alone than to go to a play by myself here in Minneapolis. Mary and I used to have season tickets at the Guthrie. It's funny though, I've never minded going to movies by myself. But I'd love it if you'd join me sometimes."

Kathryn was quiet, observing Ellie. "You know," she said, "this is the third time since I arrived that you've massaged your elbow. Is it bothering you?"

"A bit. I aggravated an old injury playing pickleball."

"What's the injury?"

"It's called cubital tunnel syndrome. I spent way too many hours leaning on my elbows while studying in grad school and then as a teacher correcting papers. I aggravated a nerve."

"For real? I've never heard of it." Kathryn made a beckoning motion with her hand. "May I see?"

"Sure." Ellie pushed up her sleeve and held out her right arm, palm up. She touched her inner elbow. "Right there."

Kathryn placed a hand behind the elbow and with the index finger on her other hand touched the spot. "Here?"

Ellie was glad she was sitting down as her whole arm ionized at Kathryn's touch.

"The ulnar nerve?"

"Yes. My chiropractor says it gets entrapped in the small tunnel it goes through. She usually massages it a little to break down the scar tissue and unstick it."

Kathryn pressed the spot lightly, cocking her head in concentration. Her eyes took on the other-worldly look cats have when lapping milk. "Boy, it is really subtle. I'm not sure what I'm feeling. Your chiropractor must have very sensitive fingers."

"She's good," Ellie said.

"Well, I won't muck around in there because I don't know what I'm doing," Kathryn said, returning Ellie's arm to her. "I don't want to make it worse. But thanks for showing me. I learned something new."

Ellie shook her arm, a privileged appendage now. "It feels better, whatever you did. Thanks." She pulled her sleeve down and started to gather the dishes. "Let's clean up here and be on our way . . . if you're still willing."

"I am. The question is, are you?"

"I'm never ready . . . ." Ellie closed the dishwasher and took a deep breath. "And just to warn you, shopping always makes me crabby."

"It'll be fun—for me at least."

Ellie raised her eyebrows in wonderment.

"Okay," Kathryn said cheerfully, "let's go get you some clothes!"

CHAPTER 8

*T*he first stop was Macy's at the Southdale Mall.

"Walking through a department store is like being in a museum of women's oppression," Ellie observed as they passed through a spritz of cloying perfume by the make-up counters. "The purpose of everything here is to exploit women, to make us sexually attractive to men, and to tell us we're not good enough as we are. We have to look young. Hide our wrinkles, hide our blemishes. But imperfections give a face character."

"You're preaching to the choir."

"And don't get me started on the sexual politics of high heels," Ellie said as they passed the shoe department.

"Maybe this wasn't such a good idea after all." Kathryn twisted her mouth into a pout.

"No, no, we're here, and I do need new clothes."

As they descended the escalator to the women's department, the ocean of clothing spread before them like Dante's Eighth Circle.

"Here is the cavern of hell," Ellie said, shaking her head, "where exploitation and deception are commercialized, not punished. Well, let's wade in to see if any monsters bite . . . but I'll tell you right now, I don't see a thing that appeals to me."

"Follow me," Kathryn said. She made for a rack in the Calvin Klein section, like a bee to the sweetest flower. She tracked her fingers along the tops of the hangers, pulled out a blue collarless top, and held it up. "What do you think?"

Ellie's brow furrowed. "Hmmm. I like it. How did you know to come right here, to this very rack?"

"Instinct. Now go try it on. Here, take both the medium and large."

While Ellie was in the dressing room, Kathryn found several more items. "How did the top work?"

"Good."

"Which size?"

"Medium."

"Okay. Here are a few more things to try on."

The wooden door creaked open and Ellie reached for the new batch. "I should have worn a bra," she said.

"Do you usually wear one?"

"No."

"Then you shouldn't wear one when trying on clothes. Now see how these fit while I round up some pants and capris for you."

"Make sure they have good, deep pockets," Ellie said, shutting the door.

Kathryn turned to re-enter the sartorial forest. "Lord help me," she muttered.

After twenty minutes, four items had met with Ellie's approval.

"Okay," Kathryn said, pushing the hair off her damp forehead. She took in Ellie's unhappy face. "Mind if I step inside?"

Ellie's eyes, peeking from behind the door, grew large. "Umm, sure."

Kathryn quickly entered the large corner dressing room and shut the door. Ellie had moved back against the wall mirror, slump-shouldered and defeated, standing in her sleeveless undershirt and a pair of black capris with the tags hanging from the side. Kathryn's gaze never left Ellie's face with its creased brow, alarmed gaze, and crabby droop to her mouth. Kathryn could see so much of the petulant eight-year-old in Ellie that she wanted to laugh.

But the bruise on Ellie's left triceps stopped her short. "Good lord, what happened?" Kathryn stroked the angry black mark.

"Oh, pickleball. I ran into the post going after a wide shot." Ellie glanced at the bruise, a dark patch now with its own pulse.

Kathryn wagged her head. "You jocks." She moved her hands to Ellie's almost bare shoulders, placing her face close, "Okay, dear friend, you're miserable because you're resisting this experience. Can you think of it as playing ... or creating art?"

"I don't know." Ellie's expression had changed completely. She had snapped out of her funk but was in a different sort of daze.

"Or think of it as writing a poem." Kathryn turned Ellie toward the mirror and reached for the try-on tops hanging on a hook. She held one after another in front of Ellie. "See. Just like you try to fit words together, we're fitting clothes together. One top. One bottom. Maybe a jacket. You're assembling your look, your own style. Your color palette is winter, so that's why I'm bringing you clothes with bold colors. Look at how wonderful you look in red and black ... red emphasizes your dark eyes ... gosh, they're beautiful."

Their eyes met in the mirror and held for a moment too long.

Kathryn stepped back, quickly taking in Ellie's broad back, the spray of faded freckles across her shoulders, the soft hairs on her neck. Fighting the impulse to stroke them, she hung the tops back on the hook.

"Are you on board?"

Ellie nodded.

"All right." Kathryn smiled. "I'll take the winners and wait for you at the checkout counter. Then it's time to shift gears."

"How so?" Ellie asked meekly.

"We're going to the men's department."

CHAPTER 9

*J*udith Epstein waved to Kathryn from the back of an upscale Italian restaurant off France Avenue. "Over here!" she called. She was one of Kathryn's old country club friends, a retired lawyer, the wife of a radiologist, and a big booster of the Twin Cities arts and philanthropic scene. Although she was a couple of years older than Kathryn, she looked years younger given the scalpel work on her face and her highlighted hair. She always looked like a million bucks, or a million and a half, she would have probably preferred to say.

Kathryn gave Judith a peck on the cheek and collapsed in the chair across from her.

"I'm at your beck and call, Kathryn. You know that. Now, what's up? Why did you want a quiet corner?"

A waiter delivered water to the table and left menus.

"Wait, don't tell me," Judith said, smiling brightly. "You are absolutely glowing. You've met someone."

"Am I glowing?"

"I practically need sunglasses."

"Well, I have met someone . . . but I'm not sure what's happening."

"Tell me," Judith said, scooting forward, her dark eyes sharpening in anticipation.

"I've met a woman, a retired college teacher, and I really, really like her." Kathryn paused to gauge Judith's response.

Judith nodded in comprehension, her face revealing nothing except eagerness.

"She's a lesbian."

"So I figured."

"Her partner died three years ago . . . and, I don't know. I really like spending time with her. But I don't know if I can go where she might want to go . . . romantically and physically."

"Has she made a pass at you?"

"Not a hint of one."

"What would you do if she did?"

"I don't know."

Judith broke into a grin. "Well, that says it all right there, my dear."

"Not to me."

They paused while the waiter returned and took their orders.

"If you don't know how you'd respond, there's a possibility that you'd say yes."

"I could say no. I don't want to hurt her. She is such a good person."

"Are you in love?"

"It's more like infatuation. But I think I could fall in love, if I let myself."

Judith beckoned the waiter to the table. "Two glasses of Prosecco."

Kathryn ran her fingers through her hair and gave Judith a knowing look. "Are you plying me with alcohol to loosen my lips?"

"No. To celebrate your coming alive." Judith leaned forward. "Now, listen. Wait! I assume you've done your due diligence with this person. What's her name?"

"Ellie Belmont. And, yes, I've looked her up on the internet and checked her Facebook timeline. Lots of good things about her."

"She's a catch then? Okay, listen. Kathryn, you're approaching seventy. Time is short, and the list of suitable men is even shorter. Those two blind dates Rita set you up with—they were just rich old coots looking for a nursemaid in their dotage. You deserve better."

"What I'm hearing you say, Judith," Kathryn said carefully, holding the gaze of her friend, "is that my prospects aren't very good, so I should give this new experience a try. I'd like to frame it a little differently: I'm fortunate to have lived long enough to explore and enjoy a new facet of myself."

Judith considered her friend. "You are spot on. As usual. I think the idea of a woman is marvelous. Ellie is very lucky."

"I am, too."

A shadow of pain crossed Judith's face. "Well, you couldn't have fallen in with a better person. You know what I think of lesbians."

"I do."

"How they took care of my brother . . . we were all clueless. Heartless, really."

"No one knew what was going on, Judith."

"But the whole family turning away? My parents so ashamed they forbade his name to be spoken?"

"It was ignorance. At least you visited him in hospice."

"But I was afraid to touch him." Judith snorted. After a moment, she brightened. "I remember this tough little butch . . . she couldn't have weighed more than ninety pounds . . . dressed all in black leather . . . she'd spoon soup into his mouth as though Ben were a baby bird. She'd talk to him in the sweetest, dearest tone, and then turn around and spew every curse word imaginable at Reagan and the rightwing. And at my family. God, she was tough."

The waiter delivered the sparkling wine with a flourish and poured two glasses. Bubbles streamed from the bottom of the flutes in happy chaos.

"Your Ellie doesn't wear leather, does she?" Judith kidded.

"No, she doesn't."

"Give me three words that describe her."

Kathryn thought for a moment. "Sweet. Sensitive. Good communicator."

"You feel quite protective of her, don't you?"

"I do. It's odd."

"No, it's tenderness and it's an expression of your love. You're falling in love, Kathryn. You won't admit it. But, here," Judith said, seizing her glass of Prosecco, "let's make a toast to being alive."

The women's eyes met in their salute, and with it an exchange of caring that had been nurtured over the decades.

Judith pushed the breadbasket toward Kathryn. "Here, have some calories. I have a feeling you're going to need them."

Kathryn laughed and sipped the sparkling wine. It tasted of joy. "I think I may have another shopping project on my hands. I took Ellie to a few stores yesterday to buy some outfits. I noticed her clothes were looking rather worn and thought she probably hadn't had one new item of clothing since before her partner died. She doesn't have much sense of style . . . ."

"Neither did Joe. You had to dress him, too."

"That seemed a lot easier," Kathryn said grimly, then burst into laughter. "Every heterosexual woman should have the experience of shopping with a lesbian feminist. It was . . . it was . . . ." Kathryn set her elbows on the table, put her hands to her forehead, and guffawed.

"What? What?"

". . . it was like trying to dress a porcupine." Kathryn dabbed at her eyes with a napkin. "No scooped necklines, spaghetti straps, off-shoulder tops. Nothing stiff or flimsy or uncomfortable. No little peek-a-boo holes, frills, or anything with any whiff of femininity."

"What does that leave?"

"Polo shirts."

The women roared with laughter.

"And she didn't want anything made in sweatshops . . . at which point I told her she'd have to remove all of her clothing and walk home naked."

"Stop! Stop! My makeup is running!"

After the women had regained their composure, Kathryn said, "Actually, Ellie was rather accepting and appreciative of my labors, thank god. I think I would have strangled her otherwise."

"You managed to find something other than polo shirts, I hope."

"Yes. We wound up at the shops at 50th and France. Title Nine saved the day. She has a whole new wardrobe that she can mix and match. I think she looks quite nice."

"Attractive?"

"Yes, very." Kathryn couldn't suppress a smile. "And even though we were both exhausted by the end of our shopping, she had a face like a kid who had just gotten the biggest lollipop in the candy shop." Kathryn paused. "And you know, I learned something. I saw department stores through different eyes, and I was shocked at how oppressive to women they can be. I've been a feminist for a half a century, Judith, but with Ellie, I felt as though I were in first grade."

Judith leveled a serious look at her friend. "Look at you. Look at you and tell me you're not falling in love. Now here comes our food. I want you to tell me all about her—every detail!

CHAPTER 10

*A*s Ellie carried the last of the plastic bags filled with clothes down the stairs and onto the front porch, the phone rang.

"Is this a good time to talk?" It was Kathryn. No one ever asked Ellie if it were a good time to talk except Kathryn, and she liked that she did. It seemed respectful and good-mannered, and it was now a habit Ellie herself had adopted.

"Perfect timing," Ellie said. "I just cleared out the last of the old clothes to make room for the new."

"What are you going to do with them?"

"Give them to Goodwill."

"Hmmm . . . ."

"Are they too shabby?"

"Worn is the word I'd use."

"Some of Mary's are in pretty good shape."

"Oh, I didn't realize you were dealing with her clothes, too."

"Yes," Ellie said, suddenly feeling a little sheepish. "When I was cleaning out my closet, I thought it was time to face her things, too. I can't believe they've been hanging there for three years."

"How was that for you, Ellie?"

"Hard. And wonderful."

Kathryn was silent, waiting for more.

"Hard because it's just one more stage of letting Mary go, and wonderful because it lightens my load physically and emotionally."

"Did you cry?"

"I shed a few tears—not as many as I once would have. There were a couple of T-shirts from our trips I couldn't bear to get rid of."

"Like what?"

"A white T-shirt with a picture of Athena emblazoned on the front. It's a souvenir from our trip to Greece. We were there three months before her diagnosis, before our lives got ensnared in the medical system." Ellie paused, thinking how cancer had turned their days into a surreal labyrinth.

"Are you still there?" Kathryn asked after several moments of silence.

"Oh, sorry," Ellie said. "I was just thinking about those times. Mary's clothes definitely go to Goodwill. I can't bear to put them in the garbage."

"Of course not."

Ellie knew Kathryn understood. She did not need to say more.

"I put away all the clothes we bought," she said cheering up. "I can't tell you how much I appreciate your helping me. I'm sorry I was such a pill."

"You were brave to let me see you in a challenging situation."

"I don't know about that, but I think I'm a new woman with my new wardrobe!"

"With a lot more closet space!"

"It's good timing, all these new clothes," Ellie said. "Just in time for my trip."

"Have you started packing?"

"No, I'll get to it next week."

"Ellie," Kathryn said, a sudden hesitancy in her voice, "I have something to ask. It feels quite forward, and please answer honestly. You won't hurt my feelings."

"Okay."

"Would you consider taking me along on your trip? I've been on the West Coast more times than I can count, but I've never driven there. My daughter lives in Sacramento, so I could stay with her a couple of days and give you a break from my company. What do you think? I won't feel hurt if you say no. I understand that people sometimes prefer to travel alone."

After a moment of stunned silence, Ellie said, "Gosh . . . why, I'd love to have you along." A hot and blinding happiness cut through her. "But are you sure? It's a long drive."

"I'd love to get away for a while, go someplace green and warm and appealing. With someone interesting."

"Well, I don't know how interesting I would be. I usually take along some podcasts and audio books. I have a course on the chamber music of Mozart I was planning to listen to. Could you tolerate that?"

"I'd love it."

"You said your daughter is in Sacramento?"

"Yes, she, her husband and two children. It would be a real treat to see the grandkids."

"Of course."

"Was it a niece who lives in Nevada City?"

"Out in the country, yes. Mary's niece. Mine, too."

"What does she do?"

"She has a small organic farm."

"Do you stay with her?"

"No. She and her husband have a pretty small house. I get a room in town."

"Well, we can figure out the logistics later, but I'm thinking maybe you could drop me off in Sacramento while you see your niece."

"I'm open to anything. Could you be ready a week from this Sunday? We'd be gone two weeks tops."

"That's fine. Ellie, let's sleep on this and touch base tomorrow or Sunday. Does that work for you?"

"Fine, Kathryn. I'll talk with you soon." Ellie clicked off her phone, joyous and terrified. "Oh, god," she said, "how is this going to work?"

"Gaaaah!" Kris shrieked at Ellie during Saturday morning brunch. The dachshunds yelped and scampered out of the kitchen, their toenails clicking on the tile floor. "You're doing a *Carol*! Gaaaah! Run, Ellie, quick, while you can!"

Ellie laughed and buttered her pancakes. "It's not as though I'm absconding with a virginal teenager."

"No, in the movie, it's the other way around. *Kathryn's* Carol, a rich suburbanite divorcée and woman of the world, absconding with you, a sweet, innocent . . . ."

"Schoolmarm?"

"Come on, Kris," Sandy said, forking a couple of cakes onto her plate. "Ellie's a big girl. She's been around the block. As has Kathryn."

"Yes, but for the first relationship after Mary?" Kris looked from Sandy to Ellie and back again. She pushed her wavy hair away from her reddening face.

Ellie did not like the implication. It sounded as though there would be a string of relationships now that she was entering the field again. That's what she was doing . . . dating, whether or not Kathryn was aware of it. Maybe dating was too strong of a word, though. Don't both parties have to know they're dating? If only one person considered it dating, it couldn't really be a date, could it? She was *seeing* Kathryn, then. *Seeing* if there might be the possibility of a relationship.

"God, you two, I don't know what I'm doing," Ellie said.

"See!" Kris cried. "That's a line right out of *Carol.*"

"It's not the exact line," Ellie said.

"You should know. You've only watched it, what, twenty, thirty times?"

"Eighteen . . . and Carol says it, not Therese." Ellie poured more maple syrup. "Oops. Too much."

"Here," Sandy said, holding out the platter of pancakes, "have another to sop it up."

"I will. They're delicious. Thanks for making them, Kris."

"You're welcome, El," Kris said with sudden warmth. "You know how much I love cooking for you."

"I do." Ellie took another dripping forkful.

Sandy considered her friend for a few moments and asked, "Seriously, have you fallen in love?"

"I'm not sure. When is the moment when the falling becomes the fallen?"

"When you get a grin on your face every time her name is mentioned."

"Am I doing that?"

"Yes," Sandy and Kris said in unison.

"Okay, I've fallen in love, god help me. But I'm being a perfectly contained lady about it when I'm around her. Jane Austen would be proud."

"Oh, now we're moving on to *Pride and Prejudice*. Well, I know you, Ellie, and you'll be the impeccable Darcy, suppressing all passion until you explode."

"No, Kris," Sandy said, "Kathryn would be Darcy—the rich land baron worried about marrying below his station. Like Carol."

"For god's sake!" Ellie cried.

"Okay, okay," Kris said, "all kidding aside . . . and Ellie, you know I want only the best for you. Despite all my worry, you know I'm thrilled that you've found someone, and you're going on this trip together. But does Kathryn know why you're going?"

"No, I didn't see a way to bring it up, but I will. It could be a showstopper." Ellie frowned. "On all fronts."

"I don't want you to risk what could turn out to be a great relationship because of this. It's not worth it. We can find other ways. I mean it."

"I appreciate it, Kris. But I've been giving it some thought. If Kathryn can't accept this part of my life, then it's better to know it now, before things get serious . . . if they ever could."

"Of course, they could," Kris said. "Who couldn't help falling in love with you?" She reached over and tousled Ellie's hair. "My little heroine."

CHAPTER 11

$\mathcal{K}$athryn was reading *Yes!* magazine when her phone pinged with an incoming text from Ellie.

Need to talk. May I stop by?

This afternoon at 2? How about a walk in the neighborhood?

Needs to be a sit-down face-to-face. See you at 2.

Oh, boy, Kathryn thought nervously, here we go.

She continued with her magazine, but found it hard to concentrate, and at times, startled herself by exclaiming "Damn!" out loud. She was not ready to deal with her feelings toward Ellie; she needed time for them to ripen, to sort themselves out. She chastised herself for initiating the tag-along to California. What had she been thinking?

Kathryn popped a yoga DVD into the player in the basement work-out room. She spent an hour on the floor, stretching and sweating, being present in mind and motion, so that by the end, she had calmed herself and had reset to her natural state of poise and acceptance of what was and what was to be.

Promptly at two o'clock the doorbell to the side door rang, and Ellie was on the step, holding the vase Kathryn had given her.

"Here," Ellie said, extending the gift to Kathryn.

"Yellow roses!" she said. "My favorite!"

"Keep the vase. I'm downsizing."

Kathryn scrunched her face and laughed. "Come on in." She placed the flowers on the kitchen table. *Roses. The wooing begins in earnest. Oh, boy.*

"How are you?" she said.

"Doing well. And you?"

"Fine." Kathryn smiled at the sudden formality. Hoping to diffuse the awkwardness, she said, "There's hot water on the stove. Tea?"

They carried their ceramic mugs into the den. Ellie went directly to the stuffed chair, leaving the sofa to Kathryn, who settled at the end closest to Ellie.

The butterflies had started once again in Kathryn's stomach and now radiated out to her limbs. She set her teacup on the side table, not trusting herself to hold it steady. "What's on your mind, Ellie?" Kathryn said, a calm demeanor hiding her turmoil.

Ellie set her drink on the side table. Her eyes were round and serious. Kathryn detected a challenge in them.

"I want to be upfront and clear about something, Kathryn. It would be pretty easy for me to hide what I'm doing, but that wouldn't be honest or fair."

Kathryn did not break her gaze, but inside she was screaming, *she's going to ask me to be her lover!* Oh, god, what can I say? It'll have to be no. But look at those eyes. That mouth. How could anyone resist them?

"Okay," Kathryn said softly.

"I have to tell you the reason for my trip because I'd be exposing you to some risk. Not much, but a little."

Kathryn's head tilted slightly in confusion.

"I'm making a cannabis run."

Kathryn blinked twice, not taking in the information. "You're what?"

"I'm picking up cannabis oil to bring back to Minnesota."

Kathryn burst into shocked laughter. "Oh, my god!" she cried. "Cannabis! Are you kidding?"

Ellie smiled, clearly baffled by Kathryn's amusement.

"Oh, my god," Kathryn repeated, wiping a tear from her eye. "I'm shocked."

"I know," Ellie grinned. "I don't seem the type. I could be someone's grandmother."

"Tell me the whole story." Kathryn relaxed, relieved and surprisingly disappointed in the turn of conversation. Romance obviously was not on the table. At least not yet.

Ellie settled back in the leather chair, her face relaxed now after the confession. "It's not for me. It's for a friend—Kris."

"But CBD is available in health food stores or on-line. Why can't she get it there? Why do you need to drive to California?"

Ellie's face darkened. "Well, that's the thing. Rick Simpson oil—or RSO—is a full-spectrum extract. It can contain high levels of THC, unlike CBD which is not a psychotropic. RSO is illegal to sell anywhere."

"But someone sells it to you."

"Yes, Mary's niece Trisha."

"The organic farmer?" Kathryn pursed her lips in comprehension.

"It gets tricky. People can make RSO in their homes, but the process is complex and requires a lot of cannabis, which is illegal to grow in Minnesota in the amounts needed."

"Since it's full spectrum, I suppose it's pretty potent."

"Way potent. And far more effective than over-the-counter CBD."

Kathryn nodded thoughtfully.

"Trisha was raising marijuana long before it was legal in California. When Mary got cancer, Trish drove here with a stash of organic weed Mary could smoke for nausea and pain. She also brought RSO."

"But it didn't save Mary."

"No, I'm not sure even RSO could beat metastatic breast cancer, especially after all the damage chemo and radiation had done, but it helped with pain. After Mary died, I had a supply of RSO left so when Kris was diagnosed with Lyme disease and doctors wanted to put her on all sorts of toxic pharmaceuticals, Trish recommended she take Mary's remaining capsules. Within a month, all of Kris's symptoms disappeared. On top of that, she found it relieved her arthritis pain significantly and helped her sleep at night, so she's stayed on a nightly maintenance dosage."

"How about you?" Kathryn's face was now pensive, the eyes curious and nonjudgmental. "Do you use it?"

"I keep a small amount. Pain from old sports injuries occasionally keeps me awake. RSO helps."

"How often does that happen?"

"Maybe four, five times a year."

"I had several patients who smoked pot and a few who used medical marijuana," Kathryn said, "but I've never heard of RSO."

"It's not common knowledge, which is a shame because the oil is so effective especially against some cancers such as melanoma. Kris takes it in capsule form—just an odorless drop. I feel pretty safe in making my run."

"What happens if you get caught?"

"I'm banking on my white hairs . . . ."

"I don't know if you have enough . . . ."

". . . to get me some leniency as well as the relatively small amount I'd be carrying. Worst case, I suppose, my car gets confiscated, I pay a fine, and maybe go to prison for a while . . . where I could teach writing to the inmates."

"You'd risk all that?"

"If the odds were greater than miniscule, I wouldn't do it. But people travel all over with cannabis products. I've made the run twice, and it feels safe. Kris is still working, and the trip would be hard for her physically, so I do it." Ellie sighed. "So, Kathryn, that's the story. I'd love to take you along, but if you want to reconsider, I understand."

Kathryn remained still, contemplating this turn of events. "This is a lot to process," she said at last.

"You don't have to give me an answer now."

Kathryn rose from her seat and began to pace the room, touching the bookshelves. Those shelves must hold a hundred stories of adventure and bravery, love and loss—just like Ellie's confession. At the far side, she paused to spin the large floor globe until the outline of North America turned into view. She had been excited about this trip. Why? With her finger, she traced a route from Minnesota to California. She wanted to escape the confines of her life, to roll across the countryside, over plains and mountains, to breathe a different air. She wanted an adventure with Ellie.

As she gave the globe another twirl, she thought of Magellan and Cook and Old World sailors. "Circumnavigation," she said, suddenly unsure if she had spoken aloud.

"What?" Ellie said, rising to join Kathryn.

"Circumnavigation. It's a favorite word of mine. Voyages of discovery in a few syllables."

"It's a great one," Ellie said, letting her fingers brush the oceans and continents as they rotated past, "but it's a little farther than I was planning to go."

Kathryn laughed. "Do you have a favorite word?"

Ellie paused. "Ninnyhammer."

The women hooted.

"Saying it always makes me laugh. It means silly ass. Which is what I feel like after hearing your sophisticated word!"

As their laughter died down, Kathryn watched Ellie, standing on the other side of the world awaiting a decision, her dark eyes tracking her. Ellie's expression of patience and curiosity signaled an acceptance, no matter the answer. But Kathryn knew her response would set the course of their friendship. A negative reply would douse the sparks; an affirmative one would inflame them.

Cannabis? The country was awash in it. The risks were small. Love—now there's a real risk.

Kathryn knew she should say *Let me think about it*. Instead, she smiled. "Yes, I'll go."

"Are you sure?"

"I am."

"Well, I'm delighted," Ellie placed her palms on the globe as it came to a stop.

The women held each other's gaze: they were committing themselves to the trip. And, they tacitly understood, to much more.

CHAPTER 12

*T*he following Tuesday, Kathryn rang Ellie's doorbell at precisely five-thirty.

When Ellie answered, Kathryn thrust the same vase filled with daisies at her. She smiled. "Keep the vase."

"You're downsizing." Ellie laughed. "Come on in. Kris and Sandy will be here soon. They're anxious to meet you." She carried the flowers through to the dining room and placed them on the table.

"Likewise." Kathryn gave Ellie the once over. "I like your outfit. That black top looks even better than in the store."

"Thanks," Ellie said sheepishly.

"Something smells good," Kathryn said as she walked into the kitchen. The aroma of curry and cardamom enveloped her.

"It's lamb vindaloo, my special recipe." Ellie poured a big bowl-ful of chopped vegetables coated in olive oil and herbs onto a baking tray covered with parchment paper. "Could you open the oven door for me, please?"

Kathryn did as requested.

Ellie slid in the tray and set the timer.

"Do you have time to show me the rest of your house?" Kathryn asked. "I love seeing older homes, especially after looking at so many sterile condos."

Ellie wiped her hands on the kitchen towel. "Sure. Come this way."

As they ascended the stairs, Kathryn wondered what it would be like climbing these steps on the way to making love. She quickly put that thought out of her mind.

"This is my office." Ellie pointed to a small room with a roll-top desk, a computer table, a cushy chair, and floor-to-ceiling shelving crammed with books.

Kathryn paused at the doorway. "Do you mind?" she asked.

"Not at all."

Kathryn flipped on the light, revealing the womb of words that daily surrounded Ellie. She scanned a few titles, an eclectic assortment of books, novels, poetry, and nonfiction, hardcover and paperback.

"I see how you'll have a challenge downsizing."

"Yes, books. I love them all."

"How many of these would you say you've read?"

"All the way through—maybe sixty-five percent."

"Impressive!"

Ellie continued down the hall. "Here's the guest bedroom. I use it as a staging area for my trips."

Kathryn noticed a pair of black socks sitting at the bottom of the otherwise empty bed. "I see you've started packing."

Ellie laughed. "I haven't gotten very far, have I?"

"It's a start."

"The bathroom," Ellie said motioning toward the small room as they walked past, "and here's the master bedroom."

They walked into a large, neat room with a queen bed, a matching oak bureau, and a couple of upholstered chairs. The hunter green walls and the cream-colored woodwork gave the room a touch of classy British tranquility. Small Persian rugs were scattered on the shiny maple floor.

"Look," Ellie said, opening a closet door. "My new clothes, with space between each piece."

"Very impressive."

"You deserve the credit."

As they turned to leave the room, Kathryn paused to consider the bed, the darkly patterned comforter covering all the history lying underneath. This is where Mary had been so ill. How many hours had Ellie waited on her, nursed her, cried with her, rejoiced at any good news or glimmer of hope? Right here. How many sleepless nights, dashes to the bathroom, and trips to empty a basin? How had the last morning been when Mary, left alone, had departed?

"Do you ever feel Mary's presence here?" Kathryn asked.

"Except for right after her death, no. I thought I would, but she's flown away. The silence was disappointing at first, but I've accepted it. She's on her own journey now."

"Were Kris and Sandy part of your support group at Mary's death?"

"Yes, they were the first to arrive. They were angels. They took away the meds and changed the sheets. A few more intimate friends came, and we washed Mary's body with lavender water and dressed her. It was a sacred ritual."

"One women have performed for millennia."

"Until the funeral directors took over."

"It's kind of like midwifery," Kathryn said as they turned from the room. "Women were doing it forever until the medical industry claimed childbirth as their territory.

"And in both areas, women are stepping back and reclaiming our power." Ellie switched off the light. "I love how we tended to her. Having her body here at home was such a comfort. I know it's not for everyone, but it helped immensely with my grieving."

Back downstairs, Kathryn set the table under Ellie's direction, while Ellie turned the vegetables roasting in the oven. Soon Sandy and Kris appeared at the door bearing homemade bread and a bottle of pinot noir.

After introductions and the pouring of wine and water, the four settled around the dining room table and began to pass the serving bowls.

"Ellie says you're a retired psychotherapist," Kris said to Kathryn, who sat across from her.

"Yes, I am."

"Did you have a specialty?"

"No, I was in a neighborhood wellness clinic. I saw any referral. I was the only therapist who could prescribe meds, though, so I was assigned the cases that on the surface called for them."

"Does that mean you weren't quick with the prescription pad?"

Kathryn ladled tender lamb chunks and rich gravy on her plate and passed the bowl to Ellie. "Yes. I like to look for the underlying cause, not just medicate the symptoms."

"Did you deal a lot with depression?"

"Depression, troubled marriages. Abuse, incest, self-esteem."

"PTSD? Grief?"

"Yes, and yes."

"Any couples counseling?" Sandy chimed in. "We may need it after tonight."

Everyone laughed, except Kris. "I'm just asking," she said.

"I appreciate your interest," Kathryn replied and winked at Ellie.

"Are you packed yet, Kathryn?" Sandy asked.

"No. I'll start tomorrow."

"I checked Intellicast, El," Kris said. "You might hit some snow in the Sierras.

Kathryn shot Ellie an amused sideways glance. *El.*

"I haven't checked the forecasts yet. Well, if we can't make it over Donner Pass, we'll just wait out the storm."

"You don't have chains, do you?" Sandy asked.

"No, and I don't intend to buy any. If it's bad enough to use chains, I'm—we're—staying put. I don't want to risk an accident, especially when there's no hurry. I'll get to Trisha's when I get there."

"I'm glad you mentioned the weather, Kris," Kathryn said. "I wasn't planning to take any winter clothes along, but it sounds as though a heavy jacket would be good."

"Nothing too heavy," Ellie said. "I'm taking layers. Sacramento can be pretty hot in April, as you probably know since your daughter lives there."

"How many children do you have, Kathryn?" Kris asked.

"Two. A daughter and a son. Plus four grandchildren."

As the conversation drifted into the family backgrounds of the four women, Kathryn caught herself gazing at Ellie's mouth, at the finely curved lips of a delicate pink shade she could not name. And then sliding lower. She glanced at Kris across the table.

Kris stared back through narrowed eyes.

Busted. She gave Kris a lopsided, guilty smile.

"What if you two don't get along?" Kris asked abruptly, breaking away from the stare. "It's a long drive."

"We can take turns sitting in the back seat," Ellie said.

"If it gets too bad," Kathryn said, "there are several airports between here and California. If Ellie can't stand me, she can drop me off anywhere."

"I wouldn't worry," Sandy said. "Ellie has a high tolerance level. She puts up with us."

"Speaking of tolerance levels," Kathryn said, "I'd like to hear your story about cannabis oil, Kris. How is it working for you?"

Kris shared her experience with Lyme disease and her continuing use of cannabis for arthritis. "I cut way back after my Lyme cleared up. I take only one RSO at night, and in the morning I'm clear-headed. I use CBD during the day for pain relief."

Kathryn asked general and pointed questions with such skill and in such a curious, non-judgmental tone, that when she asked, "Are you concerned about developing a dependency?" Kris, who was by nature defensive and quick to take offense, responded openly.

"No. When we traveled to Europe last fall, I left the RSO behind. I didn't have any withdrawal symptoms, but my arthritis pain and insomnia intensified. Sandy and I made a side trip to Amsterdam for some marijuana and CBD, but it wasn't as effective as what Trisha provides."

"How did you determine the correct dosage?

"I experimented until I got the minimum level I need. Trisha can adjust the strength in the capsules, too. Really, I owe her my life. With Lyme, I thought I'd have to go on disability—I could hardly walk, and I was so fatigued I couldn't even drive to work. Luckily, I have a very supportive manager. I could work at home—from my bed, usually."

"What is it that you do?"

"I work at the University of Minnesota Press. I'm an editor."

"And you, Sandy?"

"I'm an administrator in the Minneapolis City Planning Office."

"Well, an accomplished crew around this table," Kathryn's gaze swept the three companions and came to rest on Kris. "That's an amazing story."

"The laws around cannabis are so stupid. I wish Minnesota would get on board."

"They'll change eventually," Sandy said. "They are everywhere else."

"Is medical marijuana something you can prescribe, Kathryn?" Ellie asked.

"No. I'm not certified to do that."

"How do you feel about carrying an illegal drug across several states?" Kris asked.

"A little nervous, but a bit of danger heightens the excitement of the trip."

They passed around the dishes once again for second helpings and Sandy refilled the wine glasses. Kathryn held a hand over her glass. "That's a nice wine, Sandy, but I'm going to say no to another glass. One is the limit when I drive."

"More for me!" Sandy cried.

"How did you two meet?" Kathryn asked. The question was already out of her mouth when she remembered Kris had once lived here with Ellie and had left her.

"We played softball on an all-lesbian team," Ellie said, "and Kris, the pitcher, decided that a catcher—namely Sandy—was a better fit than I was on second base."

"It was all the time we spent looking at each other," Sandy said.

"Wasn't that awkward, playing together after the breakup?" Kathryn asked.

"Oh, sure, especially for me," Ellie said. She shrugged. "There were a few tears . . . ."

"More than a few," Sandy interjected.

"... a few gushers," Ellie said, "but we dealt with it."

"How did the rest of the team deal with it?" Kathryn asked.

The three women looked at each other dumbfounded. "We don't know," Kris said at last. "I guess okay. We won the league championship that year."

"Is that common on all-lesbian teams, that type of re-partnering?"

"It happens. Or I suppose we should speak just for our generation," Kris said. "I don't know what kids are doing nowadays. Things seem much more fluid with them."

"Boy, it would make a great study for a sociology student," Kathryn said.

"It may be too late," Ellie said. "I don't know if there are even any lesbian teams anymore. The Lesbian Nation is fading like Avalon."

"I don't know what that means," Kathryn said.

As the three old friends cleared the table and cleaned up, they described the culture of the Seventies and Eighties—the women's music, the coffeehouses and concerts, the lesbian magazines and novels, the women's bookstores, the fine art of a rising Amazon Nation.

"And by Amazon," Kris smirked, "we mean the tribe of women warriors, not the online retailer."

"At least the travel business is going strong," Sandy said.

Seeing Kathryn's puzzlement, Ellie said, "A couple of travel companies cater to lesbians. Olivia is the biggest."

"Yeah," Sandy said, "they rent whole resorts—like Club Med—and whole cruise ships just for lesbians."

"Those were the cruises you were on, Ellie?"

"Yes."

"There's nothing like being surrounded by two thousand dykes." Sandy smiled.

"Isn't that a pejorative?" Kathryn asked carefully.

"No, we've reclaimed the word," Kris said.

"Well," Kathryn said, looking around at the clean kitchen, "this has all been very illuminating, but I need to run. I'm stopping by my son's place to pick up a few things for the trip."

"Where does he live?" Ellie asked quietly.

"Not too far from my house. I want to get there before they go to bed."

"Sorry you have to go," Kris said. "I've enjoyed meeting you."

Kathryn gave her a high wattage smile. "Likewise, Kris. And Sandy. It's been really nice meeting the two of you. I appreciate all you shared."

Ellie walked Kathryn to the door.

"Thanks, Ellie, I had a nice time," Kathryn said. "I really like your friends."

"I can tell they like you, too. Let's talk tomorrow or Friday about final arrangements for the trip. If you still want to go."

"Of course, I do."

They hugged, a full body press, and then peeled away slowly, as though their bodies had become magnetized.

"Goodnight, *El*," Kathryn said softly, teasingly.

"'Night, *Kay*." Ellie laughed.

"Kay and El," Kathryn said. "Sounds like a railroad." She gave Ellie a broad smile, pecked her on the cheek, and was gone.

CHAPTER 13

*W*hen Ellie returned from the doorway, she found Sandy and Kris sitting in the living room, all wine glasses refilled.

"My god," said Kris, "is she ever impressive. Totally crush-worthy."

"Pretty cool, huh?" Ellie said.

"She's intelligent, good-looking, and rich. Total trifecta. You hit the jack pot, kiddo," Sandy said.

"Well, it's too early for the bells and confetti."

"I hope we didn't scare her off," Kris said.

"She was pretty big-eyed at the end, with all our talk about the Lesbian Nation." Ellie reached for her wine but did not drink. A spot of depression was spreading as she reflected on Kathryn's visit. They had come on too strong, like an exclusive club, members speaking their private lingo.

"I see a potential problem," Kris said.

"You would." Sandy took a healthy sip.

"I know what you're going to say," Ellie said, "but say it."

"There's a big cultural difference," Kris said. "You've been a lesbian your entire life. Kathryn has always been straight. She doesn't have one iota of a lesbian sensibility."

"You're forgetting," Ellie said, "people come out at every age. They make it work. Besides, lesbians live in the mainstream world and function quite well. I can meet Kathryn where she lives, and she can move a little in my direction."

"Her world is the country club, not the dug out."

"You're being classist, Kris," Ellie said.

"I'm being realistic. I think the class difference is going to bite you one way or another. Listen, I really, really like her. I can see why you're gaga over her. I'm just cautioning you about a potential problem. How is she going to explain you to her hoity-toity suburban friends?"

"Well, Mary came from a family with money, too. It was never a problem with her."

"Mary was salt of the earth," Kris said. "Kathryn is high class."

Ellie opened her mouth to reply but nothing came out. What Kris said was true.

"Besides, El, you're idealizing your relationship with Mary."

"Ladies, it's getting warm in here," Sandy said with her referee voice.

"As I recall, you and Mary were at loggerheads over buying the Lexus. Mary wanted comfort and luxury. You wanted another Subaru dyke-mobile."

"I don't see how that . . . ."

"Thank god, you relented. It gave her so much pleasure—she'd always wanted one," Kris said.

"She did?" Ellie had a tick of shock at hearing this new detail. How could she have been so oblivious?

"And you know what? I think it thrilled her even more to know she was leaving you with that car. You would never buy it for yourself. You're too frugal. But you love it, don't you?"

"Yes," Ellie said, sheepishly.

"Yeah, I noticed you didn't run right out and trade it in for an Outback."

"Okay, okay."

"Ellie, let's not argue. I'm in your corner."

"I know you are. But every relationship has issues, Kris. When they arise, we'll deal with them." Ellie stopped and smiled ruefully, her confidence wavering. "God, listen to me. This is not a done deal."

"Are you kidding?" Kris said. "Do you see the way she looks at you? Up and down and sideways. She's smitten."

"As she should be," Sandy said. "Look at you all dressed up."

"Yeah," Kris said. "You were wearing new clothes the other day, too. What gives?"

Ellie's cheeks grew warm. "Kathryn took me shopping."

"Now she's dressing you!" Kris screamed. "Gaaaah!"

An hour later, just as Ellie was about to slip into bed, her phone pinged. A text from Kathryn:

Did I pass inspection?

Ellie whooped in relief. Kathryn was being a good sport about Kris and Sandy's reconnaissance. She hadn't been scared off. She was made of stronger stuff than that, no doubt, and her text confirmed it.

Flying colors.

I like your friends.

Ellie smiled at the screen. *So do I.*

They care about you very much.

I'm lucky.

So am I, El. Sleep well.

Grinning, Ellie turned off the phone and then the light.

Kathryn had been in this bedroom! The thought excited and terrified her. She understood the excitement—the thrill of discovery, of surging hormones, of infatuation, of a shot at being loved again. And the terror? Of being rejected, humiliated, and of forgetting about or dishonoring Mary.

And what was Kathryn thinking at this moment? Ellie wondered. She would never share Ellie's perspective of being lesbian, not after sixty-eight years as a heterosexual. Could Kathryn wade far enough into Ellie's life to be her partner? Cultural gaps could be bridged. It happened all the time and with chasms far wider than what lay between Kathryn and her.

The road to California, stretching before them like a river of stars, would surely reveal the answers.

PART TWO

CHAPTER 14

*A*pril, the spanner of seasons, unfolded in character. The last winds of winter were reluctant to release their chilly fingers, and the warm breezes from the south, tasting of summer, pouted on and off stage. It was the month of opening, of newness, of change, the month sacred to the goddess Venus, the embodiment of love and sexuality. It was the month in which Ellie and Kathryn were to start their journey to California.

The Thursday morning before their departure, Kathryn stopped by Ellie's home before a grocery run at the local co-op. There was nothing in particular she wanted to do other than see Ellie again and to quell any misgivings about driving with her to the edge of the continent.

The unusually warm day was perfect for an early walk along Minnehaha Creek, the twenty-two-mile tributary flowing eastward through the southern part of the metropolis. They strolled the two blocks from Ellie's home then took the steps down to the pathway along the creek. The trees were bare, the snow all gone, and the creek of Longfellow fame was burbling along briskly. They paused to decide whether to head east or west.

A risky thought popped into Ellie's mind: What better place for a first kiss than under the Lyndale Bridge with the creek splashing alongside? It would be so romantic. She steered Kathryn in that direction, her heart thrumming.

"What's that?" Kathryn said as they approached the bridge. She pointed to a large, dark lump on the concrete and sandstone embankment. A bike lay next to it.

"We'd better check it out," Ellie replied, her idea of a kiss flittering away.

It was a sleeping bag with someone curled inside. A blond tangle of hair poked out from under a watchman's beanie.

The women exchanged a look. "This can't be good," Ellie whispered.

Kathryn shook her head and approached the figure "Are you okay?" she asked, stooping over, hands on her knees.

A teenage boy stirred and blinked at her. "Whaaa?"

"Are you okay?" Kathryn repeated. Her voice had a slight ring as it bounced off the underside of the bridge.

"Yeah."

"Do you need help?"

"I'm okay."

"Did you spend the night here?"

"Yeah." The boy roused and propped himself up on an elbow, blinking rapidly at the light, which accentuated his fine bone structure and full lips. His cheeks were circles of dull red, and his dirt-smudged jaw had traces of adolescent facial hair.

"What happened?"

"I got kicked out."

"From your home?" Ellie asked, squatting next to him. The creek slapped loudly as it narrowed into the confining tunnel.

"Yeah."

Ellie wanted to ask why but refrained.

"Do you have someplace to go?" Kathryn said. "A friend's house? A relative?"

The boy's shoulders lifted and dropped again.

"My name's Kathryn. What's yours?"

"Shawn."

"Nice to meet you, Shawn. Now, let's be realistic. You can't stay here. It's not safe and someone is going to report you to the police. I know of a place where you could live for a while. If I arrange it, will you go?"

Another shrug.

"Do you have a phone?" Ellie asked.

A nod.

Kathryn gave Ellie an of-course-he-has-a-phone look and stood up. "Okay. Give me a minute." She stepped out of the tunnel to make a call.

"Hi, Shawn. My name is Ellie. How old are you?"

"Seventeen."

"Are you in school?"

"No, I quit."

"I'm sorry to hear that."

Another shrug.

"Shawn," Kathryn said, returning, "I need your phone number so my friend can text you."

"Who's your friend?" he asked, his eyes narrowing.

"Judith. She's on the board of a safe place for homeless teens."

He gave her his number.

Kathryn turned away once again and continued her conversation for a few more moments.

Ellie extracted an energy bar from her jacket pocket and held it out. Shawn snatched it and tore off the wrapper.

Kathryn rejoined them a few minutes later. "How are you feeling?"

"Sore."

"I'm not surprised. This is a cold, hard place to sleep." She handed him a business card with something written on the back. "This is the name, address and phone number of the place where you need to go. Judith is arranging a space for you. If I call an Uber, will you get in the car and go there?"

Shawn examined the card.

"It'll be a lot more comfortable than another night here . . . or in police custody," Ellie said, hoping the shelter would have room for him.

"What about my bike?" The boy started to emerge from his bag.

"Uber can take that, too," Kathryn said. "Okay, then, we're in business." She worked the app on her phone for a few moments. "Northwest corner of the intersection of Lyndale and Minnehaha Parkway, right?" she verified with Ellie.

Shawn had his bag rolled up by now and had finished his bar. A heavy truck rattled overhead on the bridge.

"Your ride will be here in five minutes. Let's go up to the street level and wait." Kathryn hung back while Ellie led the boy up the stairs to the street carrying his sleeping bag. The bike rested on his narrow shoulders. She observed the boy's walk, his gait, and his handling of the stairs as he trudged upwards.

As they waited for Uber, Kathryn said, "Do you live around here?"

"A few miles away."

"Do you want me to call your parents? I'm sure they're worried."

"No fucking way."

"Okay." Kathryn said. "Shawn, I admire your resilience. You made it through a freezing night under a bridge. You're a survivor. You'll get through this rough patch."

"Yeah." Shawn looked at Kathryn from under his long eyelashes, his brown eyes a blur of confusion and pride.

"Do you have money?" Ellie asked.

"A little."

Ellie pulled a couple of twenties out of her jeans and handed them to the boy. "Here."

When the Uber van pulled up, the driver got out, put the bike in the back, and hopped in ready to go. Kathryn leaned into the driver's window as Shawn slid into the back seat. She handed the driver a five-note tip and said, "Get him where he's going safe and sound." And off they went.

"Very smoothly done, Kathryn," Ellie said, stepping back to the curb. "I'm impressed."

"Well, thanks. I've had many a troubled teen come into my office, and Judith's organization has been a lifeline for many of them." Kathryn turned back toward the steps. "Come on, let's go back down and get our walk in."

The path was surprisingly dry for early spring as the women strolled side-by-side this time going west. The morning sun beamed lazily through the lattice of bare cottonwood branches overhead. The traffic noises receded as they moved away from the intersection.

"These are huge trees," Kathryn said, patting a cottonwood as they passed by.

"Minnesota sequoias," Ellie joked. "It would take three of us to get our arms around it."

"I don't suppose we'll be near any sequoias on our drive, will we?"

"No, I don't think so. But I don't mind making a side trip. I'm always up for an adventure."

They walked awhile in silence before Kathryn said, "Shawn seems like a good kid. He wasn't on drugs as far as I could tell. Just a lost soul."

"Where did you send him?"

"To a center for homeless youth called Justin's House. Judith is on the board of directors. She's a bulldog—a retired lawyer—so he'll have an ally in his corner." Kathryn laughed softly. "This is ironic. Judith has been nudging me to volunteer at Justin's now that I'm retired, but I'm not sure I want to do it. And here I go and send another teen to her."

"Why don't you want to volunteer?"

"My gut feeling is not to do it—I don't know why. Maybe because I'm enjoying my freedom right now. I don't feel any need to rush into that type of commitment."

"Do you think Justin's will have a place for Shawn?"

"I don't know. Shelters are often full. They have a great staff, though. They'll figure out what to do." Kathryn looked skyward and took a deep breath. "I suspect his family kicked him out because he's gay."

"I had that thought, too."

On a bridge over the rushing creek, they paused to lean on the flat railing of treated lumber, their shoulders nearly touching. The water tumbled over rocks as though joyous to be released from the ice.

"He could be like any number of kids who have passed through my classroom," Ellie said. "All they need is a break."

"And the kindness of matrons."

Ellie laughed and stepped once again to Kathryn's side as they made their way off the bridge. She resisted the urge to put her arm through Kathryn's. The encounter with Shawn had drained her boldness. "Was it okay that I gave him a little money? I don't do that if I think it's going to be used for alcohol or drugs."

"I'm sure it's fine." Kathryn smiled at Ellie. "We did good, girlfriend."

Ellie shifted her eyes quickly to Kathryn. Girlfriend? But it was said without charge, an affectionate term women in Kathryn's realm used with each other, as passionless as the leaves under their feet, yet as fertile.

Kathryn linked her arm with Ellie's, elbow to elbow and pulled her close as they continued down the path. "Ellie," she said, "do you believe in fate?"

"To a certain extent, yes," Ellie said, aware of the pressure on her arm.

"I believe things happen for a purpose. What seems like a disaster can be the springboard for something wonderful, although it's often hard to believe so at the time."

"Uh-huh."

"Look at Shawn. Last night may have been the worst night of his life, but it led him here, to us, and I had just the connection he needs. His life could be totally turned around."

"So, the purpose of our meeting at Starbucks was so we could be here in this spot today to help him?"

"I hope that's not the only purpose of our meeting." Kathryn smiled.

"But then would you say the purpose of your divorce was to lead you to your meeting with Amy at Starbucks so you could look for condos and thus meet me?"

Kathryn laughed, a small, rich sound that rang out like pure happiness. "That does seem to trivialize everything, doesn't it?"

Ellie remained silent.

"Actually, I prefer to think that it reveals the amazing threads that weave our lives. Now Shawn is woven into both of our tapestries, a small episode with a blond-haired boy."

"So, it was pre-destination?"

"I prefer to think that life unfolds in a fluid way, that we have free will."

"Yet some things are fated?"

"Like our meeting at Starbucks? I think," Kathryn said, "the Universe smiled on us that day. I'm very glad to have met you, Ellie Belmont."

"Likewise," Ellie said, putting her free hand on Kathryn's arm and keeping it there. "Likewise."

CHAPTER 15

$\mathcal{T}$he next day found Ellie in a quandary. She traveled simply, and a trip usually didn't require much preparation. Having made this California run twice before, she expected her packing to go quickly, even with the choices presented by her new wardrobe. But when she and Kathryn confirmed they would share a hotel room—and was there any question it would be otherwise—packing became more complicated. Most of her sleeveless undershirts were either discolored, holey, or stretched into formless blobs. The elastic in her underpants had worn through the cotton unevenly, making the waistbands look like speckled swamp asps. None of this would do.

Most perplexing, though, was the matter of nightwear. Usually Ellie slept in her undies with an old T-shirt thrown on top, and in the cold of winter, she added her pilled sweatpants. Should she buy pajamas? But if things turned out as she hoped, she wouldn't need them. But how far into the trip would they no longer be needed? And there was always the chance things would never get that far—more than one straight woman had flirted with Ellie in her youth, only to flee when things turned serious.

Oh, and what about her socks? Her Smart-Wool socks with the heels worn to near transparency? Cotton socks with holes where her big toes saw light they should not see?

All this would require another foray into the mall's maw of commercialism and exploitation. Was love worth it? Of course, it was.

But this led to the existential question of one's authenticity. As Ellie pondered the matter over a hot chocolate, she wondered if, by buying a new wardrobe and new underwear, new socks, and new pajamas to please Kathryn, she was being untrue to herself. She had always dressed for function and comfort. She was not a slob, only inattentive. But now she was seeing herself through Kathryn's discerning blue eyes, and the picture was not pretty. She had let herself go since Mary's death.

"You know," Kris said, sitting at Ellie's kitchen table, "I just want to slap you silly. But you're silly enough as it is."

"I know. I feel like a teenager."

"Okay, here's the deal. You're in the throes of infatuation. Enjoy it while you can. It won't last forever.

"I know."

"And don't wallow in your angst—what's wrong with perking up your wardrobe? Don't you feel better?"

"Yes."

"Well, there you go. You're not selling out to the fashion industry—believe me—you are just adding a bit of beauty and joy to the world."

"But who defines beauty?"

Kris leveled an impatient look at Ellie. "Shelley and Keats. Go read them."

"Okay, okay."

"As for the pajamas, here's my advice: Forget them. Do you still have those batik pants you bought at MichFest?"

Ellie nodded.

"Are they in good shape?"

"Very."

"Okay, take them as your PJ bottoms. Wear a nice T-shirt for your top. Do you have a white one that's passable?"

"My Athena one."

"From your Greece trip with Mary?"

Ellie nodded.

"That's a big NO. What else do you have?"

"Trisha gave me one last year."

"Does it say anything about marijuana on it, like 'Cannabis Cooks'?"

"I'm not totally out of it, you know. What about a bathrobe?

"No. Too *Carol.*" Kris paused, ticking through a list in her mind. "Okay, you're set with nightwear. Now, for the rest of it, don't go to the mall. Make a beeline to Target, go directly to lingerie, and get what you need. Pay for it and leave immediately. You don't need to be in the store more than fifteen minutes. I promise."

Ellie put both hands on the table. "All right. I have a mission and I accept it."

"And for your other mission," Kris said, reaching into her canvas messenger bag, "here's the money." She slid the fat, legal-sized envelope across the table.

Ellie let it rest between them. "Thanks."

Kris put her slightly deformed hand over Ellie's. "No, thank *you*, you extraordinary human being. Now be careful."

Kathryn paced in the master bedroom of her home. Her Travelpro suitcase lay open on the padded chest at the foot of the bed. She knew she was overdoing the clothes—she did not need ten outfits—but she couldn't make up her mind. Clothing was not the only challenge.

She went to the French doors opening to the balcony. The table and chairs had on their red and white striped winter covers. When she returned from the trip, it would be time to take them off, wash the furniture, and enjoy a morning cappuccino, sitting there in her robe. Who would that person be? Who was she becoming?

The reddish buds on the backyard maple tree were swollen with life. Kathryn could relate to that sensation. After realizing her feelings for Ellie, she had been in an almost perpetual state of arousal. She opened the doors and stepped outside into the refreshingly chilly westerly wind. She felt deliciously off-balance, poised for a burst of growth like those expectant buds about to reveal nascent leaves. A tree self-actualizing. Smiling, she turned back into the house.

As she stepped across the threshold, the phone rang.

"Hi, there," Ellie said, her voice soft and thrilling. "How's it going? Finished packing?"

"Almost."

They chatted for a bit regarding the pros and cons of miscellany to take on a road trip: binoculars, headphones, ear plugs, flashlights, sunscreen, slippers, and a hundred other items to weigh in the decision.

"The big decision right now is what food to take," Ellie said. "Usually I fix a couple of wraps and a batch of egg salad for lunches. Dinners I eat out. Snacks are usually a few energy bars, nuts, apples."

"Sounds good. What can I bring?"

"Nothing. I've got it covered. The hotels usually have a breakfast buffet. Are Best Westerns still okay with you? We could step it up, if you'd like."

"No, I'm fine with your usual places, and it saves us from having to search for new ones."

As they discussed their plans, Kathryn thought how different this trip already was from the ones she and Joe took. With Joe, she had had to do all the preparation—determining where to go and when. Even if a travel agency handled reservations, she still had to deal with a myriad of details—flight schedules, tour extensions, mail and phone service, and all the other chores required to shut a house for weeks. All the packing fell to her, too. Joe's concept of travel was to have someone hand him his plane ticket. With Ellie, the discussion of plans, the partnership and ownership of the trip, was eye-opening.

Later, when Kathryn closed the lid to the suitcase with a satisfying click, she lay back on the bed, looking at the ceiling, the expanse of the room, its paintings. She liked it. She imagined Ellie there beside her, in this room, in this bed she had shared for so many years with her husband. What would that be like? Pretty nice, she decided. Maybe as good as some of the lesbian romances she had downloaded to her Kindle.

It was interesting that as a therapist, she had always promoted communication between people. No matter what the relationship—parent to child, spouse to spouse, worker to boss—clear communication was essential to a well-functioning relationship. She and Ellie communicated extremely well, she thought, except for the one topic simmering at the core of their friendship: their sexual attraction. Would she counsel one of her clients to get the matter out in the open before they set off across half a continent? Of course, she would.

Then why couldn't she do it herself?

Perhaps it made the razor's edge sharper. The unacknowledged desires fed the intensity of them. If they talked about it now, before they left, a little of the thrill would be shaved off. They still had the discovery to make and confess, and the danger—though unlikely—of the attraction not being mutual. She might be reading Ellie entirely wrong. She thought not.

In fact, she had abandoned a core principle of telling the truth. She was not disclosing what she felt and what she wanted: Ellie right here in bed with her.

CHAPTER 16

"Well, aren't you a symphony of color!" Kathryn exclaimed when Ellie came through the side door precisely at eight o'clock Sunday morning. "All decked out in purple and red and black. You look very nice."

Ellie grinned sheepishly. "Thanks. It's a great top."

"No leggings?"

They were the one item of ambivalence in Ellie's new wardrobe. She approached them cautiously as a puppy might a new squeeze toy, a little intrigued, a little intimidated.

"They are terribly comfortable, but I need pockets. Ergo, jeans."

"All right, then." Kathryn motioned to a pile by the door. "I'm all set. Shall we load the car?"

The women spent the next few minutes rearranging the trunk of Ellie's light blue hybrid Lexus. Kathryn's suitcase and duffel bag fit snuggly next to a cooler and thermal bag covered with a fleece blanket for extra insulation. Ellie's two bags were pushed toward the back and nearer at hand a box of dry food: granola to supplement the hotel breakfasts, energy bars, potato chips, and several bottles of water for emergency hydration in case of a breakdown. Tote bags with books, e-readers, snacks, and other items needed for easy retrieval went into the back seat.

"We're off!" said Ellie, throwing the car into reverse and easing down the driveway. "Everything's loaded into the GPS," she said, motioning toward the on-board screen, "but we don't need to turn it on for a while. All we do is go south on Interstate 35, hang a right at Omaha and head straight for California."

"Easy-peasy." Kathryn smiled. She adjusted the passenger seat and turned on its warmer. She fished a water bottle out of her tote bag and put it in the cup holder beside the steel container with a green flexible straw. "Dirty chai latte?"

"On ice. I stopped at Starbucks on my way to your place." Ellie paused. "I always start a day of travel with a little . . . I don't know . . . intention, I guess you'd call it. Do you mind?"

Kathryn smiled with curiosity. "No, go ahead."

"I call upon the Universe to protect this car and all who are in it and all we meet on our journey today. We will be invisible to all law enforcement, who will have their attention directed elsewhere. Thank you for your guiding presence."

"Interesting," Kathryn said. "Does it help?"

"I believe it does."

"How did you come up with it?"

"Several years ago, Mary and I drove down to the Yucatán. The first two days inside Mexico we were stopped by cops for no reason other than to extort money. We realized we'd be out of cash before reaching Mérida. So, Mary devised this little invocation, and we were never stopped again."

"You two drove to the Yucatán? Good lord! Why didn't you just fly down and rent a car?"

"We wanted to see a number of sights along the way. Mary was in remission and had pretty much recovered her strength from chemo and radiation. I was on sabbatical, so a two-month trip was no problem. It was *carpe diem* all the way."

"You were both feeling the fingers of mortality rather vividly, I suppose."

"Exactly." Ellie took a sip of her drink. "We knew it might be the only chance we'd have to make the trip, and Mary had been talking about it for years."

"Are you glad you did it?"

"Definitely. It was harder on Mary than she let on, but we had a lot of fun. Our visit to Palenque made the whole trip worthwhile. The Mayan palaces surrounded by jungle, the early morning mists, the whole spirit of the place. It was magical. Have you been there?"

"No. I've only seen pictures."

"The other highlight—especially for Mary—was the *temazcal*, or sweat lodge, in a small village in the Yucatán. It didn't bring about a physical cure as we had hoped, but it helped Mary find peace with whatever was to come."

"Can you tell me what happened?"

"A Mayan shaman led a ceremony to connect us to the Cycle of Life from birth to death. We sat on the ground, naked, in a small domed hut. He brought red-hot lava stones inside and splashed water on them. He called the stones 'grandmothers' because they're older than any human and, since they come from the earth, they're female."

"Nice."

"It was dark—like a womb. As copal incense and steam filled the *temazcal*, the heat was intense, and I could no longer see Mary next to me. Sweat ran off me right into the earth. The shaman had us picture the Tree of Life, the roots going deep into the ground and the branches reaching toward the sky. We gave thanks to our grandparents, one-by-one. I felt such a connection to my grandmas and to the generations beyond them, for making my life possible. I was filled with their love and support . . . and I knew one day I would be with them."

"Sounds powerful."

"It was profound," Ellie said, teary-eyed. "When Mary's time neared, we both drew on the experience of the *temazcal* for strength and solace."

The miles clicked by in silence as the women went deep within themselves. The Minnesota farmland rushed by, a patchwork of black soil and stubble from crops harvested the previous autumn.

A car passed with two children jumping around in the back seat.

"I read the other day about the rise of hyper-activity in kids," Ellie said. "Did you notice it in your practice?"

"Yes. Parents often wanted a prescription for Ritalin, but I liked to look at possible causes first, such as diet and allergies. It's a disheartening area of my practice—so many things could be cleared up by diet."

"It's hard, though, to control a child's diet with sugar and processed food available at every turn."

"Exactly. And sometimes drugs *are* the answer to a chemical imbalance. But I've seen kids with ADHD change completely with probiotics, magnesium, and fish oil." Kathryn laughed softly. "My methods got to be a sore point between Joe and me. He's Western medicine to the tee. I've attended holistic medical conferences for years and have learned so much. I was never able to get Joe to go with me."

"Was that difficult?"

"We butted heads occasionally, but I respected him. He's a brilliant surgeon, and a lot of people are still alive because of him." Kathryn paused, studying Ellie's profile, taking in her quick glance. "Joe wasn't much for spirituality, but I believe that healing spirit is the essence of what I do . . . opening troubled people to a Divine or Inner Wisdom."

"That sounds like some sort of shamanic soul retrieval."

Kathryn laughed softly. "You know, in a way that's about right. Most of us need to reintegrate parts of ourselves that got lost along the way. We can't change what happened to us, but we can find a new perspective, change our story, and let our light shine."

"Instead of resenting what happened?"

"That's right. Accepting reality, saying 'yes' to what is."

"People are amazingly resilient," Ellie said. "Some of my students had extremely difficult lives, yet there they were, the first person in their family ever to go to college, to reach for their dreams."

"Sometimes, a person just needs a little help—like a caring teacher," Kathryn said, giving Ellie's arm a little bump.

Ellie threw her a quick smile. "Or a caring therapist."

Kathryn returned the smile.

"Teaching in an urban college, I had a lot of student diversity. People think of composition class as 'ugh,' but putting something on paper—describing what one feels about a topic—requires inner work. Some of the essays I received were about survival—refugees coming from war zones or adults with abusive childhoods. I felt very—content—

is that the word I want? —about giving people tools to express them-selves with."

"Maybe the word is 'purpose-filled.'"

"I'll accept that."

Kathryn reached for her water but changed her mind. "May I have a sip of your drink? I'm curious."

"Help yourself." Ellie lifted the large thermal cup from its holder.

Kathryn's lips encircled the straw and drew up a column of dirty chai latte. "Yum. I get just a touch of coffee flavor."

"I don't like coffee by itself, but I love a shot of espresso in chai and milk. The jolt of caffeine is a great way to start a day." She took the cup and placed her lips where Kathryn's had been moments before. The thrill lasted for miles.

The women stopped at an Iowa rest area next to a flat, barren field. The warm days of the previous week had drifted to the East Coast. Now cold westerly winds battered the remaining dry stalks of harvested corn and blew leaves through a cluster of forlorn picnic tables. Ellie and Kathryn zipped on their jackets before walking to the nearest table.

"Here are the fixings for our lunch," Ellie said as she pulled containers and baggies from a soft-sided thermal carrier. "Egg salad, seven-grain bread, and iceberg lettuce. Dill pickles, coleslaw, and potato chips on the side."

"Looks like a feast." Kathryn took the paper plate and plastic utensils Ellie offered.

Ellie quickly spread the egg salad across the face of two pieces of bread. She carefully positioned a crisp leaf of lettuce on the bright yellow topping, but as she lowered the crowning slice of bread, the wind snatched the let-tuce, sending it tumbling across the lawn. Ellie jumped up to retrieve it just as the zippered bag of lettuce skittered down the table.

"Oh, no!" Ellie cried. She snagged the bag, but let nature claim the grounded leaf. "Okay," she said, regaining her seat, "let's try again."

"This needs a team effort," Kathryn said. She held the lettuce in place on the two sandwiches as Ellie topped them off with bread.

"Want some chips?"

"Just a few."

Ellie tipped the bag downward. In an instant, the chips were scuttling over the grass towards the parking lot like crabs to the sea. Ellie managed a half-hearted laugh. "Thank you, Mother Nature, for saving us from temptation."

The women ate with a sandwich in one hand, the other clamped on their paper plate when the cole slaw and pickles could no longer weigh them down. Their concentration was so focused on getting the food where it was meant to go, they had no time for conversation. When finished, they quickly packed leftovers in the thermal bag, put dirty utensils in a separate bag, and tossed the plates and a few captured chips in the garbage, all as efficiently as if choreographed.

As they were leaving the restroom, Kathryn said, "My turn to drive."

Ellie plopped into the passenger seat. "What a disastrous lunch."

"Not for the liberated chips." Kathryn smiled. "And thank you, Ellie. I haven't had a picnic in ages. Certainly never one in gale force winds."

Ellie watched Kathryn adjust the seat and mirrors. She felt oddly dislocated, like a boulevard bush that finds itself transplanted to the side yard. "If you press the Set button and number three," she said, pointing to a panel on the driver's door, "you store all your seat and mirror settings so you won't have to adjust them every time we change drivers."

"Number three it is," Kathryn said. "Which number are you?"

"One."

"And two?" Kathryn asked, although she knew the answer.

"Mary's. I used it a few times after Mary died. It was a silly way I could connect with her."

"Not silly."

Ellie smiled wistfully. "I'd forgotten about it . . . until now. You're the first person to merit her own setting since then."

"I feel honored," Kathryn said. "Ready for take-off?"

Ellie adjusted the shoulder strap across her chest. She chafed a moment longer at being in the passenger seat. But she was sharing space with Kathryn and that made all the difference. "Aye, Captain. Let's go."

CHAPTER 17

"What are you smiling about?" Kathryn asked several miles down the road.

"I was smiling at the exit sign we just passed. It said *Waterloo*."

"What's the significance?"

"You must not have seen the movie *Carol*."

Kathryn shook her head. "No."

"It's one of my favorite films. It should have won an Oscar for Best Picture in my opinion, but it wasn't even nominated. Anyway, a crucial scene takes place in Waterloo."

"What's it about?"

"Two women in the early 50s. Carol is a divorcing socialite, the other, Therese, is sort of a New York bohemian working as a store clerk. They meet by chance and become lovers, but Carol loses custody of her young daughter."

"Sounds sad."

"It's hopeful. The Patricia Highsmith novel it's based on—*The Price of Salt*—was ground-breaking back in the Fifties. It's the first book where a lesbian relationship has a happy ending. I taught *The Price of Salt* for years, so I was thrilled when it was made into a movie."

"Do you own the DVD?"

"Of course. I think you'd like it." Ellie was relieved Kathryn did not question her further. She did not want to explain the Waterloo scene of lovemaking that might foreshadow their own consummation.

Ellie looked out the window at the fields where the earth lay black and moist waiting for the plow and seed to bring life to the land. The grass in the ditches was starting to green—they had come far enough south for the full hand of spring—and the world itself seemed to sparkle with joy.

"How do you set the cruise control?" Kathryn asked.

"This lever right here." She leaned over and touched the black handle. The energy between the women fairly crackled. "Just press down to set it when you're at the speed you want."

They stopped for gas at Shelby because Ellie wanted to keep the tank at least half full. She picked up the driving responsibilities once again.

"Do you mind if I take a nap?" Kathryn asked.

"Go ahead. Will it bother you if I have the radio on?"

"I'll let you know if it does."

Ellie listened to the love station, identifying with every sappy song, while Kathryn, her head dropping, slept. When she stirred and woke, she took a drink. "What did I miss?"

"The roadside grass is totally green now. We've entered spring for real."

"The sun is deliciously warm." Kathryn pulled off her sweater and tossed it in the backseat.

The Carpenter's song *We've Only Just Begun* came on the radio. "Oh," Kathryn said, "we played that at our wedding. It's bittersweet to hear it now."

"Should I turn it off?"

"No, I'd like to listen."

After the last note, Ellie turned down the radio. "How did you meet Joe?"

Kathryn settled more deeply into the leather seat. "We met at Southdale Medical Center. He was a resident. I was working in ICU. We hit it off."

"What did you like about him?"

"Oh, golly, let's see." Kathryn paused a moment, thinking. "He was intense and bright, a passionate doctor with lots of potential. We fell in love—at least I did. I came to believe he loved his work more than anything."

"He was an inattentive father?"

"Like many of his generation. Child-rearing was my responsibility. Luckily, we could afford some help at the time, like a cleaner to come in once a week. I put my career on hold for eight years. Once Nate and Jenn were both in school, I went back. Actually, it worked out quite well because it gave me time to think about where I wanted to go with my career. I decided on the mental health field, so I went back to school while the kids were still young."

"What did you and Joe do for fun?"

"We traveled a bit, oftentimes to conferences. We golfed, skied, and played some tennis. Sometimes we went to the theater, but more often than not, I'd wind up going with a girlfriend because he'd be caught up in an emergency. After the kids left home, I thought we'd travel more, but he was consumed with his work and we grew apart. I've learned in my practice that it happens quite often. Couples spend their thirties and forties building their careers and raising a family, thinking the marriage will get back on track once the kids are gone, but instead they find they have little in common except their home address. With some couples, retirement is a time for a renaissance in the relationship. Not in my case, though."

An eighteen-wheeler whooshed past the car in the passing lane, rocking the Lexus slightly. The landscape had transformed into hills rolling to the horizon.

"How did you learn of Joe's affair?"

"I was at a three-day conference in Boulder and when I returned, he had moved his clothes out. He handed me the divorce papers, apologized, cried a few guilty tears, and drove away."

"Good lord, no warning at all?"

"Oh, there were warning signs, but I never saw them except in hindsight. Total cognitive bias: I assumed our marriage was good—or good enough—so I dismissed or made excuses for the red flags. Like his disinterest in sex and unwillingness to get help. I chalked it up to his getting older, to a drop in testosterone. My mind wouldn't consider the possibility of infidelity."

"It must have been traumatic."

"It was. I had to do a lot of soul-searching to see how I had contributed to my failed marriage."

"And?"

"I tolerated more than I should have. And I think I was bored myself with the marriage. We were in a rut that had deepened over decades, but I was so content in other areas of my life—my own career, spending time with friends and the kids and grandkids, decorating the house—that a less than vibrant marriage was bearable. But I had to accept my own advice—deal with the reality. Joe was done with the marriage. He had moved on, and I needed to do the same. Maybe the most difficult thing of all was having a chunk of my social circle break off like some calving glacier."

Kathryn focused on the road's painted lines, one broken, one solid, and their car speeding toward the ever-receding horizon. The road she had traveled, the decisions she had made, seemed in some odd way to belong to someone else. "But you know, really, he left in the kindest way possible. One clean break. Not the days or weeks of sharing a bed—or maybe just the living space—when you know the person is leaving the relationship. I've seen so many couples linger. But when Joe makes up his mind, it's done. And our marriage was definitely done."

"I-80 coming up," Ellie said. She eased the car onto the interstate.

"I'd like to hear more about you, Ellie. For instance, when did you know you were a lesbian?"

"When I was three years old, I became aware that it was girls who interested me, not boys. Then, I always seemed to get crushes on my female babysitters or the cheerleader who lived next door. But it wasn't until I was fifteen and learned the term 'homosexual' that I was able to name what I was feeling."

"How precocious."

"For that time, yes. I had my first relationship at college—one of the women on my dorm floor. It was awkward and wonderful and short-lived. But then came a serious love, another English major. The grand passion bowed to career ambitions, though. She got into Stanford's Ph.D. program and I was history."

"Ouch."

"Yeah . . . but meant to be, I guess."

They rode for a while in silence, listening to the radio. When the opening chords to Bread's *I Wanna Make It with You* sounded, Ellie cried, "Oh, I love this song!" and turned up the volume. Suddenly realizing the implication of the sensuous lyrics and melody, she began to blush. Ellie glanced at Kathryn, who was sneaking a peek herself. They gave each other a tight-lipped, self-conscious smile.

"What a great song," Ellie said. It took all her self-restraint to keep from reaching for Kathryn's hand. No, from screeching off the road and kissing her there and then.

"They don't make them like they used to," Kathryn replied, her voice almost a whisper.

When the song ended, they talked of their favorite music growing up, the memories evoked by certain songs, and their current tastes. "I bet you've never heard any women's music," Ellie said.

"What do you mean? Joan Baez? Lady Gaga?"

"Ah. Look in the console, Kathryn, for *The Changer and the Changed*. You're about to hear the gold standard, the album every lesbian over fifty knows by heart."

For close to an hour, Kathryn listened closely to the soaring melodies and women-loving-women lyrics. As the last note faded, she said, "This music hits the chakras, doesn't it?"

Ellie laughed. "That's one way to put it."

"It's beautiful—the melodies, the words. It's really powerful. I'd like to hear it again."

Many songs later, they pulled into a westbound rest stop off Interstate 80 to use the restrooms and take a stretch. When they returned to the car, Ellie called up the GPS on the navigation screen, while Kathryn settled into the driver's seat. "I'm going to put in the route to the Best Western in Lincoln. Things can get a little tricky going through Omaha, and once we get to Lincoln, it's easy to drive right by the exit."

Within ten minutes of getting back on the freeway, Ellie dozed off, slumping a little in her seat, her mouth relaxed, her breathing regular.

Kathryn turned to look at her and was struck by the absurdity of being in this car, with this woman, streaking across the roadways of America's heartland listening to lesbian music. How preposterous, how improbable it all was!

Ellie's vulnerability touched Kathryn deeply. Ellie had talked casually of her life, but at so many junctures there must have been acute pain and loneliness. She, herself, had had a golden life in comparison, floating along in the mainstream. Yet her career had wound through a land where so much human misery could be seen on the sloping banks. Cruelty, abuse, dishonesty, betrayal. But resilience, compassion, and love could be found on those very same shores.

The GPS alerted her to keep to the left, but did not wake Ellie. Kathryn followed the instructions, glancing at the road guide on the screen, until she had made it through Omaha.

Ellie slept for another twenty minutes, and when she awoke, she gazed out the window, disoriented. The flat land of eastern Nebraska moved past, unfolding like a dreamscape, and she was in the passenger seat. Kathryn beamed an intimate smile her way.

"Was I snoring?"

"Just a few snorts. Don't worry. They were quite endearing."

"Oh, lord."

"It looks like we're about a half hour from landing," Kathryn said, checking the GPS. "Do we need to stop for anything before we arrive at the hotel?"

"No, let's check in, get settled, and go out for dinner."

CHAPTER 18

"*D*o you mind if I get horizontal for ten minutes?" Kathryn asked once they had hauled their gear into the large room with two queen beds and living area. She folded back the light cover, blanket and top sheet, took off her canvas sneakers, and climbed onto the mattress. "Ahhh," she murmured, stretching out fully, "this feels good."

Ellie set up a recharging station on the desk and hooked up her phone and tablet. She followed Kathryn's lead and went to the other bed, the one close to the bathroom. She lay face up, but she wanted to roll on her side, to put Kathryn in her sight. Would that be too bold? When she finally turned, she found Kathryn staring at the ceiling, hands laced together under her head.

"Kathryn," Ellie whispered, "are you awake?"

Kathryn slowly turned her head. Her blue eyes pierced Ellie. "I'm awake."

"I'd like to take a shower before going to dinner," Ellie said. "I'm feeling a little grimy."

"I know what you mean. Go ahead. I'll take one after you."

An hour later they were in a nearby Ruby Tuesday's perusing a menu. What a relief to be sitting across from Kathryn, able to look at her directly. Car conversation served sometimes for intimate conversation when one is a little embarrassed—and eye-to-eye lent itself to going deep in other ways.

They both chose the salad bar, mainly because it would be the fastest. Neither wanted to linger in a restaurant.

As they began to eat their greens, Kathryn said, "How about a little check-in, Ellie. How do you think our first day has gone?"

"It's been wonderful having you along. At first it was a little disorienting being in the passenger seat, but I got used to it." Ellie held Kathryn's gaze. "No issues on my end. What about you?"

"None. I'm enjoying myself."

"Really?" Ellie looked frankly at Kathryn. "I hope that's true. I have been a little concerned that my style of travel is a little . . . déclassé for your tastes."

Katherine tilted her head. "Can you say more?"

"I'm sure you're used to traveling in style. With me, you get homemade egg salad sandwiches and potato chips at a cold picnic table, and a hotel without chandeliers and 600-thread count sheets."

"It's fine. My surroundings are less important than the company I keep. I tend to be comfortable no matter where I am, Ellie," Kathryn said. "The hotel is fine—in fact, I'm rather impressed at the quality—and the lunch, well, I love picnics and your sandwiches." She set down her fork and leaned in. "Do you realize what a treat it is for me to have someone else take care of the meals? To plan them and make them? I can't tell you how thrilled I am to be tended to this way. Thank you."

"You're welcome," Ellie said with some surprise.

Kathryn had put on a teal tunic for dinner with swirls of gold and green. A small, decorative bow at the cleavage beckoned Ellie to reach over and pull one of the strings. She tried not to look directly at it.

"No matter how much a woman wants to be modern, it's almost impossible when it comes to food. I spent two decades providing almost every meal for the kids—there was no getting around it unless I was willing to let Joe order in pizza and Chinese take-out—his version of meal preparation."

"You sound resentful."

"I try hard not to be," Kathryn said, and then added with a smile, "especially since it's all in my past. It's a theme that runs through my practice, though. There's another grievance about men, too, of nearly equal intensity. Can you guess what it is?"

"Lack of communication?"

"That's a big one, too. But a complaint I hear often is that men come to bed stinky."

"Are you kidding?" *We both took showers, thank god!*

"It's true. Luckily, I never had to complain about Joe—he always took a shower at the hospital before he came home." Kathryn snorted playfully. "I realized later, of course, that his showers also hid his infidelity. Golly, it feels good to be able to laugh about it."

Ellie had a sudden image of Kathryn in bed with her husband. She did not like it one bit. She took a sip of mineral water. "Do you like to cook?"

"Less so than I used to, probably because I live alone. I enjoy eating well, though, and by that I mean organic and local. I lean toward vegetarian, but not totally."

"Me, too," Ellie said. "We really cleaned up our diet when Mary got sick. Less sugar and processed foods. But I'm not fervent about it, obviously, because here we sit with plates full of non-organic produce."

"Moderation in all things, including moderation?"

"Definitely."

"You mean you'll splurge once in a while?"

"Occasionally, yes. A good bottle of wine. Staying in a four-star hotel." Ellie paused. "Given what happened with Mary, I regret sometimes that we didn't live it up more—stayed at fancier places, eaten out more. She would have enjoyed it."

"But we never know, do we?"

Ellie caught herself looking at the bow and the cleavage it guarded. "Teal is your color, isn't it?" she said, trying to cover up her glance. "It makes your eyes look like pieces of sky. They're . . . lovely."

"Thank you."

The women ate a few more bites of their salad.

"It's complicated, isn't it?" Ellie said, returning to the subject. "I learned my values from my parents, I suppose. They were both high school teachers and quite frugal, although I never had a sense of deprivation. I want to be spiritual about money, yet I want to be comfortable."

"They don't have to be mutually exclusive."

"No. It's a matter of finding balance."

"As is everything," Kathryn said. "Does it bother you that I live in the burbs in a big, fancy house?"

"No. I don't envy you your lifestyle."

"How would you define my lifestyle?"

"Tasteful. Quietly elegant."

"Nice description," Kathryn said with a smile. "And I like what you've been saying. I come from a family of doctors and nurses, so I was raised quite comfortably. My mother didn't work outside the home. She always told me to be content with what I had."

"Have you been?"

"For the most part, yes." Kathryn set down her fork again. "You know, Ellie, I think with aging comes a certain honing of what's important. My friend Anna had a lifestyle similar to mine. A big house. Fancy car. Beautiful clothes. But when she was dying, she said it was all unimportant. She could live happily in a hovel if she had her loved ones with her. I believed her then, and I know in my bones it's true for me now, too. My family, my friends, you . . . that's what's essential. The rest is decoration."

You? Me? Essential! Trying to keep her voice calm, Ellie said, "Downsizing is exactly that—honing our lifestyle to the essentials." A sharp heat rose in her.

"It is. Of course, I still enjoy the decoration," Kathryn said, her eyes flickering in self-deprecation. "I'm content with our style of travel, Ellie. I don't want you to spend another minute worrying about it. Promise?"

CHAPTER 19

$\mathcal{A}$ little past eight o'clock, the women returned to the warm browns and golds of their room. Kathryn closed the drapes on the bright lights of the parking lot below as Ellie settled on the sofa to check her messages.

"There," Ellie said with satisfaction as she hit the send button with a flourish. "Kris always wants a report at the end of the day when I'm traveling."

Wearing an expression of inquisitive concern, Kathryn sat close to Ellie, angling to face her. "Before we get any further into the evening, there's one more thing I'd like to check out with you."

Ellie placed the phone and her reading glasses on the coffee table before turning to Kathryn. "Yes?"

"It has to do with what I sense is happening between us." Kathryn spoke slowly, carefully. Her fire-blue eyes did not leave Ellie's. "I think perhaps more than a friendship is developing. I'm not misreading you, am I?"

Ellie gave her head the slightest of shakes.

"Or where we could be heading?"

Ellie added a barely perceptible smile to the head shake. Her lungs suddenly required a conscious effort to breathe.

Kathryn waited for Ellie to say something, but as the silence stretched, she said gently, "I've noticed you're not wearing your wedding band on this trip. Do you want to talk about that?"

A shadow passed across Ellie's face, a mix of sadness and vulnerability. She looked down at her empty finger and then back into those eyes that demanded truth. "It didn't feel right to wear it when I'm falling in love with someone else."

"I see."

Ellie scrunched her eyebrows at Kathryn, while a tiny, self-conscious smile tugged at the corner of her mouth.

Kathryn found Ellie's *help me!* expression endearing. She cleared her throat and adopted a clinical tone, undercut by a mischievous smile. "And does this person know how you feel?"

"I think she suspects."

"But you haven't told her outright?"

Ellie shook her head. "I'm in the process."

Kathryn's smile softened into more serious territory. "What if I told you that I know for a fact this person feels the same way about you? How would you feel about that?"

"Thrilled. Terrified."

"It's a little scary, isn't it?"

"A little. Maybe a lot."

The seconds ticked by as they let their eyes drift down to each other's desirous mouths. Watching. Measuring. Barely breathing.

"Well, Ellie, what do you think the next step should be?" Kathryn said, her voice nearing a whisper.

"I think," Ellie replied, her confidence growing, "I should pinch this little bow that's been tormenting me all evening . . . ." Her finger brushed Kathryn's cleavage as she sought the bow.

Kathryn gasped softly.

". . . and draw it toward me, pulling her close . . . ." Ellie slowly drew the bow, the tunic and Kathryn into the space between them, leaning in herself to meet in the middle. "And if she doesn't resist . . . ."

She didn't.

Their lips pressed softly together. Slowly the intensity increased, the mouths opened slightly, the pressure surged and receded in tidal rhythm, their tongues brushed together, light as sparrow wings. It went on and on as if this were the one and only kiss allotted them.

When at last they parted, Kathryn breathed, "Oh, my." Her fingers moved like a breeze through Ellie's hair. "I suppose we should talk about this."

"I suppose we should."

But their mouths quickly rejoined. Kathryn slipped her tongue into Ellie's mouth and moaned as Ellie drew it in deeper. As though responding to the lift of a maestra's baton, their breathing deepened and the kiss became urgent and relentless, unshackling their bodies—arms free to embrace, hands to roam and caress.

"I like how you process," Ellie murmured.

"I like how you kiss." Kathryn's fingers tightened in Ellie's hair as the kissing resumed and deepened.

"El," Kathryn whispered, "there is a bed a few steps away."

"How convenient," Ellie replied, unable to break free. But as the kissing became more frenzied, the Siren call of the sheets grew irresistible. They staggered to the bed, dumb with shock and intention, pulling off their clothing as though the clothes themselves were aflame.

They were not abashed virgins, blushing with inexperience—together they brought over ninety years of sexual history to their consummation. Nor were they self-conscious apologists, embarrassed by their wrinkles and collagen dimples. They were simply two mature women caught in a fireball of lust tempered by wisdom and kindness.

Skin tasted skin as the full length of their bodies met. For minutes they kissed and grasped and reveled in a delicious sensual downpour slaking a Saharan thirst. And then, as if on cue, they pulled back.

"Is this really happening?" Ellie whispered. "You're here?"

Kathryn nodded, her face flushed. "Yes, the two of us."

They stroked each other's hair and sought the firm land in the other's eyes.

"We're not given many times like this are we?" Ellie said.

"No, we're not."

As their eyes held, a tacit knowing arced between them that this would be the last First Time in their lives.

They breathed each other's names then, confessed their love in the treasured, intimate tones only lovers share, and interlaced their limbs in a transcendent embrace.

Alas, even sacred moments are not foolproof: The dry communion wafer lodging at the back of a celebrant's throat, the groom toppling over in a faint at the altar, the giggles erupting at a silent retreat. And so it was that before Ellie had the blessed opportunity to tap the lodestone, the gyrations of these jubilant bodies sent the lovers on a premature launch.

"Oh!" Kathryn cried, her eyes large in surprise. "I'm coming!"

"But I'm not touching you!"

"I know," Kathryn panted. "God have mercy, but don't move your leg. I'm still . . . ohhhhh. Yikes."

Laughter replaced the sounds of lovemaking. The kisses turned kittenish; the clutching loosened to featherweight strokes.

"I don't think that was right," Kathryn said. "Did I just flunk Lesbianism 101?"

"No, sweetheart. You jumped to the head of the class. From zero to *Oh!* in record time."

CHAPTER 20

*A*lthough Kathryn had never made love to a woman, she was a woman herself, after all, with a skill at self-pleasuring, and recently, in her well-appointed den and bedroom, a partaker of lesbian erotica. She acquitted herself well, with a few gentle directions, and in the process realized with shocking satisfaction that she was an active player in this bed, not just a receiver or receptacle. Had she gotten that lazy in her marriage bed? She could not have anticipated the thrill of tipping Ellie into climax. When the last echoes faded, Kathryn clasped her firmly, as though laying claim to her body.

"Kathryn," Ellie whispered as she moved to lie side by side. She explored the eyes that had so captured her from the start. "Kathryn," she repeated, a hand now stroking the graying hair, "I love you."

"It's wonderful to hear those words." Kathryn lifted her head off the pillow, her lips locking once again on Ellie's, drawing her back into a fierce and surging embrace.

A while later, as Kathryn lay in her arms, spent and satisfied once again, Ellie felt her twitch. "You're falling asleep," she whispered.

"No," Kathryn said, trying to rouse herself. "I need to make love to you again to make it even."

"I'm content, sweetheart. I'm not counting Cheerios."

"Cheery Ohs?" Kathryn said sleepily.

A laugh burbled up from Ellie. "Yes, those, too, sweetheart. Now, go to sleep."

Ellie stood in the light of the bathroom, a light meant for hygiene and makeup, not post-coital examination. She looked a fright—her hair going in a thousand directions, her cheeks red with sexual blush, her lips cherry. Her body felt tight, the skin smeared with dried sweat, saliva, and juices both she and Kathryn had thought incapable of flowing again. She was a wonderful, unbelievable mess.

She found herself brushing her teeth because it was ten o'clock and that's what she did at this hour. Her hand trembled. It had finally happened. Now what?

She contemplated the sag in her abdomen that all the crunches in the world would not reduce. The creped neck, the fine hatch work around her eyes and mouth. This is what she had to give to Kathryn, bless her. Plus all that resided inside, the stuff that really counted.

She turned off the bathroom light and, as she made her way to the bed, took a detour to pick up and fold the clothes strewn on the sofa and floor. As she doubled over the sleeves of the tunic Kathryn had been wearing, she lifted it as carefully as a relic. Kathryn had been inside of this, her body, her breasts, her arms, just hours before. And now she had shared everything. But one day it would all be empty, just as Mary's clothes had been, and all this, all this wonder would be gone. Ellie could have wept from happiness and anticipated grief, but instead, she clicked off the bedside lamp. She slid quietly next to Kathryn, who stirred and turned to her.

"Where have you been?"

"The bathroom. Are you awake?"

"I am now."

"I'm sorry. I woke you."

"I'm not. My bladder is full . . ." she said, a hand finding its way to Ellie's thick hair, "as is my heart."

Kathryn's stream sounded from the bathroom, a startling note of intimacy to Ellie's ears. When she returned Ellie asked, "Which side of the bed do you prefer?"

"The left. And you?"

"The right."

The very sides they were on.

"How convenient."

They squirmed into a comfortable cuddle. Ellie looped a strand of hair over Kathryn's ear. "When did you know—or at least think—we'd end up like this?"

"I thought there was a possibility the day I took you shopping for clothes."

"Oh, lord. I was so awful."

"You were precious and vulnerable. I felt very tender toward you." Kathryn traced a line along Ellie's collar bone. "Or, maybe, even before that on some subconscious level, when we had lunch at Highland Meadows, and you told me about Mary. I liked how you could open yourself up emotionally. And I realized how much being with you made me feel alive."

"You were so good with me that day."

"But for sure, really-really, I knew we would be like this the day you came to tell me the reason for your trip."

"I was so scared."

"So was I, but for a different reason."

"Really? Tell me."

And so they talked late into the sweetness of night, turning over their memories, examining them through a new prism, their first meeting, standing together on the bridge over Minnehaha Creek, the dinner with Kris and Sandy, listening to love songs in the car. They kissed for a while again, body on body, tenderly, sensuously, without going further. Finally, they fell asleep, not in each other's arms, but apart because that was their habit after all their time alone. But they were close, very close, and together at last.

———ⴲ⴨ⴲ———

Kathryn woke. She lay on her side, Ellie snugged behind her, her arm encircling her ribs, her hand cupping a breast. Had they fallen asleep this way or had Ellie moved over during the night? Here they were, together, skin touching skin, living sheets of neurons communicating at the primal level. Kathryn stirred slightly just to feel the sensation of shifting touch.

Touch. She remembered how she had missed it when Joe left. She had been suddenly cut off from the easy contact of two intimate humans, the hand thrown on a thigh in the car, fingers grasping in unconscious connection. She felt Ellie's sparse bush against her. Scratchy. Arousing.

This is what she had wanted. To be lovers with Ellie Belmont. Her lust had been satisfied in its temporary way, and here it was again. That was a good sign. Especially now she knew what it was about. Their bodies played together well. Their selves fit together, well, too. They could laugh; they could cry; they could share. They could go deep and surface back into the light.

CHAPTER 21

he morning light seeped into the far end of the room where the drapes failed to join completely, a luminous bar into a changed world. Ellie's eyes adjusted to wakefulness, and she remembered where she was and what had happened. Kathryn stirred beside her.

"Good morning," Ellie said. "Welcome to a new day."

Kathryn angled soft kisses on Ellie's check and around to her mouth.

"Wait until I brush my teeth," Ellie cautioned.

"As you wish," Kathryn said, running her hand along Ellie's arm. "Thank you for last night."

"Thank you for initiating it."

"I couldn't have stood one more day sitting beside you in the car and not being able to reach over and touch you."

They were quiet for a while, stroking each other lightly.

"How do you propose we start this day?" Kathryn asked.

"I don't know about you, but I need to fuel up. How about we shower and go downstairs for breakfast?"

An hour later they were finishing the last morsels in their room, having brought plates of scrambled eggs and bacon from the breakfast bar off the lobby. A nearly empty bowl of fruit was perched at the edge of the coffee table.

"I think we'd better have another check-in," Kathryn said.

"You think?" Ellie speared the last chunk of cantaloupe and popped it into her mouth. "Whatever for?"

Kathryn smiled.

"I think last night went well."

"I'd say so." Kathryn leaned back on the cushions and brushed a muffin crumb from her pant leg. "So, how serious is this, Ellie?"

"For me, very."

"Me, too." Kathryn's eyes had a new luster. "I'm not sure what to think of all this—I never thought a serious relationship would come my way again, and frankly, I wasn't sure I wanted one. And, yet, here you are. Here we are. Two women."

"Yep, that's how the lesbian world works."

"Who would have guessed?" Kathryn picked up Ellie's hand and laced their fingers together. "I love that you—we—can share openly. That's important to me."

"I know it is."

"So, can we just see where this takes us?" She kissed the back of Ellie's hand.

"Yes, of course," Ellie said, her voice low and serious. She took a sip of hot chocolate to fortify herself. "I do have a couple of concerns."

Kathryn's head tilted a fraction, as though listening for underworld rumbles.

"The first is . . . well, I don't know how to put it without sounding offensive . . ."

"That I'm straight?"

"Yes. I want to trust you . . . but . . . it's not uncommon for lesbians to be an interlude between men. We get our hearts broken a lot . . . and really, we have no one to blame but ourselves."

Kathryn accepted this news quietly without defense . . . or offense. "I'm aware such 'interludes' happen, Ellie. You know me well enough to know I don't play games. Last night we made love. It wasn't experimental sex."

"I know. I trust you're not doing a Margaret Mead and sleeping with me for anthropological research." Ellie placed her free hand atop Kathryn's. "But it's an insecurity that's in the tribal DNA. I just want to be upfront about it."

"Thank you, I appreciate it." Kathryn kissed the back of Ellie's hand. "And your second concern?"

"I've been alone for three years and I'm afraid I may be set in my ways."

Katherine smiled. "Our rough edges will appear as we spend more time together. And the more we communicate, the more we will find things to disagree—and agree—upon." She kissed Ellie's hand again. "Love doesn't require us to be clones, you know. We can celebrate our differences."

"You're right."

"Those are things we'll work out over time."

"Okay." Ellie took in the measure of Kathryn. "So, what do you want to do now?" she asked, her eyes wide with invitation.

Kathryn leveled a playful grin at Ellie. "Yes."

Ellie called the front desk to extend the room reservation another night. They did not want to feel rushed.

The drumbeat of lust had softened. Now they were able to make love leisurely, to enjoy the stirrings of passion, to explore each other's bodies and marvel over the delights and scars, to pluck memories from all the decades they had not shared together and share them in the telling.

"I've known other lesbians, but you're the first I've become friends with," Kathryn said at one point. "And here we wind up in bed."

"Uh-huh."

"Well, how does that work in your world? You meet someone and you click and become friends and then you become lovers?"

"That's usually how it works."

"But then don't you all wind up in bed, everyone sleeping with everyone else because you're all friends?"

"Sometimes it seems that way." Ellie laughed. "Like with Kris. But there are different chemistries and, of course, boundaries."

"Ah, boundaries."

"When Mary and I got together, we promised to tell the other of any crushes we were developing. It's amazing how just that bit of sharing would diffuse the feelings, put them in the context of our relationship. If we had kept it a secret, the crush could have fueled itself into something larger and more difficult to control."

"So, no secrets."

"No secrets, Kathryn. For us, too. Okay?"

"Absolutely."

"Didn't you experience something similar in your marriage? What did you do if you found some guy attractive?"

"I could appreciate them on an intellectual level . . . ."

"Come on!"

"And, yes, occasionally there would be some totally studly guy, and I'd say, 'Gosh, Joe, so-and-so is really hot' and Joe would grunt and say, 'There's no accounting for taste' and that would be it."

"Well, that's similar to what I'm talking about."

"I guess so. I'm trying to understand all this." She ran her fingers through Ellie's hair and clutched a handful. "It's been a long time since I've felt hair like this. Thick and luxurious."

"Not as much as it used to be."

"It's wonderful. An advantage of women, I suppose."

"Sounds like a comparative study, Ms. Anthropologist."

They kissed. And kissed some more.

As Kathryn's hand traveled over Ellie's hip and circled around to the front, Ellie said, "See, that's where my hair is thinning out."

"Mmmm-huh. Well, no need for a Brazilian."

"I hear all the young women are getting them these days."

"I think it comes out of porn—making women look like prepubescent girls."

"I wonder if Brazilians would be as popular," Ellie said, starting to laugh, "if young women knew it would make them like old ladies."

CHAPTER 22

It was the afternoon of The Day After. Yesterday they had been friends. Today they were lovers. Now would come the negotiations of how to be in the world. Or even alone together.

Ellie lounged on the sofa listening to Kathryn blow-drying her hair in the bathroom. Would Kathryn be okay with an affectionate swipe across her butt or a buzz on her cheek in passing? A palm on the nape of her neck or on her thigh?

She had not been skittish last night. Ellie smiled at the thought. She had been surprised at Kathryn's ferocity. She had taken Ellie without hesitation; she was not intimidated. She may have been a novice with women, but not one in the art of lovemaking.

Kathryn seemed comfortable sharing her personal space within the confines of their room. And even downstairs at the breakfast bar, she had winked when Ellie had touched her arm to point out the hard-boiled eggs as an option to the scrambled ones.

But now they would be going out into the big world. How would that be?

"Why are you smiling?" Kathryn asked, crossing the room.

Ellie looked up from her reverie. "You." She rose and walked into Kathryn's arms. The kiss was slow and steady.

"Oh," Kathryn said, "kissing upright. A new position for us."

Ellie laughed and stepped back to look Kathryn full on. "Tell me, how do you feel about PDAs?"

"I haven't thought about it. Oh, okay, I suppose. I don't want you pushing me up against a store front and doing a pelvic grind on me, though."

"Of course. I just don't know that I can keep my hands off you."

"Ellie, let's do what feels natural. We'll see how that works. And we need to communicate."

They spent the afternoon strolling the campus of the University of Nebraska. The sculpture of a huge mammoth outside of Morrill Hall drew them into the State Museum and its collection of paleontological wonders. As they meandered through Elephant Hall past the march of skeletons from distant eons, Kathryn slipped her arm through Ellie's. "Imagine a world without humans," she said. It was Holy Week, and the museum was quiet.

"No pollution," Ellie replied, surprised at the intimate and unselfconscious way Kathryn moved with her. Anytime she was in public, Ellie had certain brain waves devoted to sentinel duty, scanning the environment for hostility. Baggage Kathryn did not have.

Yet when Ellie gave Kathryn a quick kiss on the cheek as they stood in front of the Plesiosaur skeleton in the Mesozoic Gallery, Kathryn flinched.

"Oh, I'm sorry," Ellie said. "Too much?"

Kathryn looked at her frankly. "No, it wasn't too much. I don't know why I did that. Let me think about it."

They ambled out of the winding exit and climbed the stairs to the dinosaur room. There they sat in front of the Stegosaurus skeleton, the plates on its back splayed like giant petrified rose petals. A self-consciousness had bloomed around them like a Jurassic gas, filling the space between their untouching bodies. The quiet hum of the ventilation system was the only sound.

"What's happening here?" Kathryn asked quietly.

"The ground is feeling a little shaky. I want to touch you, but I don't quite dare to."

"Is this normal?"

"Yes. We have to negotiate PDAs. That's why I brought it up back at the hotel."

"I get it now." Kathryn scooted over to place her body solidly against Ellie's.

———❦———

An hour later, Ellie was surprised when Kathryn slid in beside her in the booth of a brew bar and grill in the Haymarket district.

"The table's too wide and the background noise too loud for a decent conversation," Kathryn explained.

"I'm not arguing," Ellie said, her smile widening as Kathryn pressed a thigh into hers.

As they waited for their orders—beer cheese soup and a chicken Caesar salad to share—Kathryn brought up the kiss in the museum.

"I've been thinking," she said. "Maybe it was partly a startle reflex— I wasn't expecting it. But more than anything, I was suddenly afraid someone might see us."

Ellie was silent for a long moment, her face kind and concerned. "What's the fear in that?"

Kathryn unrolled her napkin. "That they would think we were lovers."

"Uh-huh. And they would disapprove?"

"Yes." Kathryn shook her head.

"This is what internalized homophobia looks like," Ellie said.

"Ugh." Kathryn searched Ellie's face. "This feels so odd. I'm old enough that I shouldn't give a rat's patootie what anyone thinks. And normally I don't. But today something new in me emerged. I guess I have some work to do."

"But there's also the legitimate concern for safety."

"In an empty museum?" Kathryn said ruefully.

Ellie took in Kathryn's pained expression, her misty eyes, and she was filled with tenderness. "I have a feeling you'll lean into this conundrum."

"Leaning into discomfort is part of my life work."

"We do need to be aware of our surroundings, though, Kathryn. Some situations are riskier than others. It's a matter of finding balance between spontaneity and foolhardiness."

Kathryn heaved a big sigh.

Before they went to bed that night, Ellie sat on the sofa to text Kris. Kathryn plopped down next to her. "Okay," she said, "what are you going to write?"

"'Extra night in Lincoln. Lovers now.' How does that sound?"

"Succinct."

A few moments later, the reply came.

"What's the verdict?" Kathryn asked.

Grinning, Ellie held up the phone: Twenty emojis in various states of joy.

CHAPTER 23

Interstate 80 took them west through Willa Cather's tabletop of prairie land stretching to the horizon and into the rock formations of western Nebraska. They passed arrays of windmills and undulating land, barren of all except scrub brush and tumbleweed, and stopped overnight in Cheyenne, Wyoming. The next day, they passed over the Laramie Mountains and drove the long, winding asphalt ribbons through the Rockies. Patches of snow appeared and disappeared with the changing elevation, and mountains always seemed to be hunched in the distance. They overnighted in Evanston—another relatively short day.

On the drive, the women engaged in long conversations deepening their understanding of each other, fine-tuned their California plans—Kathryn would now accompany Ellie to the cannabis farm—and they listened to love songs, Broadway tunes, and Mozart's chamber music. They ate the last of their picnic lunches at a desolate rest stop.

The stretch from Evanston to Reno proved to be too much, however. The mountains, and then the tediousness of the Great Salt Flats, although eerily mesmerizing, tired the women whose nights had been short on sleep and whose bodies had been in almost constant arousal. By the time they reached Fernley, Nevada, they were done, unwilling to push themselves to Reno. They collapsed onto their king-sized bed and slept a full nine hours. In the morning, unable to stomach another standard breakfast bar, they decided to eat at a nearby restaurant.

While Ellie was turning in the room cards at the front desk, Kathryn complimented the young manager on the décor. "These pictures are wonderful," she said, pointing to the large, framed sepia photo of a white horse.

"Thank you, ma'am," the manager said. He had a narrow face with a chin coming to a point, short brown hair parted on the side, and friendly brown eyes. "Most of them are by local photographers."

"Really? Well, you have some big talent in the area." Kathryn noticed the printed weather report farther down the marble countertop. "Snow?" she said, running a finger to the day's forecast.

"Yes, ma'am. Are you headed east or west?"

"West."

Ellie folded the receipt and joined the conversation. "What's happening?"

"Snow," Kathryn said.

"You'll need a four-wheel drive or chains to make it over Donner Pass. We had a trucker in last night who said that at ten o'clock they had the snowplows lined up and ready to go. They were expecting up to a foot. They may get more by the time the storm passes."

"I suppose Route 95 is blocked, too?" Ellie asked.

"Yes, ma'am. You're welcome to stay another night, or you might want to go to Reno. You won't make it past Truckee, though."

"How long until the roads are open?"

"Given this time of year, I'd say maybe by tomorrow morning. But you never know."

"Well," Ellie said, "we can figure out what we want to do over breakfast. Can you recommend a restaurant?"

"Our breakfast bar is complimentary," he said, pointing across the way.

"Yes," Ellie said, "but we're tired of hotel food, no offense. We would prefer a different menu."

"I understand." The young man smiled. "I recommend the Black Bear."

Ten minutes later, Ellie and Kathryn slid into a comfortable booth and ordered the breakfast burrito and veggie omelet respectively.

"Okay," Ellie said, "time to improvise." She studied a paper map while Kathryn worked her smartphone.

"I think our best bet is to stay in Reno until the roads are clear. The storm is supposed to let up by this afternoon, so maybe we can get through tomorrow."

"Uh-huh," Kathryn said. "Give me a few minutes. I'm checking on something." She put aside her phone as the food arrived. "Are you ready for my idea?"

"Shoot."

"I propose—and this is my treat, Ellie, and I mean it—that we stay the night in Reno, rent a four-wheel drive, and take a side trip to Yosemite for a few days. It'll be a bit of a drive, but it'll be spectacular with all of this snow."

Ellie's fork, laden with eggs and black beans, stopped mid-way to her mouth. "That is so far beyond my imagination, I can't even process it."

"Have you been there?"

"Decades ago. You?"

"Never. I've always loved those magnificent photos by Ansel Adams. It must be one of the most gorgeous places on earth. What better time than now? We're not in a hurry, and we won't want to dally on our way home. I can check with my daughter and you with Trisha to make sure the delay is okay with them. This is good. It'll give me a few more days to rethink my visit with Jenn."

"How convenient."

Kathryn grinned at the in-joke. "I know we could just stay tonight in Reno and head for Nevada City. But think of it, Ellie. We have a chance to see Yosemite in a fresh blanket of snow. The waterfalls will be gushing...."

"... filling up and spilling over?" Ellie winked.

"That, too." Kathryn laughed and blushed at the erotic reference to the Cris Williamson song. "We're at the beginning of our own magical journey. Let's celebrate by going someplace magnificent."

Kathryn's eyes sparkled in excitement. Ellie looked at her hair, the lights of the restaurant deepening the contrast between the honey and silver and knew she could not refuse. She would be an idiot to do so. Yosemite. Even the name sounded like magic. This could be their honeymoon, a spontaneous one better than any they could ever plan. "Let's do it," she said with a grin. "*Carpe diem.*"

CHAPTER 24

*I*f Ellie and Kathryn weren't already in love, Yosemite in April, muffled with fresh snow under a brilliant sapphire sky, would surely have done it. The bank of windows in their room at the Ahwahnee Hotel looked out on snow-dappled pines. The plush drapery and bedding, the Native American artwork, and the comfortable leather sofa gave the room a rustic, yet elegant panache. On the coffee table a glass ice bucket held a bottle of champagne and two flutes. A plate with cheese and fruit sat alongside.

Ellie set up a charging station on the small corner table while Kathryn arranged her clothes tidily in the chest of drawers.

"You're unpacking?" Ellie said as she cracked open a window.

Kathryn glanced up. "Aren't you? We'll be here a few days."

"No. I thought I'd just get things out of my suitcase as needed."

Kathryn raised an eyebrow. "I see. Well . . . different styles . . . ."

"Speaking of style, did you order this?" Ellie picked up the bottle of champagne and examined the label.

"I did." Kathryn rolled her suitcase under the bed and checked her phone. "Oh, good, I'm getting a strong signal . . . and a text from my daughter." She sent a quick reply and joined Ellie on the couch.

Ellie popped the cork and poured them each a glass. "Speaking of your daughter . . . I'm curious about something."

Kathryn's gaze snapped into focus.

"You've told me about Nate, his pulmonology practice and his family. But you've never said much about Jenn. Why is that?"

"You've never seemed that curious about my children. I know people can get bored by parents going on and on about their kids and grandkids."

"I'm sorry if you were waiting for me to ask. Of course, I want to know about them—they're your family." The unspoken extension was that they were on their way to becoming *her* family. "What's Jenn's story?"

Kathryn centered a wedge of brie on a whole grain cracker, as though precision with her food would carry over to her answer. "It's a somewhat painful topic these days."

"Maybe you'd like to wait until another time to discuss this," Ellie said, tipping her flute toward Kathryn, who smiled wistfully. "Let's celebrate now." They clinked their glasses, but a sour pall had settled in the room, one even the fresh breeze from the Sierras could not dispel.

"I want to talk about Jenn," Kathryn said, "and now is a good time with champagne in hand and food to fortify me."

Ellie settled back to listen.

"The divorce hit her hard. Even though Joe left me for another woman, Jenn blames me . . . that I wasn't attentive enough or maybe I'd put on a few too many menopausal pounds.

"No!"

Kathryn held up a hand. "That's Jenn. Or, as she's fond of pointing out, as a therapist I should have seen the danger signals in my own marriage and done something to save it. There's some truth in that, as you know."

"Grrrrr . . . I want to defend you."

"Jenn is complicated. She's a strange and wonderful mix of strength and dependency, braininess and naiveté." Kathryn popped a grape into her mouth, chewed slowly, and swallowed. "She's had her share of challenges. She lost her first baby at about five months. A boy. She went into a depression that, frankly, I don't think has ever totally subsided. She loves her girls, but I sense a primal yearning for her lost son."

"Sounds difficult." Ellie sipped her champagne and set the glass down quietly.

"It is. I've tried to suggest counseling or a support group for her, but she resists anything I have to offer. She accuses me of trying to psycho-analyze her." Kathryn chuckled. "Her self-image is of a cool and logical woman, but in truth she's temperamental and quick to flare. I'm not sure where the anger comes from. But she can be good-hearted. I never know which Jenn will be present on any given day."

"Do you have to walk on eggshells around her?"

Kathryn smiled. "No. I don't give her that type of power. If she gets angry, I deal with it—usually by letting her spout. I don't get sucked into a fight."

The women sat quietly for a several moments savoring the champagne and canapes. From what Ellie had heard from friends, children always seemed to bring complications. Nurturing students for a semester or two was the closest she had ever come to child-rearing. How would this moody daughter respond to her mother's glide into lesbian territory? A ping of alarm struck Ellie for the first time.

"The divorce was another loss for Jenn—if nothing else, the loss of her vision of our ideal family."

"Reality can be harsh."

"She was quite angry with Joe and me for not working things out. She thought we should have tried harder, but you know, when one party says it's over, nine times out of ten there's nothing to be done. It takes two to make it work."

"Does she have a career?"

"She's an accountant. She took a break after the second child was born, and now she has a few clients. I adore her kids—Gena and Maddie. Things have changed, of course, as they've gotten older. They're teens now and past the tea and crumpet parties we used to play."

A tea party with kids? Ellie couldn't think of a worse way to spend an afternoon. She drained the last bit of champagne from her glass. "Kathryn, how are you going to explain me to your family?" A small knot of worry began to tighten in her stomach. "I'll let you call the shots."

"Thank you." Kathryn's face softened. "I'm not sure how to approach it. But there'll be no lies, Ellie. Ever."

Ellie nodded.

"I think the best thing is to call Jenn and tell her about us. We can't just show up at her door and spring the news on her."

"Sounds reasonable."

Kathryn sighed. "I'll call her in the morning when I'm fresh and have my wits about me."

CHAPTER 25

To make manifest her promise of total honesty, Kathryn made no pretense of their relationship when they went for dinner. They strolled arm-in-arm, fingers entwined, through the three-story dining hall to a small table in the rear alcove. Kathryn ordered the salmon and Ellie the grilled striploin.

Ellie ran her hands along the top of her head. "My hair is dry. I stepped out of the shower . . . what? Ten minutes ago?"

"It's the alpine air."

"And my fingers are getting rough already." She rubbed the sensitive tips together.

"When we get back to the room, I have something you might like."

"I know you do."

Kathryn's eyes lit with mirth. "I love you, Ellie."

"I'm so glad I'm not in this alone."

"Me, too. Unrequited love is one of the saddest things in the world."

Ellie leaned in. "Tell me three things you believe, not counting what you just said."

"Let me think a moment."

While she waited for an answer, Ellie took in the warm colors of the room the golden light of the gothic chandeliers high overhead, the rich pine beams awash in the glow.

"I believe every communication can have healing energy. I believe this wonderful thing we have—you and I—has the power to last. And I believe I'm too tired to think of a third."

Ellie smiled. "I definitely believe in your second point, I honor your third point, and I'm curious about your first. What do you mean communication can have healing energy?"

"Well, it follows on from what we talked about the other day in the car. It's twofold, actually. It's being truthful and forthright. Authenticity is a powerful way to go deep with someone. Think about our first meeting, Ellie. We didn't have to share what was really happening with us—we were both recovering from loss. We were being real; we didn't keep things on the superficial level. And look what it led to."

"But I don't usually talk with strangers like that."

"No, of course not. We have to trust our intuition."

"It's the same with writing, isn't?" Ellie said. "Good writing is authentic. I always tried to get my students to dig deeper, get the details, find their truth."

"It's crucial I remain authentic with Jenn. I have to state my truth. She may not like it, but I can't live for a daughter's approval, can I?"

"No."

"If I'm truthful about what's happening, perhaps Jenn and I can come to a place of understanding." Kathryn took a sip of her wine. "Of course, it's never worked in the past . . . ." She made a goofy face.

Ellie laughed at the expression she'd not seen before. "You said your answer was twofold. What's the second part?'

"It's communication that's more on the therapeutic level—bringing to light the pain we feel about something. By talking about it we give the wound air, diffuse its power, and give it a chance to heal. For instance, children can have a lot of anger toward parents. Sometimes, if they can just state their truth—your anger frightens me, your drinking scares me, you let Dad hurt me—it can open the way to a deeper relationship. Or a more distant one. But at least the effort has been made. The truth is out."

"And illumination can begin."

"Yes."

The waiter approached with their orders. "Looks wonderful," Ellie said, leaning back as the plate was placed in front of her.

The women ate silently for several minutes.

"Ellie." Kathryn put down her fork. "Speaking of truth, there's something on my conscience I'd like to tell you."

"Sure." Ellie stopped cutting her steak and laid down her knife.

"The day after we went clothes shopping, I had lunch with a friend, Judith—she's the one who helped us with Shawn. I regaled her with tales of our trip, and I felt bad later because I had made fun of you, of your inattention to style . . . something that, really, is quite endearing. I'm sorry I did that."

Ellie's growing smile erupted into laughter. "I'm so glad you can make sport of me, Kathryn. Please, don't hold back. I love you for it."

"But it's not kind."

"It's not intended to be mean. We have to laugh at our foibles."

"But not behind your back. I don't like it when two people connect by wounding others—making fun of them or gossiping. I want my bonding to be on a positive plane."

"Was there anything you said that you wouldn't say to my face?"

Kathryn thought for a moment. "No, I guess not."

"Well, there you go. Now tell me what you said that was so funny."

They finished the meal as Kathryn replayed her conversation with Judith, leaving them both weak with laughter. A bit tipsy from their second glass of wine, they eschewed a walk around the Great Lounge as they had planned and headed directly to their room.

The bed was king-sized, the sheets luxurious. They fell into it blissful and exhausted from a day of driving on treacherous mountain roads that had finally morphed into the snow-laden fairyland of Yosemite Valley.

"Thank you for a wonderful, magical day," Kathryn said as she settled her full length and weight on Ellie.

"Are you going all brute force on me?" Ellie said, smiling. Their fingers were laced together and their hands, resting on the pillow above Ellie's head, touched the cedar headboard.

"Yes, I am, my love. I have two inches and at least twenty pounds on you."

"So, you're saying size matters."

"In this instance, yes."

"Well, I love every ounce of you on me."

Ellie searched the eyes inches from her own, the little gold and black flecks in the pools of blue, the pupils that seemed like a portal to some place not of this world. She lifted her mouth to Kathryn's. They kissed for minutes, passionate and deep, their pelvises moving against each other in a matching rhythm.

They were familiar with each other's bodies by now, the curves, the tender and erogenous spots. They had even sorted out some of their disinclinations. Ellie had told Kathryn that she sometimes scratched her, and she didn't like it. Kathryn was careful not to do it again. And Kathryn didn't like Ellie playing with her ears—kissing them or even tickling whispers of "I love you" in them.

Ellie's hands stroked Kathryn's lower back, farther and farther down. And then Ellie's fingers inched toward her wet pool.

"You're cheating!" Kathryn cried.

"Just a different path to enlightenment, sweetheart."

Kathryn laughed and shifted down to Ellie's chest, moving out of range. Ellie opened and wrapped her legs around her. The carnal embrace thrilled Kathryn to her core and fed a sexual ferocity and possessiveness unknown to her. Alcohol had loosened Kathryn, and she slid down farther with Ellie's encouraging hands in her hair. She was blind now, in a forest so ancient even the owls hooting outside the window had no memory of its beginning, no knowledge of its ending, and when she felt the shudder and heard the cries, she gently rose up into the night and covered Ellie with her body, totally and irrevocably.

CHAPTER 26

*A*fter breakfast the next morning, Ellie wandered from the dining hall to the main lounge, newspaper and cup of hot chocolate in hand. Meanwhile, Kathryn returned to their room to call Jenn.

Kathryn meditated for twenty minutes. Afterwards, she set a glass of water on the coffee table along with a notepad and pen. She placed the call and put the phone on speaker. "Hi, honey," she said. "Is this a good time to talk?"

"Sure. Paul took the girls to a soccer match. You said in your text you're in Yosemite?"

"Yes. It's gorgeous here, as you can imagine."

"It's gorgeous even without snow. We haven't been there in years."

"Well, amazingly, it's my first visit."

"So, when are you getting here?"

"It looks like we'll be in Sacramento toward the end of the week. Friday, maybe Saturday. Does that work for you?"

"We're flexible."

Kathryn took a deep breath. "Jenn, there's something I need to share with you before I visit. I want to give you time to process it."

Silence. "You're seeing someone," Jenn snapped at last, an aggrieved tone in her voice.

"I am. There's been a big change in my life, and I'm happier now than I have been in years."

"Well, good for *you*, Mom."

"I know it isn't easy, honey, but I'm asking you to keep an open mind and support me." Kathryn flicked a piece of lint off her black pants.

"There's more to the story, Jenn. You know the friend—Ellie—with whom I'm making this trip . . . ."

"Yes, you've mentioned her."

"Well, she's the one I'm in a relationship with."

A stunned silence followed. "Are you kidding me? You mean, like, you're with a woman?"

"Yes."

"Mom!!! Have you lost your mind? When did this happen?"

"On the drive out."

"For godsakes, Mother."

"I know it's a big shock. It is for me, too."

"Is this Ellie a lesbian, or did it just happen?"

"Both."

"So, she seduced you?"

"No. It was mutual."

"Stop, Mom. I can't wrap my mind around this."

Kathryn remained silent.

"I suppose you want to bring her here to meet everyone."

"I'd like her to meet the family, yes, but only if she would be welcomed."

"What's her full name? I wanna Google her."

"Eleanor Belmont." Kathryn rose and walked to the window while she heard Jenn spell the name into a search engine. The world outside was sunny and the snow sparkling. "We'll be staying at a hotel while we're in Sacramento after we spend a few days in Nevada City where Ellie's niece lives. If you'd feel more comfortable, you, Ellie, and I could meet somewhere first for lunch."

"I don't know."

"Well, why don't we talk in a few days after you've had a chance to think about this and discuss it with Paul."

"Oh, that should be fun. I'll tell you right now he'll say you can come for a visit but not your . . . *girlfriend.*"

Kathryn pursed her lips. Jenn was putting her words into Paul's mouth. As usual. "Talk it over, think about what meets your comfort level," she said, her equanimity beginning to thin. "I'll be in touch in a few days. We can discuss plans then. Or you can call me. Anytime, you know."

"Right."

"Talk with you soon. Love to you, Paul, and the girls. Bye now."

Kathryn clicked off the phone. She breathed intentionally for a full minute. By the end of it, she was able to smile to herself. *That went about as well as could be expected.* Just as she was about to text Ellie to come back to the room, she changed her mind and placed another call.

"Well, I've been wondering when I was going to hear from you," Judith said directly, no preliminaries. "How are things going?"

"With Ellie, fabulously. It's beyond what I could have imagined."

Judith laughed with delight. "See. I told you. But there's an 'and' in here, isn't there?"

"I just got off the phone with Jenn. You know how she can be."

"Please."

"It's a lot to take in."

"More so since sex is involved. Children can't think of their parents as being sexual, especially their mothers."

Kathryn began to laugh. "I could hear in Jenn's tone *sleeee-azy,* my giving in to lust in hotel rooms."

"You couldn't contain yourself," Judith joined the laughter.

"No, I couldn't."

"So, tell me, how is the sex?"

Kathryn dug for the perfect word. "Joyous."

The women laughed again and then caught up on other news, including Shawn.

"He's still in Justin's House. Getting along well, from what I've heard. You were right. He was kicked out of his home for being gay. I don't think his parents are coming around anytime soon."

"If you want me to talk to them, I'm happy to do so."

"Does that mean you're willing to come on board as a volunteer therapist? At last?"

"I walked into that one, didn't I?" Kathryn smirked. "Let's discuss it when I get home."

"Okay, dear friend. Happy trails . . . and good luck with Jenn."

CHAPTER 27

*K*athryn found Ellie in the Great Lounge perusing a National Geographic park map, running her finger along a thick black trail line. The light poured in through the huge windows catching an illustrated guidebook splayed open on the cushion next to her.

"How did it go?" Ellie asked, moving the guide to the coffee table and patting the now empty space.

"I'd give it a B minus. Jenn's shocked, but at least she didn't hang up on me. I don't think she could handle me in a heterosexual relationship either." Kathryn smiled unhappily. "Well, at least the issue is out there. We'll see which way she runs with it."

"And, how are you?"

"A bit shaky, but I'm used to Jenn's snark." Kathryn brightened. "I had a good chat with Judith afterwards."

"Moral support?"

"Yes. Come on, let's go for a walk. I'll tell you all about it."

"Good. I've just the route for us."

They spent the day among the pine and cedar trees in the valley, hiking the flat trail around the meadow. Lingering on the bridge over the Merced River, swollen with the melting snowpack, the women recalled another time they had stood shoulder to shoulder over water. This time they could touch as lovers. At the nearby waterfall, they even kissed as the roaring water sprayed them with a fine, cold mist.

After lunch, they wandered through the Indian Village of the Ahwahnee, and explored the museum and various shops. Kathryn bought a couple of small prints at the Ansel Adams Gallery.

"This is silly, I know," she said to Ellie as they left the shop. "I'm trying to downsize and here I buy pictures I don't have wall space for."

"They give you pleasure in this moment. Maybe that's enough." For Ellie, this was enough, walking alongside Kathryn. Life was taking on the contours of John Muir's sanctuary, a granite and forested temple on a scale beyond comprehension. Where once she had once been leading the way—planning the trip and marking its destinations—now she and Kathryn were partners, their decisions joint and unhurried.

At the afternoon tea in the Great Lounge, Ellie and Kathryn settled near a massive stone hearth with their Earl Grey and chocolate chip cookies. Warming air curled in through propped open side doors. They sat close, poring over the guidebook and maps, deciding on a trail to hike the next day. At one point, Ellie glanced up and caught two women giving her and Kathryn the once over.

"Who are you smiling at?" Kathryn asked.

"A couple of sisters just strolled into the room."

Kathryn followed Ellie's line of direction and spotted the women who appeared to be in their early forties. "They don't look alike . . . Oh! Gay? How do you know?"

"I just do. It's instinct, like your going to the exact rack in Macy's with the perfect shirt for me. Those two have me pegged, but you," Ellie said, admiring Kathryn's Italian printed skirt, yellow sweater with the colorful scarf, and lightly coifed hair, "you confuse them."

"Well, good. I like to surprise people."

❦

That evening, as Ellie and Kathryn walked arm-in-arm into the hotel bar for a light dinner, they spotted the women again, who motioned them over to their table.

Sally and Dee, from Walnut Creek, were indeed a couple and invited them to share their table. Shortly after the introductions, Sally mentioned she was a chiropractor and Dee a commercial lighting engineer.

"Could you explain your profession to me?" Kathryn asked Dee.

"Sure. I design the lighting systems for new buildings and rehabbed ones, including sports arenas and hotels." Dee gazed only at Kathryn. "I determine the type and placement of lights from the parking garages to the penthouses."

"What an interesting—and important—career." Kathryn smiled. "Lighting is so crucial to our well-being, isn't it?"

"Yes," Dee replied, her voice touched with pride. Her intense, dark eyes continued to linger on Kathryn. "But I can't take credit for my career. I was destined for it."

"What do you mean?" Ellie said.

"Her parents are from India," Sally replied. "They named her Deepika. It means Little Light."

"How convenient," Ellie said, shooting Kathryn a wry look.

Once the women had placed their dinner orders, Ellie asked, "What brings you to Yosemite?"

"This is our spiritual home," Sally said. She pushed her blond bangs to the side and gave Ellie a forgive-my-wife-for-flirting-with-your-girl-friend look.

"We come to the Ahwahnee on every fifth anniversary," Dee added.

"Congratulations," Ellie said. "How long have you been together?"

"Fifteen years. And you?"

"A week."

The Californians gaped dumbfounded at Ellie and Kathryn. "A week?" Sally repeated, taking in their big, sheepish grins.

Kathryn's infectious guffaw set everyone to laughing.

"Well, that's thrilling," Sally said. "How long have you known each other?"

"Oh, much longer," Kathryn said. "What, Ellie? Almost a month?"

More laughter.

"Of course," Sally said. "You have the glow about you. And here you are in Yosemite on your one-week anniversary. How did that happen?"

Ellie and Kathryn shared their stories of meeting at Starbucks, bonding over downsizing, and Kathryn inviting herself along on Ellie's cannabis run.

"So, you had your eye on her?" Sally asked Kathryn.

"I did, but it took me a little while to realize it."

"How many days will you be here?"

"Four," Ellie said. "We were lucky. There was a cancellation because of the weather. We arrived yesterday."

"Have you had a chance to see any of the park or are you mostly . . ." Sally made a little cough . . . "in your room?"

"Actually," Kathryn said, blushing, "we spent the day wandering around the valley. This afternoon at tea, we were going over some options for tomorrow."

"Yes, we saw you with the maps," Dee said.

"Do you have any recommendations?"

Sally and Dee suggested some beautiful but not strenuous hikes. "We're driving to the Tuolumne Grove Trailhead tomorrow to go snowshoeing and see the sequoias. You're welcome to join us. And," Sally smiled, "we'll give you honeymooners plenty of privacy."

"It's a two-and-a-half-mile trek with a 500-foot drop in elevation," Dee said. "You go down at first, but then on the return you have a bit of a climb."

"Have you ever snowshoed, Kathryn?" Ellie asked.

"Yes, on the North Shore. It's been a few years."

"Same with me. I haven't done it in, gosh, at least a decade."

Ellie and Kathryn raised their eyebrows at each other and looked for confirmation in the other's face.

"Let's give it a try," Kathryn said.

"We'll take our own car," Ellie added, "in case we poop out."

"Sounds like a plan!" Sally grinned. "I'll give you my phone number in case you change your mind. We can check at the front desk about renting snowshoes and poles for you. We brought our own."

After their soup and sandwiches arrived, Sally said, "We're lucky that cannabis is legal in California. Eventually it'll be nationwide. I have several patients who are on it."

"For pain?" Kathryn asked.

"For pain, muscle spasms, anxiety, and depression."

"Do you prescribe it?"

"Oh, no. But I can usually tell when someone is using—I can feel it in their muscles."

"Really? What does it feel like?"

"The muscles are more relaxed and pliable."

"Do you two use cannabis?" Ellie asked.

"No," Dee said. "I'm a recovering alcoholic, so I stay away from it."

"I do, too, for the most part, to support Dee," Sally said. "I might have a couple of puffs at a party, but that's all. And I'll have a rare beer or glass of wine."

Dee hadn't taken her eyes off Kathryn. "Did you deal with substance abuse in your practice?" she asked.

"Yes, but I usually referred patients to the substance abuse program."

"My addiction had a strong physiological component," Dee said. "I had my first drink in high school and couldn't stop."

The four women shared their stories and at the end of the evening, made plans to meet in the lobby at nine the next morning.

CHAPTER 28

"Want to give it a try?" Kathryn asked, holding open a jar of expensive moisturizer.

Ellie, sitting on the toilet lid, leaned forward to examine the milky white substance. It looked like liquid silk, so unlike the homemade aloe vera and almond oil mixture she sometimes used. "No, that's okay."

"Go ahead. I won't report you to the Butch Police."

Ellie froze.

"Oops. Was that politically incorrect?"

"Well, no," Ellie said. "I'm just surprised you'd use that term. And, besides, *butch* and *femme* are sort of old-fashioned . . . and kinda not."

"Really?"

"It's true that one person in a lesbian couple may be more masculine or feminine than the other . . . but that, of course, just plays into male/female stereotypes."

Kathryn screwed the lid back on and leaned against the sink, facing Ellie. "Compared to you, I look like a femme, but that's not the way I feel toward you sexually. I feel quite aggressive, as a matter of fact . . . ."

"I've noticed."

". . . but there, look what I'm doing: I'm labeling 'aggressive' as masculine and, by default, 'passive' as feminine."

"Exactly. It's assigning gender to behavior. It's sexist quicksand."

"Well, I spoke without thinking. I'm sorry."

"Come here." Ellie rose and wrapped Kathryn in her arms. "There's nothing to apologize for. I don't want a censor sitting on your shoulder. Besides, who knows how long those terms will be around. So many young butch lesbians are becoming transmen." Ellie made a face and stepped back. "God! Let's not even go there!"

Kathryn reached into her toiletry bag and withdrew a tube of lotion. "Come on," she said, leading Ellie out of the bathroom. "Here, put your head on a pillow at the foot of the bed." She sat against the headboard, placed one of Ellie's feet on her lap, and began to knead the soft tissue of the arch.

"Ahhh, that feels good," Ellie said.

The radiator clattered to life, and cheerful sounds of hotel guests returning from dinner came through the heavy door. As Kathryn massaged a knot, she said, "I'd like to go there, Ellie."

Ellie's eyes snapped open. "What do you mean?"

"I'd like to know what you think about the trans issue."

"It's a difficult subject for me."

"So I sensed. All the more reason to shine some light on it."

"Oh, lord."

"Why is it difficult?"

"Because it's painful... because... because feminists are called transphobic if we even question the concept of gender."

Silently, Kathryn enfolded Ellie's ankles, squeezing and rubbing. Waiting.

"Thank goodness I grew up when I did. Nowadays, if a girl says she wishes she were a boy—as I did because I wanted to wear jeans and play football—her parents could cart her off to a doctor and she'd be on her way to transitioning." Ellie scowled. "A kid consigned to a lifetime of powerful drugs, and who knows what health complications."

"Sounds as if you disapprove of transgendering."

"No." Ellie flinched as Kathryn touched a tender spot near her heel. "People should control their own bodies—feminists have been on the front line of that battle for decades. Personally, I don't care how anyone dresses or presents themselves. But why can't behavior simply be human behavior? The only reason to assign a gender to it is to enforce a patriarchal stereotype."

"So you're saying behavior should not be associated with a gender?"

"Exactly," Ellie replied. "Women—especially lesbians—have been at the bottom of the heap for millennia because of prescribed gender roles." Ellie adjusted the pillow. "During my last year of teaching, ten lesbians started the fall semester in the LGBTQ student group. By spring, all had decided to transition except two who called themselves non-binary or genderqueer or some other godawful deconstructionist term."

"Why does that bother you?"

"Because young butches are buying into the patriarchy. They're becoming men, for Pete's sake! Lesbians are an endangered species. My culture, my identity are being erased by transgender ideology. They're being sacrificed to *gender fluidity.*"

Kathryn paused at the tears in Ellie's eyes. "Are you feeling threatened?"

"Of course I am! People say it's just the younger generation establishing its own norms. But they're laying waste to ours. We were despised in my day. Reclaiming the word 'lesbian' helped us own our power and build communities. Now kids scorn the word . . . and us."

"This *is* a painful issue."

"You have no idea. Transactivists derailed the whole Michigan Womyn's Music Festival—which is an excruciating story I don't want to get into. And then . . . ." Ellie looked out the window into the darkness beyond. "In my last year of teaching, I accidentally referred to a transwoman as 'he.' Mind you, Roberta looked and sounded totally male except for dangling earrings and a skirt."

"Oh-oh."

"All hell broke loose." Ellie grimaced at the memory. "I apologized immediately, but Roberta was enraged. Not a single student came to my defense. After berating me up and down, Roberta stormed out of class. I was shaking with fear. In my three decades of teaching, I had never had a complaint, but the next day I was sitting in front of the Dean having to explain my misgendering a student."

"Sounds traumatic."

"It was awful." Ellie's eyes began to tear again.

Kathryn tapped Ellie's other foot. "Next one," she said. She kneaded in silence for several moments. "It can be challenging to get the language right. I ran into that issue in my practice. I slipped up occasionally, but I never encountered the type of anger you did."

"I've found the young generation to be impatient and unforgiving regarding pronouns."

Kathryn gazed quizzically at Ellie. "Shouldn't people be able to call themselves whatever they want? Why should it matter to anyone else?"

"Because to say that transwomen *are* women entitles them to women's sports and shelters. If anyone objects, transactivists accuse them of hate speech. I believe in collaboration, and I want good-faith discussions, but it feels impossible in the face of such entitlement and rage."

Kathryn fingered the top of Ellie's foot. She sensed the bones and tendons under the moistened skin, living tissue that supported her lover as she walked upright in a world that had repeatedly tried to beat her down. The wounds went deep. "I can't fully appreciate what you're going through, Ellie, since I haven't lived my life as a lesbian."

"True."

"Neither can *we* fully appreciate what trans people go through since we haven't had their experience, much of which is deeply painful, too. But to have so much anger and resentment, Ellie, is spiritually corrosive. Perhaps someday you can forgive those who have injured you and your community."

"Maybe. But the vitriol . . . the misogyny!" Ellie caught her breath.

Kathryn gently laid Ellie's foot aside. "Come here," she said, and invited Ellie into her arms. She held her cautiously. "How are you doing?"

"Can we drop it?" Ellie pleaded.

"Of course, sweetheart," Kathryn said, gently kissing the top of Ellie's head.

CHAPTER 29

A thick mantle of glittering snow muffled all sound in Tuolumne Grove. Kathryn and Ellie soaked in the magic of the surrounding sugar pines and Douglas firs as they trudged along the path zigzagging down through the forest. Only the clink of their aluminum snowshoes striking each other broke the silence, ringing with startling clarity though the forest. Sally and Dee had set off before them and were now out of sight. It was as if Kathryn and Ellie were alone in the world.

They took their time, pausing for water breaks and to check on each other's well-being. By the time they reached the loop through the stand of sequoias, their muscles ached. They rested awkwardly against a fence, perching on a fat wooden slat. The Red Giant soared upward behind them into the brilliant sapphire sky, snow clinging to its branches and needle bunches. The crevices of the rust-colored bark held patches of snow.

Ellie slipped off the daypack on loan from Sandy, extracting energy bars and apples. "Here," she said, handing one of each to Kathryn. "Sustenance."

"Thanks." Kathryn tilted her head back. "My god, this tree makes me feel small."

"Me, too." Ellie thought for a moment. "And a little embarrassed that I got so worked up last night over gender politics. Nature on this scale puts everything into perspective, doesn't it?"

"It does."

The women stood for several moments in reverent admiration of the sequoia.

"This tree is probably thousands of years old," Kathryn said. "It'll be here long after we're all gone, no matter our sexuality, no matter our gender."

"Death, again. Is there any escaping it?"

"None. But death hardly seems possible in a moment like this."

"Sometimes I think it doesn't exist at all—we all just change form, melt into this, this wonder of nature. Mary's energy is here. I feel it."

Kathryn laid a hand on Ellie's arm. "It's all holy, isn't it? Especially the silence."

For several minutes the women filled their lungs with the sharp alpine air.

Ellie said at last, "How are you holding up, Kathryn?"

"I'm tired and my legs are sore. You?"

"Same. I'd forgotten how much work snowshoeing is."

"We could have covered the same distance in a tenth of the time if we had been skiing."

"Yeah, and I'd be lying halfway down the hill with broken bones."

Kathryn took a big bite out of her Braeburn. "Ah, carbs. Energy. I feel better already."

Ellie peered ahead on the trail. "Dee said this loop is about half a mile and that there are some twenty sequoias ahead. But we could appreciate this single tree and head back."

"Do you want to do that?"

"If you do."

"Okay, Ms. I'm-Not-Codependent." Kathryn humphed good-naturedly. "What do *you* want to do?"

"Call for a helicopter."

Kathryn's laugh rang like angel chimes through the forest. "Somehow I don't think air rescue is an option."

Ellie grinned and snapped off a chunk of energy bar. "Actually, I'm beyond caring. We're here. I think I could do another half mile . . . plus the mile back to the parking lot. But I'm also fine to turn around. I don't have a strong preference either way."

They listened for a few moments to the silence, deep and eerie. Otherworldly. Ellie would not have been surprised to see a sorceress with a pointed hat stepping from behind an ancient tree. The sequoia towered overhead, indifferent.

"It's beautiful here," Kathryn said at last. "Let's not be in a hurry to leave. We can take our time. I'd like to explore more."

"All right," Ellie said. "Onward and, eventually, upward."

Well over an hour later as they neared the Tuolumne Grove Trailhead, they heard a whoop. Sally waved at them furiously from behind her Subaru Outback. "Welcome back! You made it!"

"Ugh," Ellie said as she reached their car, "that last stretch is a killer."

"Here," Sally said, kneeling down and tearing back the Velcro straps of Ellie's snowshoes, "let me help you out of these things."

"Mine, too, please," Kathryn said, handing her poles to Dee who, with a shy grin, dropped to her knees to loosen the binding.

Both women stepped gingerly out of the foot harnesses.

"My thighs are burning," Ellie said, unzipping her outer jacket.

"You'll be sore for a few days. I have some Epsom salts you can soak in before you go to bed."

"I'll drop them off when we get back," Dee offered eagerly.

"Arnica would help, too," Sally added, giving her wife a private sideways smile.

"I have that already," Ellie said. "I'll need a good plop on my elbow. All that poling really aggravated it." She bent the distressed hinge back and forth.

"What happened?" Sally asked standing back up and brushing off her knees.

"Cubital tunnel syndrome."

"I'll take a look at it when *we* drop off the Epsom salts."

Kathryn broke in. "Say, am I smelling coffee?"

"Yes. We have hot coffee and lentil soup for you," Dee said, moving around to the back of her car.

Ellie and Kathryn, their legs not yet adjusted to being without snowshoes, shuffled over to the car. Two large Thermoses sat at the trunk edge. "Are you kidding?" Kathryn laughed.

"Always prepared," Dee said with a wink.

Sally poured the soup into mugs. "We have only two, so each couple can share, okay?"

"Fine," Ellie said.

Couple.

It was the first time someone had referred to Kathryn and Ellie as a couple. It felt odd, and when Ellie glanced at Kathryn, she saw that she, too, had been struck.

As the four women stood in the parking lot enjoying the soup, Kathryn said, "Were you waiting here to make sure we got back okay?"

"It didn't feel right driving off." Dee smiled.

"How long did you wait?"

"Not too long," Sally said. "We started on the loop a second time and went to the Tunnel Tree to take pictures, then we retraced our steps to the main path. It gave us a little extra workout."

"Thank you," Ellie said. "That was really kind. And thanks for the soup. It's perfect." She handed the steaming mug to Kathryn. "Here, finish up. I've got to unzip my inner jacket. I'm soaking."

Kathryn spooned the remaining soup into her mouth under the watchful eye of Dee.

"Coffee, anyone?" Sally asked, picking up the enamel pot.

She got two yeses. Ellie declined.

They savored the rich coffee aroma as a breeze sprang out of the winter-nipped forest. After finishing the brew, Sally and Dee began to organize their gear. "No need to help," Sally sang out. "Get back to the lodge and relax!"

As Ellie drove onto the main road, Kathryn said, "What a delightful pair. Waiting for us. Having soup and coffee at the ready. Wow."

"There are angels everywhere . . . including the one sitting next to me." She patted Kathryn's thigh. "I think Dee likes you."

"Yeah, the strong, silent types seem to fall for me."

"Wouldn't you know," Ellie teased, "I've fallen for a butch magnet."

The early afternoon sunlight shimmered overhead. The air was crisp, but warming, transforming the snow into rivulets and puddles on the road. They drove around Yosemite with no destination in mind, open to what presented itself. They took switchbacks up and down the mountains, stopping where they could to absorb the panoramas of jagged, snow-covered peaks and skirts of pine striped with snow. El Capitan and Half Dome loomed over the valley like huge guardians. Even as Ellie took photos on her phone, she knew the pictures would be unworthy of the experience of being in the clear alpine air with 360 degrees of nature at her most magnificent.

"My god, we did it!" Ellie crowed at one point. "We snowshoed in Yosemite. Can you believe it! I never in a thousand years would have thought of doing it."

"I'm proud of us for pushing ourselves."

"Yes, but I think it's the last time I go snowshoeing."

"Oh, come on. You may change your mind when we go to the North Shore some winter."

A warm excitement rose in Ellie. This was the first time Kathryn had mentioned plans after the trip. *A future.* It felt significant, like Sally calling them a couple. "If my body has recovered by then."

"Sounds like we need a hot bath and a massage. Let's hope my new admirer remembers to drop off the Epsom salts."

"She will."

Kathryn reached for Ellie's hand. Was this a dream, her sitting next to a woman unknown to her a month ago, but now her lover? How could this be? The break from her past life was almost too fast and too wide to be integrated into her present. Sally had called them a couple. She guessed they were now, but what did that mean? Maybe she needed to call on Anna's spirit to have a good long chat. Immediately her old friend's pure voice flashed in her mind: *You're alive, Kathryn! Be here now!*

And she was, here in the present, totally alive. The world seemed torqued into a sharper and brighter realm, the colors supersaturated, the sounds as distinct as snowflakes. "I love you, Ellie," she heard herself saying.

Ellie glanced at Kathryn, her face open and glowing. She squeezed Kathryn's hand, took it and raised it to her lips. "I return it ten-fold."

After her divorce, so much had fallen away from her life. Kathryn had thought her remaining days would be routine. She would settle, could settle, into contentment. But now her future looked as vast as the valleys spread before her, teeming with life bursting into spring.

April had changed her, washed her soul with a magic potion in Minnesota that was finding its fruition in the heights of the Sierras. This is what she wanted, someone as clean and keen as the mountain air. She embraced the world they were creating together, she and Ellie alone, in an immense universe. She could not remember when she had been so happy, yet she knew there had been times, long ago. The capping as a nurse; her wedding day; the birth of her children. But all those days were layered now with the amber veneer of decades past, and this—this passion with Ellie—was here and now, and as alive as her skin under Ellie's mouth.

And yet. And yet. In two days, they would enter the world of family: Ellie and Mary's niece, and then her own daughter, Jenn. Kathryn had heard enough in all her years of sitting across from distressed souls in a small, softly lit room to know that the magic eventually dissipates in the glare of reality. Change was inevitable, and how they—she and Ellie—responded could set the course for the rest of their lives.

PART THREE

CHAPTER 30

$\mathscr{P}$rivate Land. No Trespassing.

The red and white aluminum signs barked an unfriendly welcome as the Lexus made its way down a one-lane dirt road. Through the tall hedges, Ellie and Kathryn could catch glimpses of rolling green pastures dotted with live oaks and grazing horses. But the vegetation seemed to close in on Kathryn like an ominous forest, enveloping her in a strange anxiety.

The purpose of the trip was at hand—taking full-spectrum, high-potency cannabis oil to Minnesota—and for the first time, the truth of their adventure hit her. She and Ellie had been carried along on a current of bliss for the past two weeks. It had been easy to forget there was a destination other than a flat surface with queen-sized sheets or meals with wine and intimate conversation. But once they took possession of the Rick Simpson Oil, they would be lawbreakers.

She had a lot to lose. Her license. Her family. Her money. Her lover. Her freedom. Ellie had been so casual about the whole matter. But she, herself, had been stupidly naïve.

"Could we stop for a moment?" Kathryn said, her voice tight.

"Now?"

"Right now. This second."

Ellie braked and put the car into park. "What's wrong?"

"I don't like what we're doing."

"What are we doing?"

"Picking up drugs."

"You mean medicinal botanicals?"

Kathryn leveled a withering look at Ellie. "Don't play word games with me."

This was the first flash of anger Ellie had seen in Kathryn. She knew to keep calm. The anger came from fear, and it was the fear she needed to deal with. She paused before replying, taking in the dense hedges that seemed to encapsulate the car. "Let's get some air in here." She reached up to press the switch that opened the sunroof. Cleansing sunlight poured in as the tinted glass slid back.

Kathryn raised her face to the rectangle of sky overhead, a blue flag signaling freedom. A breeze stirred the charged interior air.

"Are you feeling claustrophobic?" Ellie asked. Kathryn looked as if she wanted to take flight, a hummingbird speeding to the southern continent.

"A little."

"What's going on?"

"The thought of transporting the cannabis oil is starting to frighten me. Why are we taking this risk?"

"I'm doing it for someone I love, and the chances of being caught are miniscule."

"But possible."

"Anything is possible. Is it probable? No. People carry this stuff all the time."

"We've both got a lot to lose."

"You're right," Ellie said. She unbuckled her seatbelt so she could turn fully toward Kathryn. "You know, after Mary died, I didn't really care what I lost. This cannabis run was as much an excuse to get away as it was to pick up medicinals for Kris. Nothing mattered very much. But now, with you . . . ." Ellie took Kathryn's hand and kissed her knuckles one by one. "I won't do anything to jeopardize what we have."

Kathryn remained taut and unappeased. "Meaning?"

"Meaning we don't have to do this. Or at least you don't. You could fly back to Minnesota from Sacramento and I could drive back alone."

"But what if you're caught."

"I'll deal with it," Ellie said, her voice hardening.

"And where is the 'we' in that response? What happens to you affects me, you know."

"Oh, lord." Ellie flopped back in her seat. "I'm sorry. Of course, it does. I've been alone for so long I'm thinking only of myself. I'm not used to being partnered again."

"Is that what we are? Partners? I don't know what that means."

Ellie shut off the car engine. "Kathryn, you're starting to scare me. What's going on?"

Kathryn's eyes started to water. "I don't know. I'm not used to being scared." She took in the sky and breathed in all the freedom it promised.

"You're scared of transporting the RSO. What else?"

"Isn't that enough?"

Ellie waited.

"Oh, I don't know," Kathryn sighed. "I'm nervous about meeting your people. I don't know why. Lord knows I've dealt with plenty of drug culture folks in my job."

"Trisha and Mark are farmers, not druggies. Their operation is legit . . . except the RSO is a little dicey. Jeez, what do you think I'm taking you to?"

"I don't know." Kathryn let the breeze wash over her and tuned into the staccato melody of a house finch. She focused on the hard nugget of fear in her diaphragm. "Things seemed fine when they were in the abstract. But now everything is becoming real."

"The honeymoon is over?"

"I don't know." A tear rolled down Kathryn's cheek.

"Oh, sweetheart," Ellie said, leaning into Kathryn and putting an arm around her. "We're not over, are we?"

Kathryn shook her head.

"Whew." Ellie put her forehead against Kathryn's. "Think of what you've gone through in a little over a year," Ellie said. "The shock of your husband's infidelity, a divorce, looking for a new home, retirement, a new relationship, expanding sexuality, and now flirting with the law. Any one of those experiences is a lot to handle. No wonder you're feeling off balance."

Tears continued to seep out of Kathryn's eyes.

Ellie stroked Kathryn's hair. "Do you want me to take you back to the B & B?"

Kathryn breathed deeply, her mind checking her gut. "No. We're almost to the farm, aren't we?"

"It doesn't make any difference. If you want to go back, we can."

"How? There's nowhere to turn around."

"This is a pretty up-to-date car." Ellie smiled. "It has a reverse gear. Or when we get to the farm, I can turn around in their yard."

"I don't know."

"Remember, we're only visiting today. We won't pick up any product."

Kathryn broke from Ellie and nudged her back into her seat. "I need to blow my nose," she said, pulling a tissue from her purse.

"We don't have to figure things out now. Let's have lunch here as planned and then go back to the B & B. How's that?"

Kathryn closed her eyes. "Okay. Let's sit here while I compose myself. Then onward."

CHAPTER 31

*T*he road took a sharp turn to the left around a copse of walnut trees and opened into a clearing. To the right a geodesic dome appeared and straight ahead four huge greenhouses, one small greenhouse, a corrugated tin warehouse, and a small parking area with several cars. To the left, an array of solar panels marched across a quarter acre like a phalanx of robots. A large vegetable garden lay near the dome. The newly mown lawn glimmered vibrant green, and purple and yellow irises waved alongside the house.

"Goodness!" Kathryn exclaimed, slack jawed.

"Impressive, huh?"

"I don't know what I was imagining, but certainly not this."

Ellie circled in front of the house and parked alongside a Toyota Prius and a Range Rover. She exited the car and stretched.

The side door of the dome sprang open and a lithe woman with a long blond ponytail emerged with a big grin on her freckled face. She wore blue-tinted wireless glasses and silver earrings. A couple of golden retrievers bounded after her, barking and with tails wagging.

"Ellie!" she cried, giving her aunt a bear hug. "So good to see you!"

"It's great to be here," Ellie said. "Trisha, this is Kathryn. Kathryn, my niece, Trisha."

The women locked eyes, gray meeting blue, and shook hands. "Nice to meet you," they said in unison.

"Welcome to Deep Haven Farm, Kathryn. Ellie speaks highly of you," Trisha said with genuine warmth after she shushed the dogs. "Please make yourself at home. We have some drinks in the fridge and there's a hammock around the side of the house if you need to stretch out for a bit. I know the road in here can be jarring. We'll get around to having it paved one of these days."

"You're very kind, thank you," Kathryn said quietly. "It's nice to be here," she added because suddenly it was—the sounds of leaves stirring and a woodpecker hammering away soothed her. "It's quite an operation you have. There are so many buildings."

"That's not by our choosing, believe me," Trisha said, the smile leaving her face, but the warmth remaining. "The cannabis industry is highly regulated, and there are different building and licensing requirements for the different phases of production."

"Do you give tours?"

"Not officially, but for you, yes. Would you like to do that now?"

"I'd love to, thanks. Does that suit you, El?" Kathryn's eyes lit with curiosity, her thirst for knowledge trumping fear.

"Sure." Ellie winked in encouragement.

"Mark is in the veg house, so let's start there. Can I get you anything to drink before we set off? The sun is pretty hot."

"I'm fine," Kathryn said.

"Me, too," Ellie put a reassuring hand on Kathryn's back.

In Greenhouse One, or the veg house, Mark was halfway down a row inspecting an eighteen-inch cannabis plant on the lower tier of shelving.

"Look who's here!" Trisha called out.

Mark glanced up and broke into a wide smile. He sported a brown beard with hints of red. "You made it!" He gave Ellie a hug and offered his hand to Kathryn. "Nice to meet you."

"Would you like me to show them around?" Trisha asked. "Or would you prefer to do it?"

"Go ahead. I'll continue with the mothers."

"Mothers?" Kathryn said. She fingered the white tag on a plant and read its varietal name: Girl Scout Cookie.

"These all are mother plants." Mark walked toward a row of clear plastic tents. "Right now, I'm selecting the ones to clip. We put the clippings in the controlled grow rooms." Mark unzipped a space-age looking cube to reveal shelves of small plants. "Once they're big enough, they go into pots like you see."

He pointed at some small-bore tubing. "There you can see our drip irrigation. Given the water situation in this state, we want to be as frugal as possible with the ol' H2O."

"Everything here is organic and pesticide-free," Trisha added. "Most of what you find in the dispensaries is dirty. We want our brand to be contaminant-free."

"How do you keep away the bugs?"

"With great care." Mark smiled the smile of someone who holds a trade secret.

Trisha showed Kathryn the flowering, drying, and processing areas as well as the nursery where seeds and starter plants were prepped to sell. In another building, four workers in white lab coats and hair protectors stood at black trays piled high with buds. The pungent smell of marijuana, intense as incense, permeated the building.

"Have you ever used cannabis?" Trisha asked.

"I smoked a little pot in college," Kathryn said with a smile.

"You don't smoke anymore?"

"No, not in decades. Back then it was mostly at parties. I never felt the effects, so it didn't seem worth the risk of getting caught."

"The product is more potent nowadays . . . and there are so many varietals to choose from. It's a matter of finding which one is most agreeable. I'll give you a couple of joints to try—that's a legal amount to possess in California."

"Thanks." Kathryn smiled.

"Well, that ends the official tour," Trisha said with a wink.

"Now comes the off-Broadway show?" Ellie asked.

"Yes. Rick Simpson Oil."

"You don't make it here?" Kathryn asked.

"No, we keep it separate from the commercial areas—it's our own private activity."

Trisha led Kathryn and Ellie behind the vegetable plot where potato and carrot tops poked up from the brown soil, along with a riot of kale, lettuce, and chard. A small, well-ventilated structure served both as a garden shed and RSO processing station. One- and two-gallon plastic pails, small vats, cedar poles for mashing, and other paraphernalia, including a rice cooker and capsule filling machine, occupied various tables.

"I have some oil in the dehydrator right now." Trisha pointed to a machine on a stainless-steel worktable. "We're reducing it to a thick sludge. Once that's done, I'll put it in capsules." She motioned to a bag holding hundreds of empty pill-sized casings.

At one end of the table, a small shoe box held two baggies. Kathryn picked up the one marked *At Night* and studied it.

"That's the order for Kris," Trisha said. "A count of 365 capsules of RSO for night-time use. The other bag has 365 CBD capsules—no THC—for the morning. A year's supply."

"But there's only a drop in the RSO capsules," Kathryn said, examining a clear gelatin capsule with a dot of tar at one end. "It's mostly empty unlike the CBD which looks like it's full of oil."

"It looks peculiar, doesn't it? But one drop of RSO is all it takes."

"Potent stuff."

"Very. As you can see, we're not talking about a trunk full of drugs here. Everything I'm sending back with Ellie fits nicely into a small box."

"Well, thanks, Trisha," Kathryn said. "I have a much better idea of what we're dealing with."

Ellie stood to the side, annoyed with herself for not painting a better picture for Kathryn. Heaven knows what she had envisioned—a backwoods, drug-running criminal enterprise that would stuff their trunk with garbage bags full of drugs?

CHAPTER 32

As they were walking back toward the house, Kathryn said, "I was expecting to see rows of marijuana in the fields, but it looks like you're doing most of the growing indoors."

"Yes, we've found it's easier to raise the crops in a climate-controlled environment. We have several acres where we used to grow other crops to hide the marijuana, but now that it's legal, we've let those acres go fallow so they can be certified organic in case we want to put in vegetables or herbs . . . or more cannabis."

Ellie went to the car to fetch a couple bottles of Napa Valley whites for lunch.

Kathryn followed Trisha indoors through the mudroom. "What about theft?" she asked.

"There's always the threat of marauders—whether feds, local narcs, or bad-ass gangs. A lot of money is involved. We have over a quarter of a million plants here, so we've installed a top-notch security system."

As they entered the living area, Kathryn exclaimed, "What a delightful home!" The dome had an open floor plan and a staircase to the loft across the way, with the kitchen and dining area to the right. Earth-tone furniture accented by colorful pillows with New Age symbols filled the bright space. "I've never been in a geodesic dome."

"We love it."

"Did you build it yourselves?"

"No, it was here when I bought the land." Trisha turned to Kathryn and laid a hand on her arm. In a lowered voice, she said, "I just want to tell you, Kathryn, I'm so glad you and Ellie found each other. Mary's death

was painful for us all . . . and Ellie has been so alone. She deserves someone special."

"Thank you. I'm sorry you lost your aunt. She must have been
extraordinary."

"She was—and a lot of fun even after she got sick. I don't know if
I could have been in such good spirits in her situation." Trisha opened
the refrigerator and took out a large salad bowl filled with a variety of
greens. "Fresh from the garden!" she said, mostly succeeding in returning to cheerfulness.

"It's beautiful!" Kathryn said.

"There's a quinoa and nut salad, too. We're pretty much vegetarians,
although we never pass up barbeque ribs."

"Who can?" Kathryn smiled. "Should I set the table?"

"Already done."

The two couples gathered on the cedar deck at the southwest corner
of the house. A large tree provided dappled shade. A slight breeze stirred
the branches and marijuana-scented air.

"I imagine legalization has made your lives a lot easier," Kathryn ventured after the food had been passed around.

"Far from it," Mark said. "We don't have to worry about state officials
as much, but we don't trust the feds and, really, there's always some gov-
ernment bureaucrat itching to do us in."

"Our big concern," Trisha said, "is big ag monopolizing the industry.
Already they're shooting for hundreds of acres of cultivation, and with size
comes economy of scale. We could eventually be priced out of the market.
We've spent a ton of money to be legit—and organic—but now we don't
know if it was worth it. Luckily we have a loyal client base."

"Doesn't making RSO put your enterprise at risk?" Kathryn asked.

"Well, that's an issue, but we make it only for our family's use, so that's
okay" Trisha looked like she wanted to say more, but refrained.

"That's right. It's illegal to sell, so we don't." Mark's smile said,
I'm lying.

"How on earth did you get into this?" Kathryn asked.

The young couple exchanged a look. Mark scooted his chair back and pulled up a pant leg to reveal a palm-sized patch of pale skin on his calf. "Skin cancer. Ten years ago."

"How did it get so big?"

"I was an oblivious nerd programming games 24/7. I never paid attention to it until it was the size of a quarter. The doctors wanted to cut off my calf. That was not an option for me. I went into full internet research mode and stumbled on Rick Simpson's website and gave RSO a try. That's how I met Trisha."

"I'd been growing the indica cannabis strain for several years here with my ex," Trisha said. "Mark needed a lot of bud to boil down for the oil. We figured out how to make RSO, create a salve to put on the cancer, and fell in love doing it. Mark moved in and turned this place into what you see now. We kept making RSO on the side—it's the only hope some people have."

"I made a lot of money—I mean a lot—from the gaming world. It was fun . . . but this life I have—we have—is rewarding. I wouldn't trade it for anything." Mark kissed the back of Trisha's hand.

Over a dessert of peach cobbler, Trisha said, "Are you nervous about driving back to Minnesota with the RSO?"

Kathryn tapped her nose with a finger. "Yes. In fact, I almost had a meltdown on our way here."

"I'm sorry," Trisha said. "I won't tell you how to feel, of course, but the amount I'm giving Ellie is relatively small. Even if you are stopped by cops, the chances they'd discover it are tiny. Besides, who can tell by looking at a drop of oil in a capsule that it's RSO. I wouldn't worry."

"But I do."

"It's not like you're traveling with a brick of bud," Mark said. "Its odor can be picked up by dogs—and people—very easily. But folks travel all the time through airports with cannabis oil. Now, I wouldn't recommend keeping any joints in the car on the way home. Cops seem to take a perverse pleasure in finding them."

"Law enforcement is confused these days," Trisha said. "There's such a patchwork of regulations."

"The states where cannabis is legal are reaping huge revenues," Mark said. "You'd be amazed at the products coming online and all the processing, packaging, and distribution that's involved—and that means jobs as well as tax revenue."

"That's just the economic part," Trisha noted.

"Right," Mark said. "Eventually the medical establishment is going to have to accept cannabis when they can no longer ignore its benefits."

"Nurses and naturopaths may be our wedge," Trisha said. "They do direct patient care and can see the results of cannabis and RSO. They really are the ones who have the patience and skill to come up with a workable—and legal—dosage for patients. There's even a national organization of cannabis nurses. If Mary had lived, I bet you anything she would have become one."

"All I can say is that I'm stunned," Kathryn said. "I had no idea about any of this."

Ellie eyed Kathryn. Enough! "Let's move to the lounge chairs," she suggested, "and get more comfortable." And away from the harangue before their hosts could start in on big pharma. She longed to settle her glutes, still sore from snowshoeing, on softer cushions.

CHAPTER 33

*N*evada City was the quintessential Old West town with brick and clapboard buildings from the gold rush days lining the main thoroughfare. But now, instead of Forty-Niners lusting for yellow nuggets and flapjacks, weekenders from the Central Valley and the Bay Area came seeking a getaway in one of the charming inns serving gourmet breakfasts.

Ellie and Kathryn landed in one of those B & Bs, a large Queen Anne mansion with Deer Creek burbling along in the back yard. After spending the afternoon at the farm hearing anecdotes about the healing powers of cannabis, they were relaxing on a bench by the creek, wine glasses in hand, and triple cream brie and whole grain crackers on a small plate between them.

"I used to sell Girl Scout cookies," Kathryn said. "I never dreamed I'd be smoking them." She took a pull on a joint and, coughing, handed it to Ellie.

"Oh-ho! You were a Girl Scout!"

"Yes, and a den mother for a few years."

"Did you ever fall in love with a camp counselor?"

Kathryn stared at Ellie. "Guitar-strumming Cindy Sanders," she said at last. "I do believe I had a crush on her. First thing I did when I got home was have my parents buy me a guitar."

"So not quite a straight line to your marriage."

"Maybe not. I haven't thought about Cindy in decades."

"Interesting varietal, this Girl Scout Cookie. I like it . . . though my experience with dope is somewhat limited. That shows my age right there. Dope. Weed. Grass. Lesbians. All of our old nomenclatures are gone. We're antiquated, Kathryn." Ellie took a hit on the tightly rolled joint.

"The professionalism of Trisha's operation impressed me and seeing all the products in the store downtown—wow, it normalizes cannabis. I don't feel so nervous now about driving back home with it."

They sat quietly for a while, watching the creek splash by, listening to a crow family squabbling in the trees across the way, taking turns with the potent roll.

"I think the last time I smoked was when I was a senior at the U," Kathryn said. "It's appropriate because I feel like I'm back in school taking courses—in sex and cannabis."

"Sounds like my undergraduate years," Ellie said, laughing.

"I'm sorry for my meltdown in the car this morning."

"I'm the one who should be apologizing, Kathryn. I didn't explain things very well."

"I didn't ask enough questions, either."

"I can still drive back alone if you'd prefer."

"No, I want to be with you. Partner."

"What was *that* about?"

"I don't know." Kathryn listened to the burbling stream. "But you were wise to open the sunroof. It gave me an escape hatch. You're so good for me."

Passing the joint back and forth, they left the stone upturned, the darkness exposed to light and air.

"Do you have any interest in a career change," Ellie asked, "as in becoming a cannabis consultant, perhaps?"

Kathryn shook her head and blew out a stream of smoke. "I've already changed my career. I'm an orgasm doula now."

Ellie laughed. "Really? How's that going?"

"Excellent. I have only one client, but one is enough."

"She must pay well."

"In cash, not so much, but the perks are mighty fine," said Kathryn.

As Ellie took Kathryn's hand and kissed it, they heard an ethereal ring tone. Kathryn squinted at her phone lying on the table. "Busted," she said with a laugh. "It's my son. Do you mind?"

"Go ahead."

"Hi, Nate," Kathryn chirped.

"Hi, Mom. You're sounding cheerful."

"I'm here, too," said another voice. It was Nate's wife, Sarah.

"Both of you on the line? This must be important."

"Well, Mom, we got a call from Jenn. She's worried about you."

"Of course she is. That's her nature. To worry."

"But what's happening?"

What's happening is I'm sitting by a stream in the Sierra Nevadas smoking a joint with my lesbian lover. Instead she said, "What isn't happening? It's true. I've fallen in love with a woman—Ellie—and I couldn't be happier." *Or higher.*

"You must be. I've never heard you sound so . . . giddy."

Kathryn made an I'd-better-get-sober face at Ellie.

"Have you told the boys yet?"

"No," Sarah said, "but I can predict the response. They'll say 'cool' and a minute later, they'll have forgotten it."

Kathryn laughed. "Harsh and wonderful."

"Is Ellie there with you now?" Sarah asked.

"Yes."

"Could you put her on the line?"

Kathryn mouthed to Ellie, *they want to talk with you. Okay?* With Ellie's nod, she switched on the speaker. "Okay, here she is."

"Hello, Sarah and Nate," Ellie said. "How are you?" She quickly extinguished the joint and set it aside.

"Hi, Ellie," Sarah said. "We're fine and we want to tell you how happy we are for you and Kathryn."

"Thank you. We feel very lucky to have found each other," she said, making goo-goo eyes at Kathryn.

"Where are you now?" Nate asked.

"We're in Nevada City, sitting by a stream, enjoying a glass of pinot noir."

"Sounds heavenly."

"It is."

"Jenn has filled us in about you," Sarah said. "She's exhausted Google and can't find a thing to criticize, other than you were a tough grader."

"I make no defense. It's true." Ellie put a smile in her voice. "Tell me, Nate, how are you feeling about this development with your mom?"

"It was quite a surprise, as you can imagine. But I love her, and I want her to be happy. It's just that it seems so out of character, so . . . impulsive."

"It was sudden."

"Oh, come on, Nate," Sarah said. "Don't you believe in love at first sight?"

"Was it like that?"

"For me it was," Ellie said.

"It took me a little while," Kathryn said.

"You met at a Starbucks?" Sarah asked.

"Yes," Ellie said. "Fate brought us together and let the magic work."

Sarah laughed. "Well, that's wonderful. When you two get back, I'd like to have you over for dinner."

"You're on," Kathryn said. "Text me a couple of dates that work for you."

After the good-byes, Kathryn took a sip of wine. "You can see why I love Sarah so much. She's a gem. At least we won't have any problem with that branch of the family."

CHAPTER 34

The walk to the heart of Nevada City was a bit challenging with its streets twisting over the hilly terrain like the veins of ore that once brought riches to the city. Ellie and Kathryn chose an Italian restaurant off the main thoroughfare and took a quiet table near the rear.

As they studied the menu, a waiter approached. "What can I get you young ladies to drink?" he said breezily.

Ellie caught the young man's eye and held his gaze until he realized he had done something wrong. "I know your intentions are good," she said, "but we are not young ladies, and to be called young disrespects our age."

"Oh, gosh. I . . . I . . . I'm sorry. I didn't mean to be disrespectful."

"I know you didn't." Ellie gave him a warm smile and turned back to the menu.

They placed their orders—fish and a glass of chardonnay for both. After the waiter scurried off, Ellie said, "I hate it when people call me young. I'm not young. It's considered a compliment because old is seen as undesirable."

"Do you have some feelings about this?" Kathryn said, an affectionate glimmer in her eye.

"Yes! I want to be proud of my age—out and proud, old and bold!"

Kathryn laughed.

"The crazy thing is, ever since I met you, I've been feeling like a teenager. I'm full of energy, my libido is off the charts. Love songs scroll through my head like there's no off button."

"I know what you mean."

"But those feelings aren't just for teenagers," Ellie said. "I'm—we're—experiencing them and we're in our sixties. Falling in love doesn't have an age limit."

"Do you think we just associate those feelings with our younger selves?"

"Maybe, but ageism is so deeply embedded in our culture. When I say I feel young, what I mean is I feel vibrant and alive." Ellie shook her head. "Why can't I just say that? It's all internalized ageism."

"The first time we made love, I wished I'd had my young, firm body to give you. As though, what? I was better then? You'd love me more? Desire me more?"

"This knee-jerk loathing of old people is corrosive to our self-esteem, Kathryn."

"At Highland Meadows, I remember looking around at all the people in their eighties and nineties, and thinking, *Thank God, I'm glad I'm not that old.* But I will be one day—soon, actually—and so will you. Where will we be with our self-esteem then? We may have rich, passionate lives, but we'll be dismissed as ugly and useless."

"It's odd, isn't it, that of all the isms, ageism is the one everyone can experience—it's a condition we all grow into. So why do we disparage growing old when it's everyone's fate?"

The waiter came with their plates. "Ladies," he said, "I'd like to offer you another drink on the house."

"Why, how kind," Ellie said, suppressing the impulse to point out that *ladies* is classist. "I'd like another chardonnay."

"The same for me, please," Kathryn said.

As they began to eat, Ellie said, "I'll give him a generous tip to show I don't hold his comment against him."

"I doubt he'll make that mistake again," Kathryn said. "Anyway, going back to what we were saying, I think ageism is fear-based, like any ism. Fear of the other. Fear of death."

"When we're young, we're indoctrinated to see old age as distasteful, so by the time we're old, we turn it against our peers—I look younger than she does, I can walk farther, better, faster than he can. It becomes competitive."

"And then what, especially if our health is compromised? How can we accept the changes with grace, to say yes to the challenges and losses?"

"How do we break free?"

"By doing what we're doing. Talking about it. Educating ourselves. Calling ourselves and others on ageism. And then at some point, we'll just have to say to the world, 'Piss off!'"

Ellie raised her glass in a toast. "To us, Kathryn. May we embrace our journey to the end of our days . . . ."

Kathryn leaned in. "And go at it like bunnies until then."

———— ○∞○ ————

Later that night they lay in bed, their limbs woven in a tapestry of spent desire.

"Not bad for two young ladies," Ellie said.

"Yes, but this young lady can't keep it up," Kathryn said.

"What do you mean?"

"I'm exhausted, still sore from snowshoeing, and probably on the verge of a urinary tract infection."

"Well, so much for being bunnies."

"Their lifespan is what? Three, five years? No wonder they screw like maniacs." Kathryn brushed the hair back from Ellie's forehead. "How would you feel if I stayed here tomorrow while you went to the farm?"

Ellie repositioned herself up on one elbow to make eye contact with Kathryn.

"That would be fine."

"I like Trisha and Mark, but I could use some alone time."

"And maybe not so many stories of cannabis miracles?"

Kathryn smiled. "I appreciate their passion, but cannabis is not a cure-all. Their certitude gives short shrift to so many healing modalities. I'll stick with functional medicine which deals with the source of disease, not just treating symptoms."

Ellie traced a finger along Kathryn's eyebrows. "I love it when you talk scientific."

Kathryn's eyes narrowed. "You're not patronizing me, are you?"

"God! Never." When Ellie realized Kathryn was teasing, she gave her a little jostle.

"What do you plan to do at the farm?"

"Probably just hang out, help out in the garden or whatever else."

"When will we get the RSO?"

"I thought Friday after we check out. We can go to the farm for lunch and then drive directly to Sacramento. Any word from Jenn?"

"No. I'll call her if I haven't heard anything by morning."

"I think," Ellie said, settling back into Kathryn's arms, "my day may be more fun than yours."

CHAPTER 35

$\mathcal{K}$athryn texted Jenn the next morning asking if it was a good time to talk. The immediate answer was no, call after lunch.

After an hour of yoga and meditation, the rest of Kathryn's morning was free. While the funky shops of the town beckoned her, she remained awhile at the B & B with coffee and a sketchbook. The other guests had checked out or were off on their day adventures, so Kathryn was by herself on the back deck. She sat at one of the round tables looking past the white balustrades toward the creek, whose comforting murmur rose up over the gardens. The sketchbook remained unopened, the soft-leaded pencil by its side.

The coffee was delicious. Kathryn smelled it. Tasted it. Let the heat of the ceramic mug warm her hands. Life vibrated around her and in her. It felt good to be alone. To think alone. To breathe alone.

Kathryn had been alone for over a year and, in fact, had been alone long before that. Now another relationship had rolled in like a fine, replenishing mist. She and Ellie had talked about forever, but at their age they knew there was no such thing. Time was not limitless, and she needed to choose wisely how to spend it.

She had always thought she would die for her children and grandchildren. But would she give up Ellie if those relationships were threatened? Jenn was capable of such a demand. The prospect did not frighten her, only saddened her.

She would keep Ellie. Her own life and her own happiness were separate from those of her children, who had long ago made their own way in the world. She didn't know how many years she had left, and she did not want them to be lonely. But Ellie was more than a bulwark against isolation. She had her heart. Kathryn would not trade the joy and excitement and passion she now had for some dour existence that would please a discomfited daughter . . . as if anything she could do would find approval in Jenn's eyes.

To be truthful, the disappointment ran both ways. Kathryn had hoped for a daughter who would be strong, not wayward; perceptive, not self-centered; loving, not judgmental. Jenn had a gift for annoying people, and often that annoyance was aimed at her. But at her heart, Jenn was a good person. She loved her children, and they were turning out to be fine young women. Kathryn could and would love her daughter just as she was. She always had.

⸎

After a satisfying morning in the garden hoeing weeds, cutting back vines, and picking lettuce, Ellie and Trisha now lounged on deck chairs sipping a post-lunch iced tea. The sun tracked into the afternoon sky, and the westerly breeze stirred the leaves of the nearby oak tree.

"What are your plans, Ellie?" Trisha asked. Her blond hair had deepened into a lustrous gold in the shadow of the house.

"For what?"

Trisha smiled. "Life in general. For you and Kathryn. Are you thinking of living together? Getting married?"

"It's a little early."

"Is it?"

"Are you implying we don't have time to waste?" Ellie laughed, rousing from a languid torpor. "And if so, you're probably right."

"I always thought of you and Mary as the perfect couple. You were so kind and respectful of each other. I've tried to model myself after you two, but Mark is no Mary." Trisha paused. "We've got a great marriage, don't get me wrong, but with a man there's always a bit of an edge. Men—no matter how feminist they might be—never truly understand their privilege."

"I think you're right."

"Anyway, when you told me you were seeing someone, I pictured another Mary. Kathryn's not like Mary at all."

"No, they're different in many ways . . . and alike in important ones, such as values."

"I've met many of your friends, Ellie," Trisha persisted. "Kathryn is very different."

"I think what you're trying to say is that she seems very straight." Ellie smiled. "Yes, it's true, but a lot of that is simply a matter of style."

"Don't get me wrong. I really like her. She's a lovely, sincere person. I just don't want to see you hurt."

"I appreciate your concern. I don't know quite how to explain it. We're tuned into the same frequency on a lot of levels. And not just on the hormonal one," Ellie said, making a funny face. "Does that make sense?"

"Yes, it does." Trisha glanced heavenward. "I think that somewhere, wherever she is, Mary is happy for you . . . and maybe a little surprised."

Ellie smiled at her niece—by marriage to Mary, yes, but in her heart also. "I hope so. I also know there are no guarantees. All I can say is this day is good. You know Mary is irreplaceable, and I thought I could never fall in love again. But somehow it happened, and I'm going to ride this pony into the sunset."

"Well, then, yeeee-haw!" Trisha bellowed. "You know you have my blessing . . . as though you need permission from anyone."

"I don't, but it's a comfort to have."

"How will it be for you being a step-mom and a step-grandma? You're not used to being around kids."

"I don't know. I'll settle into my place whatever it'll be—and I have no expectations. I did talk with Kathryn's son and his wife. They seem sweet."

The golden retrievers dashed past as a black squirrel leapt onto a low hanging branch of a pine tree and scampered up to safety.

"How are things here, Trish? Really."

Trisha took a deep breath and let it out slowly. "I'm struggling a bit, Ellie. This operation has grown beyond my comfort level. Mark loves it—marijuana to the masses—but I see too many red flags. We've got investors who want to see a return on their money . . . ."

"Wait. I thought Mark financed the expansion."

"He likes people to think so." Trisha smiled sadly. "But some partners are unhappy about our RSO sideline."

"Time to give it up?"

"Yeah, all it takes is one screw up. I'm outsourcing production to one of our former employees. She'll do the cooking, which is a nasty chore, and the distribution. She'll find a way to get product to you or Kris."

"Whew. Actually, I'm relieved. I've been worried about your sideline now that you're legit." Ellie watched the dogs curl up in a spot of sun. "Kathryn's jitters have given me second thoughts . . ." Ellie stifled a yawn ". . . about doing these cannabis runs."

"I'd miss your visits, but it's probably for the best." Trisha hesitated. "You look sleepy, Ellie. In fact, I've been wondering about your health. Are you getting arthritis? You're walking a little . . . ."

"Stiffly?" Ellie snorted. "Kathryn and I snowshoed in Yosemite. We're still paying for it."

"You two!" Trisha's eyes brightened in admiration. "I have some CBD drops and salve that'll help. Now, why don't you take a nap in the hammock. We can move it into the shade, if you want."

"Let's leave it in the sun."

Ellie eased into the hemp rope hammock and adjusted the pillow. She laced her fingers through the spreader bar above her head and took in the blue sky curving to forever. Two clouds far above her passed through each other, but it was an illusion, a trick of altitude. They were separate entities on different air currents, perhaps mixing a few molecules, and then they were past each other, already history.

Ellie shuddered and retrieved her phone from the back pocket of her jeans. She texted Kris: *Can you chat?*

Within the minute, her phone rang.

"Hey, Kris," Ellie said.

"What's wrong?"

"Nothing's wrong. I just wanted to hear your voice."

"I can tell something's happened."

"Well, Kathryn got a case of nerves about driving back with the products. She's okay now."

"Did you argue?"

"Not really. But I saw her anger for the first time."

"Ah, the first time is always a shock isn't?"

"It is," Ellie said, relaxing deeper into the hammock with Kris's voice a soothing balm. "But we worked it through. And, you know, she's quite attractive when she's angry—those blue eyes really blazed."

"Gah! Don't tell her that. People hate to be told they're cute when they're angry."

"You sure did." Ellie laughed softly.

"Kathryn strikes me as the type who would not be amused, either. I bet in the moment you felt more intimidated than amused."

"Somewhat. She's powerful."

"Very. Where are you now?"

"At Trisha's. Kathryn is back at the B & B."

"A little apart time?"

"Yeah. I think we're both adjusting to being in a relationship again."

"That's not surprising."

"The naming of what we have is alluding us. Someone we met at Yosemite referred to us as a couple. Kathryn looked as if she had swallowed a pickle ball."

"So, you're friends with benefits?"

"I hate that description. But the term 'partner' doesn't wear well either."

"Remember, El, she's in foreign territory with you. Her world has never needed that term—they've owned 'fiancé' and 'spouse' for forever. We've had to settle for 'domestic partner' or 'spouse-equivalent.' Barf. Now that straight terms are available to us, it stills feels weird to say 'my wife Sandy.'"

"It was the same with Mary."

"Yeah. Well, that's the way Kathryn is feeling about the word 'partner.' It's foreign."

"But we're in a relationship. What is she? My 'relater'?"

"Your lover. Now, tell me more about your fight."

CHAPTER 36

"You're looking chipper," Kathryn said as Ellie came into their room. She was sitting at a desk in the corner writing on something blue that she slipped into her sketch pad.

"I've had a wonderful day and a super, hour-long nap this afternoon. All very restorative. Whatcha doing?"

"Who wants to know?"

Ellie laughed, put her arms around Kathryn's neck, and kissed her hair. "I do."

"All in good time."

Ellie took off her sneakers and plopped down on the bed, motioning for Kathryn to join her. "Did Jenn call?"

"We finally connected this afternoon." Kathryn scooted next to Ellie and let herself be enfolded in her arms. "Here's the deal. She wants to meet me at a park near their home where we usually walk. We'll each have our say and then if she feels like it, she'll come to the hotel to meet you. Does that sound okay to you?"

"Of course."

"I made reservations for us at the downtown Marriott. It's a suite, so we can close off the bedroom."

"To protect Jenn's sensibilities?"

"Yes." Kathryn sighed. "And I'd like to explain."

"Please do." Ellie ran her fingers through Kathryn's hair.

"I'm thinking about how I would do things if you were a man."

"My imagination goes wild."

"You know what I mean. If I were introducing Jenn and her family to a boyfriend or new husband, say, I would want a suite then, too. Jenn is overly sensitive, and if the girls were along, they would be confused by their mom's upset. If it were Nate and his family, I wouldn't need to do that."

"Jenn has a lot of power, doesn't she?"

"I like to think of it as choosing my battles."

"Are you worried?"

"It will be what it will be."

They were quiet for a while, content in each other arms. Ellie took in the golden light of the ground floor room and the heavy European style furniture. A car door slammed in the distance, probably a guest arriving. She thought Kathryn had drifted off to sleep, but then she heard her say, "I love being like this with you. Being held, actively listened to. Being seen. Consulted."

"I believe what you're describing is called 'partnership.'"

Kathryn gave Ellie a playful elbow. "Maybe. It sounds a little weak for what I'm describing."

A stillness held them then, two women sharing their aliveness.

"Judith called a little while ago. She wanted to tell me that Shawn seems to be doing well and has moved back home."

"Really? How did that happen?"

"One of the therapists at Justin's was able to persuade his parents to come in for some family counseling. Everyone signed a contract for their behavior going forward. We'll see what happens."

"A step in the right direction at least."

"I hope so." Kathryn let out a sigh. "Judith has been at me for some time to come on as a volunteer therapist at Justin's. I've always turned her down, but now I'm thinking it might be a good idea."

"Why?"

Kathryn readjusted herself, drawing Ellie closer. "Being with you has opened my horizons. In dealing with my family, Jenn in particular, I have an inkling of the disapproval you and others have lived with all your lives. It might give me a little more insight into LGBTQ kids."

"What about helping older women who are expanding their sexuality? Women like yourself. There are more and more of them, you know."

Kathryn thought a moment. "That's another option. But, right now, I'm here with you, so I think I'll let the future take care of itself."

CHAPTER 37

"*Y*ou've gained weight," Jenn said as she approached her mother in Sacramento's Glen Park. "You're eating too many carbs." She was a slender woman of thirty-six wearing tight black jeans and a white, flute-sleeved tunic. Her mouth had its typical firm set registering disapproval of the world. Her shoulders, though, bore a deflated slouch.

"Well, hello to you, too," Kathryn said cheerfully. She ignored her daughter's jab with the well-honed sense of a submarine commander of when to engage and when to let pass. She gave Jenn's arm a quick squeeze.

They strolled to the levee along the American River, Kathryn waiting for Jenn's burst, which she knew was coming.

Finally, Jenn kicked a stone out of the way and said, "I'm really angry with you. You can't imagine the hell I've been through these past few days."

"No, I can't."

"Well, how did it happen, you and this Ellie?"

Kathryn smiled inwardly and took a deep breath. "Life is full of miracles, Jenn."

"Oh, Mom."

"But I've been thinking maybe I set things in motion before Ellie and I even met."

"What do you mean?"

"After your dad and I divorced, I drew up a list of things I wanted in a partner. I had twenty items or so: honesty, good communication skills, sensitive, fun, curious, adventuresome."

"You've always been big on lists."

"Well, there was one thing I omitted: gender!" Kathryn laughed.

Jenn did not. "Who would think you would have to include that."

"Exactly."

"Did you have these feelings before?"

"Not consciously."

"Well, subconsciously?"

"Who knows." Kathryn observed an egret perched on a low-hanging branch. The white plumage caught the sun and glowed like a baptismal robe.

"Is that why you and Dad broke up—because you're latently that way?"

"No, darling."

"How do you know?"

"I just know," Kathryn said firmly, not wanting to discuss her and Joe's sex life nor his infidelity.

They walked for a while in silence, taking in the spread of the river muscling its way down from the Sierras, the last vestiges of the winter's snowpack flowing into the Sacramento watershed. A month ago, the river was sloshing on the flood plain. Now the grass was a rich green and the mud hard in the steady beat of the sun.

"How do you know that this Ellie isn't using you? You're a pretty rich divorcée."

"I have a good sense of her character."

"Has she asked you for money?"

"No, she has plenty of her own."

"Well, how are you handling money on this trip?"

"Really, Jenn, you don't need to worry." Kathryn paused to quell her irritation. "We're splitting expenses fifty-fifty. Except for the detour to Yosemite, which was my request and my treat."

They made their way across alluvial sand to the edge of the river where a young woman in a tank top and shorts was playing fetch with a golden retriever. Jenn hung back as though afraid of being splashed.

"Are you going to marry her?"

Kathryn shook her head. "We have no plans."

"Paul says you'd better have a pre-nuptial if you do."

Kathryn doubted that Paul would ever say such a thing. "Jenn, I know this is a big change for you. It is for me too, something I never would have envisioned. But I'm happy. I like being in a relationship, caring for someone and feeling cared for. Being in love and having a physical connection."

Jenn flinched. "TMI, Mom.

Kathryn waited for her daughter to calm.

"So, this Ellie has some of the traits on your list?"

"All of them. She really is wonderful. I hope you're open to meeting her."

"Paul is ... Paul ...."

An uncharacteristic faltering. Kathryn put her arm around Jenn's waist and guided her to the grassy slope of the embankment. "Let's sit," she said and sank to the ground. The warm and nourishing earth fairly hummed with life energy.

Jenn flung herself down beside her mother, her lower lip quivering.

"What's happened?"

"Paul. He surprised me." Jenn hugged her knees to her chest and rocked slightly as she spoke. "He seemed open to this ... development. At least to my face. He said these things happen. He didn't want me to make a big deal out of it. He said maybe it was just a phase you were going through."

Kathryn remained silent.

"But then I heard him on the phone with his brother the other night laughing. He said he couldn't imagine what two dried-up old bags could do together and whatever it was, it was pathetic."

Kathryn recalled the teeth-chattering orgasm she had had that morning and was more amused than offended.

"I really let him have it, and he apologized. He said it was just locker room talk. Which is complete bullshit. It made me wonder, what will he think of me when I'm your age? Will I just be a dried-up old bag to him?"

"He's in love with you, Jenn, and you'll age together."

"But when I'm old and wrinkled like you that could change." Jenn plucked a handful of grass and threw it into the breeze. "And then I wondered if that was what happened with Dad. That you were just a dried-up old bag to him."

Kathryn fought the urge to wrap her daughter in her arms and hug her, to welcome her to the painful world of female consciousness, but she knew Jenn would hate it. "I suppose to some extent it's true. He did leave me for a much younger woman after all."

"But it's not fair."

"It's life, Jenn. We make of it what we can . . . and so often what seems like a setback opens up a whole new wonderful world."

"But now you've wound up a lesbian. I don't call that wonderful."

"Well, falling in love with Ellie has been wonderful for me," Kathryn said. "But Jenn, I'm not a lesbian. I don't label myself."

"Of course, you do. You have all sorts of labels: mother, divorcée, therapist."

"Those are some of the roles I have. None of them are who I am at the core."

"And who would that be?"

It was an unlikely question from her daughter. Kathryn took a moment to think. The earth was shifting under her, her roles, her sexuality heaved up as in a quake, yet she remained the person she always had been. "Well, Jenn, I believe I'm a piece of Eternal Spirit. I'm in this life to learn some lessons. While I'm here, I strive to live with love and integrity." Kathryn cleared her throat. "Not that I always succeed."

Jenn stared at her mother. "Wow, Mom. You've got your engine engaged in warp ten New Age woo-woo."

"Well, my little agnostic," Kathryn said with a smile, "how would you answer that question?"

Jenn scowled. "I don't know. That's why I'm an agnostic."

"Life is baffling, isn't it?" Kathryn said quietly. "We walk along thinking we're on solid ground and suddenly a fissure opens at our feet."

"Then what do you do?"

Kathryn fingered the blades of young grass, smooth and pliable to her touch. "Then you go spelunking, hopefully with a headlamp so you can see what's there. Or you stay on the surface and navigate around the hole."

"Ha!" Jenn exclaimed. "That pretty much sums up our differences, doesn't it? You'd go down into the crevice and I'd say, 'Too much trouble, I'll go around.'"

They laughed ruefully at this truth and watched the wide water flow by. Kathryn savored this rare moment in their relationship, infused with a sweetness and companionship and depth she had once longed for, but had made peace with its absence.

"Do you think I'll be able to see the girls on this visit? I'm not banished?"

Jenn looked at her mother in surprise. "No, we wouldn't do that."

"And Ellie? Would she be welcome?"

"I'd have to meet her first." Jenn massaged the ever-deepening worry line on her forehead. "She's at the hotel?"

"Uh-huh," Kathryn nodded.

"Let's drive there now." Jenn said. "In our own cars."

Together mother and daughter retraced their steps to the parking lot where they left separately, a joining and unjoining as predictable as planetary motion.

CHAPTER 38

*T*he pocket door to the bedroom was shut, leaving the large living space in the Marriott suite separate from the suggestive room holding the king-sized bed. Ellie poked at the bouquet of spring flowers on the small kitchen table and made sure the cubes in the ice bucket in the refrigerator had not melted. She had just settled on the couch and opened her Kindle app when she heard the door lock deactivate. Kathryn entered wearing an inscrutable smile followed by Jenn.

Ellie rose to greet the daughter and had two immediate impressions. First, Jenn sported a defiant blaze in her eye, like a thousand students Ellie had seen walk through the classroom door daring her to teach them anything. They knew it all already. But, really, the disdain was a pose to cover insecurity.

Her second thought was: Vulcan. Jenn had short, glossy black hair cut in a severe style with bangs and sideburns—add pointed ears and angled eyebrows and she could appear in a *Star Trek* episode as a worthy ally to an *Enterprise* captain.

They exchanged hellos and a handshake and positioned themselves in a neat triad on chairs and the couch. Ellie and Jenn eyed each other, Ellie with a detached, but kind expression and Jenn with a cool, appraising look.

"I'm going to make myself an iced tea," Kathryn said. "Would anyone like one?"

"Yes, please," Ellie said.

"Do you have a Diet Coke?" Jenn asked.

"No."

Jenn made a face. "Iced tea, then. I hope it's not too sugary."

"It's not." Kathryn moved into the kitchen nook and opened the refrigerator.

"Your mother tells me you're an accountant. Is this your busy season with taxes?"

"The crunch is passed. And it's not that crazy for me. I work on a contract basis and accept only as much work as I want."

"I'm glad there're people like you who can deal with the constantly changing tax code. It would drive me nuts. It must be a real challenge to keep up."

"It means I'll always have work," Jenn said with a self-satisfied smile.

The sound of clinking came from the counter where Kathryn was dropping ice into three glasses.

"I would think it would be gratifying work—the numbers eventually add up. There's a definite right and wrong, whereas in my profession—teaching literature and writing—everything is open to interpretation."

Now the smile became genuine, and Ellie saw a bit of Kathryn in Jenn's features—the crinkle around her eyes, the patrician nose. "Yes, the logic appeals to me. It's very satisfying when things balance to the penny. But it's more complicated than that. A lot of analysis goes into my work, such as how best to take advantage of tax laws. With the software we have nowadays, you wouldn't believe all the ways we can slice and dice the data."

"Are your clients actually able to understand the reports you generate?"

Jenn's laugh had a pure ring, but her mouth looked stiff as though unused to the expression. "I'd say only a fraction of them. My clients are techie nerds, not MBAs. They just want to work on their projects and let me maximize their profits. I make sure to go over the essentials with them, of course. Ignorance is not bliss when it comes to a company's financials."

Kathryn set the glasses on the coffee table. "Here you go," she said, sliding the iced tea toward the two women she loved most in the world. She took a seat and gave Ellie a quick, encouraging smile.

"Thanks." Ellie took a sip of iced tea.

Jenn tasted her drink and found it acceptable. "You're not what I expected."

Ellie lifted her eyebrows and smiled, refusing to answer in the predictable way.

Jenn studied her for a moment. "So, you're a retired professor."

"College teacher, actually. Community colleges don't have the rank of professor."

"Then Mom misinformed me."

"Well, I'll take the responsibility for not making it clear to her." Ellie smiled at Kathryn, who was now sitting with a fist supporting her chin looking as though she were watching a matador pirouette around a baffled bull. "What do you think, Jenn, of this development with your mother?"

"I don't approve of it at all." Jenn ran a palm over her glossy hair as though it weren't already flattened in place. "Not that I think there's anything wrong with gays—god knows we have enough of them in this state—but, it's not right for her."

"How so?"

"It's just not. That's not who she is." Jenn held Ellie's eyes for a long moment of challenge and then looked over to her mother and back. "What are your plans with her?"

"To love her and let things unfold as they will," Ellie said.

"That's pretty vague."

"Well," Ellie said, "it's too soon to know how things will develop, but right now I'm optimistic. We have a lot in common, and we're still learning about each other. It's one of the reasons I'm so happy to meet you—it's a way I can learn more about her."

Jenn eyed Ellie with a look halfway between suspicion and curiosity. "Like what?"

"Well, what would you say has been her biggest influence on you?"

"I don't know." Jenn seemed dumbfounded. "I guess it's to always be authentic."

"What a wonderful gift, Kathryn," Ellie said, beaming at her beloved. *You accept your Vulcan daughter, offspring of another world.* Turning back to Jenn, she said, "And what would you say has been your biggest challenge with your mom?"

Jenn's gaze darted around as she thought. "I don't like the way she listens to me."

"How so?" Ellie said evenly, suppressing a burst of laughter.

"It feels like I'm in one of her therapy sessions. Kind of the way this conversation is starting to go."

Ellie laughed gently. "I don't mean it to be that way. I take it you're not a big fan of your mother's profession."

"No, I don't believe in therapy. It's way overrated. You're just paying someone to be your friend."

Ellie considered the younger woman for a moment. "I found it helpful once, a long time ago, when I was young and confused. Sometimes it's useful to have an objective outsider help you think through a problem."

"Well," Jenn said, waving her hand in a dismissive motion, "I'm glad for Mom's sake that so many people think as you do. It's kept her gainfully employed all these years."

"Do you think your mom is being inauthentic, being in this relationship with me?"

"Basically, yes. But I guess people change."

A phone rang, and Jenn seemed glad to reach for her leather bag. "It's probably Paul," she said, and confirmed it when she swiped the screen. "Just a sec." She stood and searched for a place to go. The closed door into the bedroom loomed like a temptation, but she recoiled from it. "I'm going to step outside for a moment." Out the door she went, putting the arm lock in position to keep the door ajar.

Kathryn and Ellie looked at each other and made faces of relief.

I am so in love with you, Kathryn mouthed.

"It's not over," Ellie said.

But it was. Jenn opened the door and said, "I need to go."

"Is everything all right?" Kathryn asked. "I was hoping we could have dinner together."

"Everything's fine," Jenn said briskly. "One of the soccer players got hurt and Paul has to deal with it, so I need to pick up Maddie and take her home."

"I hope it's not serious," Kathryn said.

"A broken arm. She'll live."

"Paul is a coach?" Ellie asked.

"He's an assistant coach," Jenn corrected.

"Come on," Kathryn said to her difficult daughter, "I'll walk you down to the lobby."

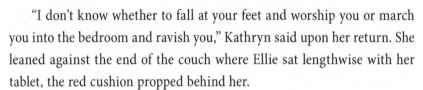

"I don't know whether to fall at your feet and worship you or march you into the bedroom and ravish you," Kathryn said upon her return. She leaned against the end of the couch where Ellie sat lengthwise with her tablet, the red cushion propped behind her.

Ellie grinned and made a V-sign. "Choice number two," she said and, seeing the shape of a rabbit's head in her fingers and fist, she made a hippity-hop motion in front of her.

Half an hour later, Kathryn and Ellie lay amongst the swirling sheets of the large bed, languid and lazy. Kathryn rested her head on Ellie's shoulder, a finger lazily circling her nipple.

"Did I pass inspection?" Ellie asked.

"You were spectacular, darling."

Ellie smiled at the old-fashioned endearment. "I thought I'd blown it there for a moment when I said I wasn't a professor. Insecure people don't like to be challenged."

"You were quite deft in immediately taking responsibility for the error . . . although, truly, I don't recall ever saying you were a professor."

"Well, Jenn would never admit the mistake came from her. As you say, you've learned to choose your battles."

"Have I ever."

"It was starting to get a little touchy at the end."

"But you kept your cool and couldn't be goaded. I would like to have heard more. Inauthentic, indeed!"

"Do you know what her insecurity is about?"

"No. Sometimes I think she was just born that way." Kathryn rolled onto her back and pulled Ellie to her shoulder, exchanging positions. "My son was an easy baby—little fuss, always happy, a good sleeper. Toilet training was a snap. We thought we were the best parents in the world. Jenn dashed that illusion. She was troubled from the get-go."

"You mean from birth? Did you have a difficult labor?"

"Sweetheart, labor is always a challenge. But Jenn was a breach birth, and she probably was traumatized in the delivery. Everything we did that was so successful with Nate backfired with her."

"I wonder just how much parents influence their kids. The acorn comes with all the traits that the oak will be."

"It certainly made me more understanding in my practice. Clients ranted about their mother or father—I'm excluding real physical and emotional abuse here—and when I met the parents in a family counseling session, they seemed exasperated, uncertain of what they did wrong, just as I used to feel with Jenn. Sometimes I think having a difficult child is just the luck of the draw. I realized early on that my influence with Jenn was about zero. She was too headstrong and combative. I just had to let her be who she is and not take anything personally. Although I admit to a crackle of pride when she said my greatest gift to her was authenticity."

"Kathryn," Ellie said carefully, "is she connected somehow to *Star Trek*?"

Kathryn leveled a sour face at Ellie. "I know. I know. My daughter is a Vulcan."

"You never told me you had an inter-species marriage."

"I didn't think it was important."

"Well, it's not. I'm not species-ist or anything."

"I know. Just anti-ruling class."

"It depends on the Ruler, oh Kathryn the Great." Ellie brushed Kathryn's shoulder with her lips. "Now, tell me, how is it that Jenn is a Vulcan."

"She became obsessed with *Star Trek* when she was in fifth grade. I thought it was a phase, but she never outgrew it. You wouldn't believe the number of toys that franchise puts out. God! She still goes to Sci-Fi conventions in full Vulcan regalia. In fact, that's where she met Paul."

"Good lord. Another Vulcan?"

"No. He's cast himself as part of the Star Fleet engineering corps."

"An inter-world marriage."

"Yes. And it works. I think it's great when a couple can share a passion. Traveling. Birdwatching. Dancing. Skydiving. Dressing up as aliens."

"Are the kids into it?"

"No. They're totally embarrassed by the whole thing. Although when they were little they were pretty cute dressed up as little Romulans in full regalia. Jenn sewed all their outfits."

"It sounds as though they have fun."

"They do." Kathryn propped up on an elbow to better gage Ellie's reaction. "You'd better brace yourself, sweetheart."

"Why?"

"We're having lunch in the Vulcan lair tomorrow."

CHAPTER 39

*J*enn and her family lived in a three-bedroom brick home. The close-clipped lawn ended in a ruler-straight edge at the sidewalk. Arborvitae and rose bushes hunkered in flawless spheres along the house and side yard.

The girls burst out of the red front door, hopped down the two steps to the walk, and threw themselves into Kathryn's arms. "Grandma! Grandma!"

By the time Kathryn stepped back and regained her height, Jenn and Paul had appeared on the porch, watching carefully.

"Gena, Maddie," Kathryn said, "I'd like you to meet my friend Ellie."

Each girl in turn shook Ellie's hand and said hello with wide, questioning eyes. Ellie voiced their names softly and returned their gaze for a polite moment. As she walked toward the house, she said, "Jenn, nice to see you again. And you must be Paul." She put her hand out for a shake as she gained the first step. "Nice to meet you."

Ellie took in the would-be Star Fleet engineer, a portly man with thinning strawberry blond hair, a clean-shaven face, and gray eyes. His navy polo shirt stretched tightly above his baggy jeans. His calm demeanor provided a nice balance to Jenn's nervous energy.

"Nice to meet you, too," he said shyly, his eyes darting away, as he shook hands awkwardly. His quick smile faded to a pleasant slant of his mouth.

"I was expecting you earlier," Jenn said to her mother as they walked into the house. "Lunch is almost ready." She was wearing the same outfit as yesterday.

"You didn't get my text? We were exploring downtown and lost track of time."

"I got it, but lunch was already in the oven."

"Oh, I'm so sorry, Jenn. You go to all the work of preparing a meal, and I add to your stress. Forgive me."

"Oh, it's all right. Have a seat while I finish up in the kitchen."

It was clear to Ellie that Kathryn's grandchildren adored her. Even though Gena and Maddie were fifteen and thirteen, they cuddled up on either side of Kathryn on the couch as though they were five-year-olds who couldn't get close enough. Their eye contact was long and loving, and the conversation breathless as they caught her up on their doings and showed her pictures on their iPhones. Kathryn responded in an animated way Ellie had never seen.

This was a new side of Kathryn, her world of family. A twinge of regret—or was it jealousy—tweaked Ellie. She had missed all those decades of Kathryn's life, of her family and its treasures and challenges. She could only know them through pictures, those ubiquitous and unsatisfying representations of times she had not witnessed. Ellie listened closely to the stories and the way the tellers told them. She watched for details that would reveal these strangers . . . and her lover.

Ellie and Paul sat in plush armchairs that could be swiveled to see the TV. The living room was dark with the shades drawn against the heat of the sun. A bookcase held shelves of *Star Trek* paperbacks and boxed video sets with bold lettering blazoned on their spines. Pictures of alien landscapes, as might be produced by street artists wielding cans of toxic-smelling aerosol paint, covered the walls.

The saying goes that the apple doesn't fall far from the tree, Ellie mused, but in Jenn's case, a branch must have heaved its fruit into the next orchard. The contrast between the elegant Kathryn and her sub-culture daughter was almost too improbable for Ellie to comprehend. And yet Kathryn sat on the couch unruffled by the science fiction world her daughter embraced. How had she come to accept it with such aplomb? Or was she just that open by nature? Well . . . look who she had just taken on as her lover!

"That's quite a collection of *Star Trek* material," Ellie said cheerfully to Paul. "I'm partial to *The Next Generation* . . . and Captain Janeway's *Voyager*. What's your favorite series?"

The blond eyelashes fluttered at Ellie as though blinking helped process the unexpected question. "We prefer *The Next Generation*."

They chatted amicably then, sharing some of their favorite characters, storylines, and moral dilemmas presented on the show. Both agreed the old movies were a disappointment, but the rebooted franchise held promise.

"Kathryn tells me you work at the state capitol," Ellie said, wishing to pivot the conversation back to Earth. "That must be interesting."

He shrugged. "It's a job. Luckily, I'm in IT, not in the legislative sausage grinder."

"Are they in session now?"

"Yes."

"Does that mean it's busier for you?"

"Not really. Any major hardware upgrade or software installation is done off-session, although we're always planning for it. Cyber security is the big issue now."

"Do you pay any attention to the political issues?"

"Oh, sure. There's always buzz about something or someone. Politics is very gossipy."

Ellie smiled. "That's true. Is there an issue you're drawn to?"

Paul thought for a minute. "Yes. Energy. It's the life blood of civilization." He leaned forward, gesturing with his large, soft hands. "We've got to be smarter about it and open to alternatives. Our kids are going to have a tough time of it with climate change."

"It seems to me California has been leading the way in solar, wind, and biomass energy for decades."

"True, but as a nation, we seem to be ceding leadership to the Chinese. And now we've got the cannabis industry gearing up for recreational sales. It's going to be a nightmare energy-wise."

Ellie started. "What do you mean?"

"I just saw a study last week. Already indoor marijuana growing accounts for one percent of total electrical use in the U.S. Hundreds of millions of plants are springing up in California alone. Where will we get the energy?"

"Aren't a lot of the growers devising ways to limit their carbon footprint? My niece and her husband in Nevada City have spent a lot of money on solar panels, and now they're thinking about wind power. Their goal is to be energy sufficient." Ellie suddenly became aware of the silence in the room. She glanced at Kathryn and read in her face *Careful*. Or was it *Courage, my truth-telling lover*?

"They grow cannabis?"

"Yes," Ellie nodded. She could see his mind calculating.

"The ones you were just visiting?"

"Yes."

"Ellie," Kathryn said, "come see this video of Maddie scoring a goal."

Ellie moved to the couch and edged next to Maddie who was holding her iPhone. "Let's see," she said, leaning in to observe. She and Kathryn exchanged a look. "Very nice, Maddie. You have good form."

Maddie blushed and played with her dark ponytail.

Jenn called from the doorway. "Okay, lunch is served."

As they got up from the couch, Ellie raised her eyebrows in a *did-I-blow-it* expression.

Kathryn shrugged, gave a wan smile, and said, "Onward."

The dining room was small and with an extra leaf in the table, there was barely enough room to walk behind the chairs to get seated. A colorful array of Fiestaware adorned the table and the side buffet held several serving dishes laden with food.

"Granny," Maddie said, "come sit next to me." She pulled on her training bra, clearly not used to the constriction.

"Okay, sweetheart," Kathryn said, her eyes brightening. "This is lovely, Jenn. You've gone to a lot of work."

"It wasn't much work at all. You know how efficient I am."

"It was a lot of work for me," Maddie said. "I peeled potatoes and now I have a stupid callous."

Kathryn inspected the thirteen-year-old's finger. "Oh, sweetie, that's a blister. It must hurt. Some tea tree oil would help it heal."

"That stuff stinks too much," Jenn said, "and it never absorbs so it makes a mess."

"What a feast!" Ellie said, "Thank you, Jenn, Paul, girls, for having us."

"Why wouldn't we?" Maddie asked. "Why would Granny be in California and not visit us?"

"Why, indeed," Kathryn said. "My favorite granddaughters!"

"Grandma, we're you're only granddaughters!"

"Yes, you are! And aren't I lucky that they're you!"

The girls beamed.

Ellie wondered if a prayer would be ensuing, and if so, to what deity. It was not, to her relief.

Jenn stood at the buffet handing one serving bowl after another to her husband. The dishes made their way around the table like the pails of a bucket brigade with much clanking and commotion but no spillage. Only after everyone had been served did Jenn fill her own plate and take a seat.

Once the family had dug in, Ellie said, "This chicken is delicious, and the mashed potatoes are perfect." Ellie picked up the basket of cornbread and took another piece. "Now, I'd like to hear more about your lives. Gena and Maddie. What do you do for fun?"

The girls recounted their exploits on the soccer field, and Gena told of her love of the piano while Maddie made a sour face at the mention of it. Paul and Jenn answered questions about their work and, to the eye rolls of their children, got on a jag about *Star Trek*.

No one asked Ellie or Kathryn anything about themselves.

CHAPTER 40

$\mathscr{A}$fter lunch, the adults were in the kitchen cleaning up, while Gena and Maddie played duets on the spinet in the living room. The flow of music paused occasionally as the girls bickered.

As Kathryn made her way toward the sink where Ellie was washing the pots, she swiped her finger along the baking pan and gathered a plop of cream icing from the carrot cake. "What's up, Paul?" she asked, licking her finger. "You're looking especially thoughtful."

"I'm just wondering," he said softly, "about this farm. Ellie's niece is raising cannabis?"

Ellie took a deep breath. *Here we go.* "Yes, that's right."

"Are you taking any of it back to Minnesota?"

"Some oil in capsules for a friend who has a medical condition. A year's supply."

"Well, be careful. You don't want to get caught with that stuff. Especially with the new federal administration."

"Wait a sec," Jenn said, the dish towel frozen in mid-swipe. "Are you dealing drugs?"

"No," Ellie said. "I'm not buying or selling."

"Just delivering." Jenn shook her head. "You know that's illegal—even for a resident to possess that much cannabis in California—not to mention the states you'll be driving through."

"I'm aware of the laws."

"Did you know about this?" Jenn said to Kathryn.

"Yes."

"Are you out of your mind, Mother?" Jenn put down the pan. "If you're caught . . ." She pivoted toward Ellie, white with anger. "What are you doing with my mother? Isn't it enough that you've turned her gay? Now you're making her a drug mule? Do you know how much she has to lose?"

"For heaven sakes, Jenn," Kathryn said.

"I understand your concern," Ellie said, "so let me set the record straight. I am not a drug dealer. I'm helping a friend who suffers from a chronic illness. And, I'm in love with your mother. I wouldn't force her into anything. As you know, she's a strong woman, and she makes her own decisions."

The piano music in the living room had stopped. Gena and Maddie stood in the doorway of the kitchen, big-eyed and somber.

"Gena, Magel," Jenn said, "go outside."

"What's going on?" Maddie asked.

"This is adult talk," Jenn said. "Go outside. Now."

They slunk through the kitchen like scolded puppies and disappeared out the patio door.

"That's just great," Jenn said. "They're still confused about your split from Dad. Now this! What am I supposed to do?"

"I think the real question is, what are you going to do with me?" Kathryn leaned against the counter, relaxed and poised, taking in her daughter and son-in-law. "With us?"

"That's always your answer, isn't it?" Jenn said. "A return question. Well, some things are a little more complicated than your verbal ploys. Have you thought of what this could do to us if you wind up in prison?"

"The impact on you would be far less than on me."

"This isn't something to joke about."

"Believe me, I'm not joking." Kathryn's face had a mix of firmness and compassion. "Jenn, I have to live my life, make my choices. Can you give me room to do that, just as I've given you?"

Jenn would not answer her mother. "Paul?" she said in a voice demanding he weigh in . . . and support her.

"Well," Paul said, slowly, "I see it as more of a cultural clash, Jenn, so it's a case for the Prime Directive. If they want to engage in illegal trade, that's their choice, and we shouldn't interfere. We don't have to like it, but our feelings are irrelevant."

The logical side of Jenn's brain came online. "Interesting," she intoned, finger-combing her Vulcan hair. "Do you see them being Ferengi?"

"Oh, god," Ellie muttered at the thought of being compared to the vile, greedy creatures.

"Somewhat. But their motive is compassion, not profit."

"Yes, I see your point."

"Besides," Paul continued, "cannabis is floating all over the place. Even at the capitol. Things are changing, but you could still get into big trouble," he said, talking now to Ellie and Kathryn. "But if you're willing to take the risk . . . well, you're big girls. I just hope you're careful . . . and have a good lawyer."

"Well, I guess I'm outvoted," Jenn said, the anger abating like a tide pulling back.

No one pointed out that the issue was not up for a vote.

"Where is the cannabis?" Jenn asked, her voice losing its harshness. "Not in your car, I hope."

"No," Ellie said. "It's in our hotel room."

"Mom, I know it's your choice, but really I don't want you driving back to Minnesota with the stuff in the car. Please stay here and fly home."

"I appreciate your concern, darling," Kathryn said, touched by the unfamiliar caring of her daughter, "but we'll be okay. I want to drive back with Ellie."

Jenn shook her head. "You always have to color outside the lines, don't you?"

"It depends on what the picture is . . . and this," she said, gesturing toward Ellie, "is a picture I want."

"It's no use arguing with you," Jenn said.

"No, it's not," Kathryn replied, giving Jenn a sad, loving smile. "Now, I'm going to go outside and see what the girls are up to." And, she thought as she fingered a silver bracelet in her pocket, she, Gena, and Ellie could welcome Maddie into her womanhood. The ritual wouldn't be around a campfire, but it would still be special.

————— ❈ —————

"I really blew it," Ellie said as she backed out of the driveway. "I'm so sorry."

The local streets were quiet on the Sunday afternoon, and the two women were relieved to be on their way.

"Well," Kathryn said, wiping her eyes from her good-bye hugs with the girls, "we'd talked about being open and honest. No lies."

"Yes, but I didn't need to bring it up. It opened a can of vipers." Ellie reached over and rested a hand on Kathryn's leg. "Will you forgive me?"

"There's nothing to forgive. It happened, now we deal with it. I know once we get back to Minnesota, Jenn will have settled down."

"I don't know. She may forgive *you*, but I have a feeling I'll be a permanent resident of the doghouse."

"You may be. But I'll be there right with you . . . where I usually am with Jenn." Kathryn's laugh was soft and knowing. "You just have to let her be who she is. And, you know, I kind of like the idea of exploding the image she has of me."

"I still feel bad," Ellie said. "I'm responsible for this breach. Would you like to stay another day so you can mend fences and spend more time with Gena and Maddie?"

"The kids will be back in school, and Jenn and Paul off to work. No, let's leave tomorrow as planned."

————— ❈ —————

During dinner at a Mexican restaurant, Kathryn reached into her tote bag and pulled out a blue envelope and a long, rectangular package wrapped in white tissue paper.

Ellie opened the envelope. It was the mystery card Kathryn had slipped into her notebook that afternoon at the B & B in Nevada City. Ellie had forgotten about it. Almost.

"What's this?" she said, happy and a bit embarrassed to receive a present for no reason, and to know that the card had been for her all along.

"Just a little something for the drive home.

Ellie opened the envelope first. The card had a picture of Half Dome in winter. Inside were the words, *For Ellie, How wonderful it is to walk by your side, to lie by your side. The now is perfect. Love, K.*

"I love it," Ellie said, noting no mention of the future. She unwrapped the present to discover a shellacked cedar board with four rows of holes. She nearly dropped it in surprise.

"I know I can't replace Mary," Kathryn said, "but I do play a mean game of cribbage."

"Where did you get this? It's gorgeous."

"A funky little store in Nevada City. I hope it's okay that I bought it."

"Totally." Ellie grinned. "You're on, partner. As soon as we get back to our room."

Kathryn's phone chirped. "Text from Jenn. I'd better read it." She slipped on her glasses, scanned the message, and smiled. "Well, it's progress."

"What?"

"She wishes us a safe journey tomorrow."

"Is this a miracle?"

"No," Kathryn said, "but it feels like we may have angels in our corner."

PART FOUR

CHAPTER 41

*E*llie and Kathryn left the next day for home, pointing the car to the rising sun. The first two driving days proved easy, the evenings languid with cribbage and conversation. At the Best Western in Rawlins, Wyoming, Ellie swam laps in the empty pool and then padded over to Kathryn in the hot tub.

Ellie stepped into the swirling water. "Ouch. Hot. Hot. Hot."

Kathryn didn't open her eyes.

"You're looking pensive."

Kathryn glanced at Ellie and sighed. "I've always found the home-stretch of a vacation a little sad. It means the fun is almost over."

"At least we don't have to go to work Monday morning."

"No. But what are we going back to?" Beads of sweat dotted Kathryn's forehead and collected in the fine grooves.

The jets of the hot tub burbled into silence. Neither woman left to reset the timer.

"I'm going to feel lonely in my house without you. I've loved being with you day in and day out. Sleeping with you. Waking to you." Kathryn waved her hand around under the water, watching the delicate surface disturbance. Action and reaction. Cause and effect. "If Highland Meadows had a unit available next month, would you take it?"

Despite the hot water, a chill passed through Ellie. "I . . . I don't know." She closed her eyes and shuffled through her emotions. "I wouldn't want to move there if it'd derail the possibility of our living together someday. I could wait for a bigger unit if you thought you might join me."

Kathryn's sub-surface hand-waving continued. "I'm not ready to talk about living together, El, but I can imagine it happening down the road."

Ellie smiled wistfully. "We just never know, though, how much road we have left."

⸻ ❦ ⸻

"We'll be in Lincoln in less than an hour." Ellie grinned. "The hotel of our consummation. I'm getting revved already."

"Me, too," Kathryn said. "I'll be sure to wear a certain tunic that seemed to drive someone I know crazy."

"I'd like that. But I'm fond of the top you have on, too," Ellie said, eying Kathryn's three-quarter-sleeve white pullover top. "It's so soft I want to cuddle you every moment."

The Nebraskan landscape, an earthen floor stretching to the horizon, rushed by. As did the traffic. The women continued to maintain a speed below the posted limit.

"There's something I wanted to follow up on," Kathryn said.

"Okay." Ellie glanced over and noted the serious expression.

"Would you tell me about the Michigan Festival?"

"The Michigan Womyn's Music Festival?" Pain sliced through Ellie, the memory as caustic as acid.

"Yes."

"Well, all right." Ellie rearranged herself in the seat. "To set the scene: For forty years lesbians and a few straight women had a place all to ourselves—six-hundred-and-fifty acres of woodland—where thousands of us camped for a week, lived in community, attended workshops and concerts, and danced. Two things bound us together: the woman-affirming music—the soundtrack of our lives, really—and the absolute safety we experienced. We had no fear of being naked out in the open or walking around at night. No rape or violence."

"Sounds idyllic."

"It was in many ways. Of course, even Eden had ants and mosquitoes. Mary didn't like it at all—the camping, the tofu, the hours peeling carrots. Everyone had to work."

"Communal living?"

"On a grand scale, yes. Anyway, eventually transactivists heard about the festival and demanded they be allowed to attend. They were women, they claimed, even if they still had their male equipment. 'Real women have dicks,' someone spray painted at the entrance."

"That must have felt hostile."

"It was hostile. Some transactivists set up a protest camp outside the gate. A few managed to get in. They displayed the same entitled and aggressive behavior we were trying to escape. Many women no longer felt emotionally or physically safe, especially at the communal showers."

"I would imagine."

"When MichFest made a policy that only female-born women could attend, the transactivists organized a boycott of any entertainer who performed there. Many of the big names had to drop out or be blacklisted and risk losing their careers. MichFest closed down."

"Painful."

"It was more than painful," Ellie said gripping the wheel tightly in anger. "It was . . . ."

An eighteen-wheeler whooshed past them. As it gained the right lane ahead of them, the entire tread peeled off a rear wheel and snaked through the air like a tear in the universe.

Ellie gaped at the thick black stripe hurtling toward her. With instincts registering what was happening before consciousness did, she kept the wheels straight, and her foot off the brake. She drove through it, hands still tight on the wheel, as though a deer were bounding across the road. The rubber glanced off the grill and bumper without setting off the airbags, hit a wheel, and skidded into the middle of the road.

Before she could even scream "Fuck!" they were safe, past the obstacle with only a thump and a shudder. But behind her in the mirror, a junk yard avalanche was rolling down the road, the leading edge a Buick on its hood. Through the closed windows the women could hear the unearthly scream of tearing metal as cars slashed into each other, skittering on the road like felled trees in a snow slide.

Kathryn turned around at the catastrophic sounds and saw the collision unfold. "Ellie!" she cried. "Stop! You have to stop! Now!"

Ellie had already taken her foot off the gas, and now eased the car to the shoulder. She was shaking. "Jesus Christ," she said as she turned to Kathryn. "Are you okay?"

"Yes. You?"

"Okay."

"I have to go back there and help. I'm a nurse."

Uncertainty flickered in Ellie's eyes, but she nodded and backed up as close to the scene as she dared.

CHAPTER 42

*N*ine cars, one van, and a motorcycle lay strewn across eastbound I-80.

As Ellie and Kathryn ran toward the jumble of metal, the stillness caught them. The moment when Nature seemed to pause, to consider the dreadful handiwork of humans. And the humans paused, too, waiting for the last of the collisions to happen from the rear, for the mass of metal to quit its forward progress and quiver to its last rattle. Then the sounds of life: the opening of car doors, the cries and curses, the diminishing whoosh of traffic across the median as the western-flowing observers slowed to behold the scene.

Broken glass dusted the highway, a crystalline gravel crunching under-foot. Among the carcasses of vehicles were torn-off side and rear-view mirrors with safety glass clinging to them like snails, the sun's reflection lasering off the facets. Pieces of plastic fenders, ceramic mugs and ther-mal cups, a cheerleading baton with tassels, a Garmin GPS screen, lay as jumbled as debris from a receding tsunami.

The survivors staggered out of their cars, bruised from the clench of seatbelts, dazed and coughing from the fine white dust spewed by air bags. Those whose wits had not left them held cellphones in shaky hands and dialed 911.

The next sixteen minutes, until help arrived in the form of the Nebraska State Patrol, the York Fire Department, and the Sherriff's Office, had an unworldly dimension of time unanchored from the clock. It could have been sixteen seconds or sixteen hours. Within whatever timeframe was given, by the time official aid appeared on the scene, Ellie—with the help of a balding salesman—had extracted a middle-aged couple hanging upside-down in the Buick, the seatbelts having held them in place, while Kathryn and others had checked all the vehicles. Everyone was accounted for, all car ignitions turned off. The traffic was stacked up behind the wreckage, blocked and unable to move.

Kathryn and Ellie shepherded some victims to a triage area at the side of the road in the shade of a crumpled Ford Econoline. They left a couple of people in place, not wanting to move them because of neck and back injuries, but made sure they were conscious and in no imminent danger.

Miraculously, the airbags and seatbelts had performed as intended, with only one fatality—a motorcyclist who had skidded into a ton of steel and snapped his neck. But the scene held an array of broken bones, sprains, and cuts.

When Officer Ronald Shaver, a ten-year veteran of the Nebraska State Patrol, appeared at the pile-up in his black trooper vehicle, he hurried past chunks of tire and knew immediately what had happened. The accident-causing semi was not on scene. Many a trucker cruised down the road unaware their rig had strewn rubber turds all over the road.

Moving around the mass of tangled cars and over metal, plastic, and shattered glass, Shaver barked into his shoulder radio, apprising dispatch of the situation and calling for medics, traffic control, and tow trucks. Spotting a blanket draped over a body, he lifted a corner and, without emotion, dropped it back over the motorcyclist's face.

In the shade of a white van Shaver found Kathryn, a first aid kit open at her side, kneeling next to a man whose pant leg had been cut away to reveal a deep slash running the length of his inner calf. He squatted down to check the makeshift tourniquet positioned two inches above the knee, a baton serving as the windlass. "Good work," he said.

Kathryn glanced at Ronald Shaver, a trooper straight out of a cop show. His short-sleeved navy uniform stretched tightly across a muscled torso, short brown hair fringed under his Smokey Bear hat, and dark aviator glasses hid his eyes.

"Officer," she said, "this man needs to be air-lifted."

"An air ambulance is on its way, ma'am," he said. "What's the situation?"

"The hemorrhaging has diminished. I hated to put on a tourniquet, but the blood was pulsing out so fast I was afraid Andy would bleed out." She eased the windlass to allow a few moments of blood flow and then tightened it again. "He passed out about five minutes ago from the pain."

"Is he with you?"

"No. Sherry," Kathryn said, nodding toward a woman on the youngish side of middle age, "is his wife. There are a couple of people with injuries still in their cars. Here we're dealing with what we can—mostly cuts, sprains, and shock."

Shaver's eyes roamed over the assemblage, past Ellie who was applying a blue ice pack to a young woman's ankle, to a body whose head was covered with a jacket. An arm stuck out revealing a silver studded leather Harley-Davidson wristband.

"One fatality," Kathryn said. She nodded toward the motorcyclist.

"Yes, I checked," Shaver said. "Are you a doctor?"

"No, a nurse." Kathryn introduced herself and pointed across the way. "And that's Ellie Belmont, the owner of the Lexus up ahead. I'm with her."

He swiveled to look at the blue car with the trunk open. "You were ahead of the accident?"

"Yes. A tire on a semi shredded and glanced off us. We stopped to help when we saw the accident behind us." Kathryn stood and faced the officer, wiping her brow with the front of her wrist, her fingers thick with blood. Large red splashes encrusted her jeans and white top. "We have at least four people who need to be in an emergency room, Officer Shaver," Kathryn said, reading the name plate over his right pocket.

"The EMTs are on their way along with a couple of wreckers to clear the road. We're going to need more though. I'll tend to the other injured if you stay with this man. You're a nurse, you say?"

"Yes. I'm a psychiatric nurse now—a psychotherapist—but I did put a stint in at an emergency room when I was young. I've done what I can here. I'll sure be happy to see the paramedics."

Another patrol car, lights blazing, bounced across the median and parked next to Shaver's cruiser. A trooper emerged just as the York County Sherriff arrived. Shaver turned abruptly from Kathryn to confer with his colleagues and coordinate the accident scene.

⌘

Ellie placed her hand on Kathryn's back. "Here, sweetheart, drink some water." She held out a bottle from the trunk. "You don't want to get dehydrated."

"Can you hold the bottle up to my mouth? I don't want to contaminate it." Kathryn took several gulps of water. "Ahhh . . . thanks."

Ellie observed the miles of flat, barren fields. Hazy bunches of trees and farm buildings dotted the land like darkened mesas. Above, the sky was robin's egg blue with barely a trace of a cloud. The air temperature was in the low sixties, but the sun beating down and the heat-absorbing roadway made the afternoon hot. "You're doing great, Kathryn. How can I help?"

"Could you make sure everyone who isn't injured is drinking enough?"

"Sure thing."

"And El. It's probably better to keep the trunk closed from now on."

"My thought exactly."

As Ellie walked back to the car to fetch more water, Kathryn caught Officer Shaver's glimpse. The curiosity and intensity she sensed behind the Ray-Bans signaled one thing: Danger.

Moments later, the air transport whirred to the scene, the helicopter setting down on the empty road ahead of the crash near Ellie's Lexus. Kathryn briefed the EMTs who jumped into action and then stepped away to let them do their job. She cleaned her hands as best she could and provided comfort and encouragement to several distraught people.

Officer Shaver checked in on Kathryn occasionally, and when she suggested that she and Ellie could be on their way, he told her they needed to stay.

CHAPTER 43

By five o'clock, the lane closest to the median had been partially cleared and traffic now inched past.

Ellie and Kathryn were impatient to leave. Both had provided IDs, insurance and registration, and given their separate statements for the accident report. Kathryn had made herself useful by chatting with folks and calming them down, especially Sherry, who had stayed by the van with her daughter after her husband had been whisked away in the helicopter.

The tow truck driver secured the van on his truck bed and made ready to go. Sherry waved a tearful good-bye from the cab, and Kathryn sent her an encouraging wave and smile.

"You ready to leave?" Officer Shaver asked, startling Kathryn. She had not heard him approach.

"More than ready."

As Shaver walked Kathryn to Lexus, he asked, "What's the relationship of you and Ellie?"

"What do you mean?"

"You two are traveling together. You have different domiciles. What's the connection? Are you related?"

"Not by blood, no." Kathryn shifted the blanket she was carrying. Plastic ice packs rattled inside the folds.

"Then what?"

Kathryn turned to him. "We're lovers."

The officer went silent for a moment. "For real?"

"Yes."

"But you don't live together."

"No, we haven't been together long. Ellie lost her partner to cancer a few years ago and I've been divorced for a year." As if that would explain everything.

"From a man?"

"Yes."

When they reached the car, Kathryn hesitated at the trunk. She didn't want to open it with the trooper next to her. She was unsure of the location of the box with SRO capsules—Ellie must have taken it out of the cooler when she retrieved the ice packs. But did she put it back in or leave it out? But then what could Shaver tell by a shoe box? Luckily the cover inserted securely into the innards and didn't just rest atop where it could easily dislodge. Kathryn sensed him waiting, curious.

"Officer Shaver," Ellie said, coming up from behind, "do you think it's worth filing an insurance claim. The dent's not too bad, and my deductible's so high I don't think it'll cover it."

"You should check with your agent. You're lucky the air bags didn't go off. Those are pretty pricey to replace."

"We were lucky," Ellie said.

"It helped that you responded perfectly, going right through the tire, keeping the wheel straight and steady. Unlike the poor guy behind you who swerved. You don't do that at seventy miles an hour. That's a guaranteed accident."

"It was all instinct."

As the car trunk swung open, Kathryn was poised to toss the blanket in, damn the ice packs. She didn't want them—dirty and contaminated—back in the cooler anyway.

The *Star Trek* fanfare, Jenn's assigned ring, suddenly blared from Kathryn's back pocket. Kathryn flinched in surprise, and an ice pack popped to the ground.

"Here, let me help you," Shaver said. He scooped up the pack and made to open the cooler lid.

"Not in there," Kathryn said. But it was too late.

The cooler lid was off, the shoebox exposed.

"What's in here?" Shaver asked flatly as he wedged a thumb under the inserted flap and quickly pried off the top. "What's this?"

"It's . . . ah . . . " Kathryn started.

"Medicine," Ellie said, stepping up. "Medicine that needs to be kept cool."

"In a shoe box?" He fingered the baggies that held hundreds of capsules. "What kind of medicine?" His tone indicated he knew the answer.

Ellie and Kathryn exchanged a look.

"It's cannabis oil," Ellie said. "I'm taking it back to Minnesota for a friend with a chronic illness."

"Is there THC in this oil?"

"That bag has simple CBD—no THC. The capsules in the other bag have THC."

"These drugs are illegal in Nebraska . . . and where you're going."

"I know."

"Are you on any of this?"

"No."

"Do you have any bud? Any joints on you or in the car?"

"No, only the oil," Ellie said, her voice tightening.

"Just the oil?"

"Yes, sir. You can search the car if you'd like. You won't find anything else."

The women stood silently. Waiting. Waiting. Kathryn's gaze never left Shaver's face. Her expression, instead of showing anger or fear, seemed calm and open-hearted. Ellie wondered how she could be so composed.

"Well," Shaver said at last, working his jaw, "you stopped to help. You didn't have to. And that one gentleman . . . he would have bled out."

"There was no question of continuing down the road," Kathryn said evenly, "although we certainly could have. Not stopping would have been a moral failure that would have haunted me the rest of my days."

Shaver froze and seemed unable to speak. He set the box back in the cooler and closed the lid. An uneasy silence unrolled as the trooper removed his hat and ran a broad, powerful hand over his close-clipped hair as though touching the brain underneath, stimulating . . . or dousing . . . some awakening. He tapped the hat back into place. "Wait here," he said at last, locking eyes with Kathryn. "I need to check with my sergeant."

As Shaver receded, his boots smacking smartly on the asphalt, the women leaned against the rear of the car, close but not touching.

"Fuck! Fuck! Fuck!" Ellie said under her breath.

Eyes shut, face a shade paler, Kathryn said quietly, "Give me a moment."

Ellie stiffened with the perceived reprimand and suddenly became conscious of standing in the middle of the continent. The vastness, the unremitting flatness, the badged men milling about—the scene had morphed into hostile territory when mere minutes before it had seemed like a land where people comforted and cared for one another.

Kathryn sought her own distance, an internal, higher view. Closing her eyes, she could hear the familiar, calming voice of Anna: *This is a gift, my dear. The path is unfolding. Trust it.* And she could. She knew, somehow, that their being here had purpose. She opened her eyes and took in the fields stretching before her, holding her as part of the great, mysterious web of being. She closed her eyes again, praying for acceptance of what was to come.

"What do you want to do?" Ellie broke in, unable to bear the silence. A frightening answer had winged into her mind. *Leave me?*

Kathryn took a few deep breaths. Her face softened and when her eyes opened, they held their usual kindness. "Let's be centered and keep our hearts open, Ellie."

"How can you be so spiritual at a time like this?"

"This is precisely the time to be so."

Ellie shook her head.

"We knew this was a possibility. We'll just have to deal with what comes. Trust the process."

"Let me take all the blame," Ellie said. "I'll say I coerced you . . . or didn't tell you about the capsules until just . . . say . . . last night."

"No, I don't want to get caught up in lies. Neither do you."

Ellie acknowledged the firmness—and the truth—in Kathryn's eyes. "You're right," she conceded. "You're right."

"Well," Kathryn said with a note of resignation, "I suppose I should get my lawyer on the phone . . . but I think I'll wait to see what happens with Officer Shaver. Meanwhile, inhale deeply a few times through your nose and out your mouth. It'll calm you."

The hot breath of the afternoon flowed across the prairie, perpetual miles of fields where newly sown seeds were awakening to become the bounty meant to feed a nation. Ellie regarded this land that stoically accepted what beat on its surface—the mammoths and the bison and the steel of plows—as well as the planetary forces that stirred and heaved beneath. Her life seemed very small now, but as she breathed in the rich country air and eyed the fringe of white clouds on the horizon, she thought of freedom. How precious it was and how foolish she had been to risk it. The wind sharpened as the sun lowered. Somehow, she and Kathryn had landed here, and they had to face its reality.

That reality was coming toward them, lumbering with alpha authority in the form of Officer Shaver.

"Okay, ladies," he said when he reached them. His words were clipped, his voice impassive. "Here's the deal. Ellie, I want you to drive ahead of me. Start off slow in case there's damage to your car we're not seeing. I wouldn't recommend going over sixty miles an hour. If you feel unsafe, pull over and I'll call a tow truck."

"Okay."

"You said you're staying at the Best Western off I-80?"

The women nodded.

"I'll follow you there. There's a Lexus dealership a couple of blocks away. You should take the car in tomorrow to have it checked."

"I will," Ellie said. *Tomorrow!* Did that mean they weren't going to be arrested?

"And you," the officer said, turning to Kathryn. "You ride with me."

CHAPTER 44

"*D*o you want me in back or up front, Officer Shaver?" Kathryn asked as she approached the State Patrol vehicle. She was wary of the man, but an inner calm strengthened her, a confidence that came from years of dealing with people in turmoil.

"The front."

Kathryn waved an assurance to Ellie and slid onto the black leather seat. A computer wedged slightly into her space gave her a moment of claustrophobia. She distracted herself by examining the busy dashboard and the camera clipped to the rearview mirror. A musky scent underlay the smell of fried food.

"Want some water?" Shaver pointed to a bottle on the floor.

"Thank you." Kathryn reached for it, noticing the wadded MacDonald's bag stuffed partway under the seat. She took a long drink and screwed the cap back on.

"Thanks for all you did back there. You made a difference."

"You're welcome." Kathryn did not add that any nurse would have done the same. She adjusted her top, stiffened with dried blood and sticking uncomfortably to her skin. "Are Ellie and I under arrest?"

"No."

"Are you going to charge us with anything?"

"No."

"Is your sergeant on board with that?"

"Didn't tell him. I just passed command of the accident scene to him."

Kathryn took another drink of water, relief washing over her. She thought of Ellie and the fear in her eyes as they parted. Kathryn wanted to text her that things were okay, but she didn't dare. "Officer Shaver, can you tell me what we're doing?"

Ellie didn't like it one bit. But what could she do except stew?

She berated herself again for getting them into this fix. A spark of anger flashed toward Kris whose needs she had put before her own security. But mostly a hollow horror gripped her innards: Was this the end? Would she—they—wind up in prison?

The Lexus had a different feel, like a dance step no longer on the beat. Maybe the wheels were, like her stars, out of alignment. The car wasn't shuddering, so she assumed it was safe enough to stay with the plan.

She kept checking the rearview mirror and the black cruiser looming in it, the nudge bars encasing the front end like a prison door. But to see Kathryn in the passenger seat, talking with the officer who had discovered their cache . . . it was unnerving as hell. Was he asking her every detail of their cannabis run . . . and then would he grill her, Ellie, and pounce on any inconsistencies? But they would tell the truth . . . and thank god Kathryn had short-circuited her insane impulse to make up a story. Where did that come from? Fear, of course.

Ellie glanced back again. Kathryn and the cop were in deep conversation.

Maybe he was harassing her, bargaining to drop any charges for money. What if he pulled off some side road and disappeared with Kathryn? What if that was what she wanted!

Bile rose up Ellie's throat, a toxic cocktail of jealousy and catastrophizing. She thought for a moment she'd have to stop the car and retch out her pathetic panic. Instead she cranked the air conditioning up to full power. She had to cool down. She had to trust the process.

Trust the process. Trust the process. Trust the process.

She spoke it aloud now, a mantra to connect her to some higher knowing.

She envisioned what Kathryn would say to her. "Everything is good right now," Ellie said aloud. "I'm safe. I'm not hurt. The car is okay. We survived. I'll get through this."

I'll get through this. But will we *get through this?*

Ellie passed a field blanketed in the green of fresh alfalfa. In the distance, irrigation rigs hovered like plesiosaur skeletons. The reflection of the lowering sun on the back windows of a passing car struck Ellie, and she had to hold her hand up against the fireball to protect her eyes. Was she driving in a dream with no way to wake?

She had an urge to call Kris, but as her fingers started to work the on-board phone interface, she realized it wasn't Kris she wanted to talk with. It was Kathryn. Only Kathryn.

Get a hold of yourself, she thought. She had to stop the disaster scenarios spooling from her fear. None of them were real. She—they—would deal with what came up. And now, be calm. Be at peace. Don't stomp on the gas and try to outrun Officer Shaver. With Kathryn in his car, there was no way she would do that. Clever cop.

Kathryn stared at Shaver across the patrol car. She considered herself a good reader of people, but Shaver's blank face and tight demeanor was as inscrutable as granite. "So, you two are lovers." Shaver stared straight ahead. "Give me a two-minute version of how that happened."

Kathryn gave him a curt sixty seconds.

He thought for several moments. "If it's serious, you should get married. You wouldn't be compelled to testify against each other in court, if that situation ever arose."

Kathryn laughed. "Now, there are a lot of reasons to get married, Officer Shaver, but that's not one that springs to mind . . . even in the circumstances Ellie and I are in."

Shaver stayed silent, eyes on the road.

"I believe marriage is the most important decision a person makes," Kathryn continued. "It impacts everything. A good choice enriches life and eases its loads. A poor choice can mean a living hell."

"You're telling me," the officer said bitterly.

Kathryn said nothing as she settled deeper into the seat.

"So, with this cannabis. You're on the level?"

"Yes. It's for a friend with a chronic health condition."

"Is this the first time you've done this?"

"Yes."

"And Ellie."

"Her third. And last, I assure you."

They rode in silence for a couple more minutes. Kathryn waited.

"You ever hear of Blue Earth?" Shaver asked.

"Blue Earth, Minnesota? Sure. Where the soil is so black it's blue."

"Yeah." A tiny hint of a smile. "At least according to the native Winnebago. That's where I grew up."

"A farm boy?"

"Yeah. My wife—my ex—is from Omaha. That's how I wound up here."

Kathryn waited.

"You're a psychotherapist?"

"I retired in December."

More silence. And then, "Did you ever work with people with PTSD?"

"Yes. Quite a few, actually."

"What's your general advice?"

"For someone with PTSD? It would depend on the situation."

Officer Shaver readjusted himself in the seat. "You know, it's tough to be in law enforcement and have a . . . problem. If you see someone . . . a shrink . . . it goes on your record."

"I can see where that would be a tough situation. Someone wants help, but to get it means exposing yourself."

"Yeah, something like that."

They rode for another minute in silence, the flat Nebraska landscape spreading before them, a patchwork of brown and green.

"You can call me Ronald. Or Ron."

Kathryn smiled. "Okay, Ron."

"Before I got this job, I was in Iraq and Afghanistan. First as a Ranger—101st Airborne Division, then as a contractor. Blackwater outfit. The pay was terrific. But what we did . . ." His jaw jutted out as he shook his head. "You heard of them?"

"Yes, I have." Kathryn vaguely recalled news stories from a decade earlier about the private military contractor involved in war crimes.

"This cannabis stuff, it's nothing compared to what goes on over there. You wouldn't believe the drug dealing, the arms dealing. The corruption. It's all . . . effed up."

Kathryn said nothing.

"Blackwater changed me. It busted up my marriage . . . which actually wasn't great to begin with."

"I'm sorry to hear that."

"I saw the really dark side of people, I mean *really* dark . . . and the dark side of myself. Things I can't make right." He paused. "I like this job. Being a trooper suits me. I can be alone all day. All night. Driving down the road wearing a gun. I have authority. But most of the time I'm just going through the motions. The truth is, I don't like people very much anymore." He glanced at her. "But you I like. There's something about you."

Empathy, Kathryn thought.

Shaver bit his lower lip. "I just got a puppy. A black lab. She stays with a neighbor during my shift. I hope she can ride with me once I get her trained. She brings me . . . I don't know . . . I just love her to bits." He shifted in his seat again causing the leather to squeak. "It tells me there's something still inside. I'm not hopeless."

"No, Ron, you're not hopeless."

"We did things . . . I did things . . ." He paused, on the verge of losing his composure.

"It sounds like you're experiencing remorse," Kathryn said, supplying the feeling word he did not have the vocabulary to express.

"I guess that's what it is."

"Ron," Kathryn said, "do you want to tell me what happened?"

CHAPTER 45

The parking lot of the Best Western on the outskirts of Lincoln hadn't changed since the last time Ellie had pulled into it. Everything else had. Then Kathryn had been beside her, both of them hot for each other, over-ripe for consummation, to be in each other's arms, on each other's skin. What a difference a horrible accident makes. And death. And the Nebraska State Patrol.

Officer Shaver's Dodge Charger, the words *STATE TROOPER*, white on black, blazoned along the side eased in next to Ellie's car. Ellie turned to Shaver, but nothing was forthcoming. Was she supposed to get out of the car? Hands up? Was she to join them? Slide into the backseat like the lawbreaker she was? Was she to sit there as the sun melted into the far reaches of the west?

Ellie's phone pinged a text.

Go ahead & register. I'll join you ASAP.

OK. How are you?

Fine.

Ellie closed her eyes, relief washing over her.

She obeyed. She checked in at the front desk, apologizing for her appearance, and asked the clerk to give Kathryn a key card when she came in. As she loaded their gear onto the luggage cart, Shaver and Kathryn, intense with conversation, ignored her. She fought down a scream that formed in her throat.

Patience. Trust the process.

The room echoed with Kathryn's absence. Ellie set to work doing her usual routine of setting up a charging station for their devices, stowing the cold items in the fridge—including the RSO capsules, and folding down the bedspread and top sheet of the king-size bed.

She undressed and stepped into the white-tiled shower. The hot water beat on her body. It would take Noah's deluge to wash away the day. The unraveling tire hurtling toward her, the tangle of cars, the motorcyclist lying sprawled like a murder victim, the blood, the crying, the cop interrogating them. The images bombarded her, but the one that overwrote them all was the one of Kathryn sitting next to Officer Shaver following in the cruiser.

And then the most wonderful and terrifying sound in the world: Kathryn's voice saying, "How long will you be?"

She was here, at last, free from the grasp of the law. But anxiety quickly overshadowed her relief. "You can join me, if you'd like."

On the other side of the curtain, silence. *Not good.* Steam rose from the shower in a steady cloud as Ellie waited for a response.

"Okay," came the reply. Kathryn's head appeared at the far end of the shower, her face a mixture of exhaustion and reserve.

Ellie could have wept.

Kathryn, stripped of her dirty and bloody clothes, climbed in. Ellie moved to let her under the stream of hot water. She reached for a washcloth, soaped it up, and gently rubbed it over Kathryn's face, then around her neck, then to her torso sticky with blood.

"How are you, Kathryn?" Ellie asked. She had wanted to say *my love*, but she was unsure of the territory.

"Beat. Let's talk later. I want to concentrate on getting clean. But first, we're not being charged."

"Really!" Ellie broke into sobbing laughter.

"Yes, I'll explain later. But how are you?"

"Okay." Ellie fought to regain her composure. "Kinda rattled."

Kathryn nodded wearily.

Ellie continued to run the washcloth over the body she had come to know so well. She washed Kathryn's hair silently and attentively. "All done. You can do a final rinse while I dry off."

When Kathryn emerged from the shower, she stepped gingerly into the towel Ellie held open for her. Ellie patted her, from head to toe, over and under and in-between. In the corner by the toilet, Kathryn's bloody jeans and top lay crumpled in the waste basket. "Ready?" Ellie asked.

"Ready."

Kathryn slipped into a thin silk robe while Ellie tossed on a clean T-shirt and shorts. They sat on the sofa, identical to the one that such a short time ago held them in their first kiss.

"How are you?" Ellie asked again. "What's going on with Officer Shaver?"

"I'm okay, Ellie. But I can't talk about Ron—Officer Shaver."

Ellie remained silent.

"I can say, he needs some . . . let's say psychological support . . . that he doesn't feel able to get without jeopardizing his career."

This piece brought the puzzle into focus for Ellie. "PTSD?"

Kathryn almost smiled. "Always the smart one."

"Not always. But I did have many students dealing with trauma—war, refugee camps, childhood abuse. Some of the essays I received from them were quite . . . harrowing, to say the least." Ellie wanted to pet Kathryn's wet hair, her face, and touch her lips, but refrained. "You heard awful things?"

"I did."

"So that's what the long conversation was about." Ellie chastised herself for the self-indulgent scenarios she had imagined. The exhaustion on Kathryn's face refocused her attention from herself. "How do you not let it affect you? How can you keep terrible images out of your head?"

"It's a professional hazard, Ellie. Therapists are exposed to a lot of toxicity."

"But how do you deal with it?"

"I could be facetious and say Lexapro is the anti-depressant of choice for my peers. But really, Ellie, part of our training is to remain emotionally stable. That's what a client needs. I can't take on their demons." Kathryn sighed with weariness, yet continued. "I have my moat of self-containment, and I have kind of a Third Eye that's always observing my sessions. If

I ever feel myself being sucked in—which is different from feeling empathy—then I check in with Anna, my old mentor. She gives me a perspective outside of myself."

"Dear Anna."

"Yes. Therapists have several ways to detoxify. I have a few practices I find helpful, including meditation. In fact, Ellie, I could use a little alone time right now to cleanse . . . and to process this afternoon."

"You got it." Ellie lightly touched one of Kathryn's hands. "What would you think if I went out and did a little hunting and gathering for dinner while you take care of yourself?"

Kathryn's eyes, tired as they were, lit up. "I'd like it. Thanks."

⸺ ∞ ⸺

When the door clicked behind Ellie, Kathryn put a hand to her chest and exhaled deeply, huffing to expel the first vestiges of the day caught in her body. As she inhaled, scenes of her life's adventures flashed through her mind—hiking the Samara Gorge on Crete, skiing the black diamonds at Aspen, exploring the spirit world with a Peruvian shaman. Never, though, had she tangled with the law. She was amazed at the chance she had taken, embarrassed she had been caught, and grateful Ron Shaver had chosen to overlook the infraction.

Leaning back into the cushion, Kathryn took another giant breath and let it out slowly. By the time the last of the air had seeped out, her mouth was curving into a smile. They had gotten away with it! The blush of triumph gathered, a thin cloud of ego she quickly swept away. She could not gloat, not after the deadly accident. Not after hearing Ron Shaver's gruesome, cruel history.

And certainly not after acknowledging that her own choices had put her at risk. Why had she given in . . . no, eagerly, blindly accepted Ellie's cannabis run? A pelvic clench told her why.

I have only myself to blame.

I let my desires override my common sense.

How could I be so stupid!

And . . . .

How could I be so brave? So wise? So amazing? Look at all the wonderful things this trip has brought into my life! Love! Passion! Connection! They were gifts, all of them.

Including the revelation that Ellie could struggle with honesty. She had been tempted for one tiny moment to keep driving, and later to lie, to claim that she, Kathryn had been a dupe in all of this. The inclination to deceit surprised Kathryn. It showed Ellie unwilling in that moment to accept the twist in their path. But she had relented quickly, somewhat abashed, knowing she was wrong. It was the first course correction they had had to make together in the territory of integrity.

Kathryn wiggled her toes and soles into the soft carpet and began to breathe deeply and slowly, eyes closed. As she sank into a calmer state, she found herself softly singing the Sa Ta Na Ma meditation. Birth-Life-Death-Rebirth. Her thumbs cycled through her fingertips with each syllable.

Anna had taught Kathryn this meditation. They had practiced it together many times over the years of their friendship. This twelve-minute chant centered her deeper than any other ritual, and after Anna's death, it held a special comfort.

Now, as her voice rang with the vibration of the last note, a serenity settled on Kathryn. She could examine her feelings, a dark, tangled woods.

Really, instead of focusing on Ellie's lapse, she should be angry at the insane drug laws, which criminalized a natural medicine. She should be angry with law enforcement officials who wasted their time making life miserable for harmless cannabis users. She should be angry at politicians and greedy pharmaceuticals and at her very own medical establishment that refused to embrace beneficial alternative therapies.

She could be angry at them all. Or she could not. It was her choice.

Kathryn knew anger was an emotion best felt and let go. Although she could work for change, she had to accept the world as it was. And she had to accept Ellie as she was, flaws and all. Relationships demanded understanding, compromise, and kindness. And forgiveness.

Kathryn rose from the couch and stretched out on the carpet. She engaged in various yoga poses, breathing, urging her mind to stillness, her soul to acceptance. She even tapped a series of acupuncture points. At last she lay quietly, her limbs extended fully, a Vitruvian woman within a circle of peace, aware of her connection with the floor, with the earth.

One could say that afternoon had been a disaster. But it had been a blessing for Ron, who had ventured into her life in search of solace. Some good, then, had come from the crash. What was the good for her and Ellie?

She loved Ellie, truly. Every relationship has its crises, usually not so enormous early on. But maybe it was better to sharpen the focus on their bond now, to test its resiliency.

With a final sun salutation, Kathryn rose from the floor. By following her heart, her path would unfold.

CHAPTER 46

*A*n hour later, Ellie spread the efforts of her foraging—take-out cartons of Hunan chicken, mixed vegetables, won-tons, and fried rice—on the coffee table. She and Kathryn sat on the couch, heaped the food into plastic bowls and dove in. The adrenaline charge of the afternoon had left them famished.

"Not exactly the meal I had envisioned for our last night on the road," Ellie said, lifting a glass bubbling with mineral water. She had been tempted to purchase a Riesling strong enough to stand up to Asian spices but had decided she needed her full wits this evening.

"No, I imagine not, although I think we'll have at least one more night here, depending on what happens with the car."

"Well, maybe tomorrow night we can pull out all the stops and go back to Ruby Tuesday's." Ellie leaned back on the couch, rubbing her belly. "Oh, I ate too fast. And too much."

Kathryn, always the slower eater, made a face that communicated *it serves you right.*

Ellie cleared a spot on the table for her empty dish. She took a big breath and let it out in a whoosh. It was time. "Can we talk about the day?" She realized she hadn't overeaten—anxiety was curdling the contents in her stomach and nausea was creeping up her esophagus.

"Yes, we should."

"How mad are you with me?"

"I'm not angry with you, Ellie." Kathryn's voice was firm and calm. "I'm an adult, and I made a decision to go on this trip. And you know what? I'm glad I did, otherwise you might be in this fix by yourself."

Ellie teared. "I feel so guilty."

"Let that go, sweetheart. It was a blessing we were at the accident site. And yes, we got caught with the cannabis, but that has led to good, too. I'm able to help Ron deal with some of his demons."

Ellie splashed a little more water into her glass and watched the exuberant bubbles roil the surface.

Kathryn snagged the last piece of chicken. She chewed slowly and swallowed. "I think it's safe to say we're not in legal trouble. Ron is letting it slide . . . not even a citation."

"He told you this?"

"Yes. Ellie, all of this should be confidential—I'm treating Ron as a patient in all reality, so he deserves discretion. His finding the drugs is part of the equation. He could lose his job if anyone found out he didn't charge us."

"I understand. The cannabis issue seems rather trivial now."

"The crash put things in perspective, didn't it?"

"All of us traveling down the Road of Mortality . . . ."

Kathryn smiled sadly. "Yes. And there's always loss on the way. As you know so well." She slipped her bowl into Ellie's empty one and pushed them aside.

"What did we lose, Kathryn?" Ellie said, fearing the answer. *Us.*

"I'm not sure. I'd rather focus on what we've gained."

They held each other's gaze. It contained a new slant, a sadness at the passing of innocence.

"As awful as things were, I have—we have—a lot to be grateful for," Ellie said.

Kathryn nodded.

"I'm so impressed with you. I saw your nursing side in action. How you took charge. Your medical skills. You were extraordinary."

"Well, thanks, but any nurse would have done the same. I felt a bit rusty for the first few minutes, but my experience eventually kicked in and I was able to go on automatic. It did remind me, though, that I'm glad I'm on the mind side of nursing, not the body side."

Their faces softened with a brush of amusement, and their eyes held in the pause.

Ellie turned fully to her. "I know I fell short today on two accounts. I'm embarrassed and ashamed. I'd like to talk about it."

"Okay."

"First, part of me didn't want to stop at the accident. The cannabis flashed in my mind, and I didn't want to risk discovery. I know you had to help, but I was tempted to get the hell out of there. You saw it in my eyes, didn't you?"

"Yes, but we stopped. Your actions speak louder than your temptations."

"Maybe, but I feel like a coward."

"You're not." Kathryn stroked Ellie's hair. "Now, what's the second issue."

"My impulse to lie to the police."

"That surprised me."

"I know. I was panicking and it popped into my head. That was cowardly, too." A chill crept through Ellie's veins. "Were these temptations 'moral failings' as you put it to Officer Shaver?"

"That's for philosophers to decide, and who wants them judging us? The thing is, I called you on your temptation and you immediately corrected your course."

"That sounds a bit condescending," Ellie said. "As though I'm a spiritual lightweight compared to you . . . um . . . which actually is quite accurate." She leveled a crooked smile at her lover.

Kathryn remained serious. "You're right. That was condescending. I apologize. And you're not a spiritual lightweight. Really, all that happened was we reacted differently to a crisis because we came to the moment with unique life experiences. For instance, I've never had to hide who I am, as you had to for decades."

"You get it, don't you?" Ellie felt her eyes moisten.

Kathryn stroked Ellie's hair again. "Remember when I told you about Anna's goal to slip up or be a little outrageous each day?"

"Yes."

"Perhaps you could say your moments of wavering over stopping and telling the truth were your errors for the day. And mine was stupidly exposing our cache of cannabis to the NSP. Can you forgive me for that?"

Ellie nodded. "So, we're okay?"

The blue of Kathryn's eyes seemed as deep as the heavens. "Ellie, did you think I would stop loving you because you're human? It's wonderful we can call each other on our foibles. It's how we grow."

"I guess so."

"Sweetheart, we did the right thing. Our 'mistakes' just put us on the path we're supposed to be on." With the back of a finger, Kathryn plucked a tear from Ellie's cheek. "I love you. You know that."

More tears flowed, and Ellie wiped them with her shirt sleeve. "Is this what it means to be involved with a therapist? I feel as though I've been analyzed . . . in a good way." Ellie smiled weakly.

"How awful! Forgive me!" Kathryn joked and then turned serious. "It's a challenge I have, Ellie. I've been known to slip into therapy mode with friends and family. Ask Jenn. But I want to understand people—you—and sometimes going deep can sound like therapy. I prefer to call it intimacy."

That night in bed, they kissed, they clung. *We could be in jail. We could be lying in the hospital . . . or a morgue. I could have lost you.*

"It's hard to stay in the present, isn't it?" Kathryn whispered into Ellie's hair. "But we're safe. We're here together." She caressed Ellie's long back, the skin soft and pliant. "Thank you for saving my life. Most drivers would have lost control."

"It was all instinct." Ellie kissed Kathryn gratefully.

"I know we'll be all right," Kathryn said with her unshakable trust in the unfolding of life. She tightened her embrace until Ellie fell asleep. One man's time had come today. Their time had not.

CHAPTER 47

$\mathcal{E}$llie started from an uneasy sleep, her heart jackhammering. Rising out of a nightmare, her mind sought to place her body, to claw her back into physical reality. She was in a hotel. Safe. With Kathryn breathing softly beside her. The details of the dream were already slipping from her consciousness, but the panic remained.

The bright red numbers on the clock read 11:11. Ellie lay in the dark. Images of the day raced through her mind, a manic montage in an unstoppable loop. The black ribbon of tire flying at the car. The thump as it hit. The accident unfolding behind them. The dead motorcyclist, his head at a sickening angle. The blood pulsing out of a man's leg, the tourniquet squeezing his thigh like a medieval contraption of torture. Officer Shaver staring from behind dark glasses, their stash discovered. Kathryn seated beside him in his cruiser. Even olfactory wraiths—hot engines and their spilled liquids, acrid sweat, metallic blood, piercing disinfectant—seeped into the room.

Would their relationship survive this trauma? Ellie eyes swelled with warm tears. Kathryn had said it was all right, but was it? In the days ahead, would her temptation to cowardice be the drop of toxic chemical triggering a lethal cancer?

Her heart thudded chaotically. Her lungs seized. Was she having a heart attack? She bolted upright.

"What's happening?" Kathryn's arm was around her. "Ellie?"

"I can't . . . I can't . . . ."

In a moment, Kathryn had the light on and was retrieving the white paper bag from the carry out Chinese food. She placed the opening over Ellie's mouth. "Breathe," she said. "Breathe."

Ellie obeyed.

"You're having a panic attack," Kathryn said. She swiped the hair back from Ellie's damp forehead. "You're okay, sweetheart. Keep breathing."

Ellie's dark eyes, large and confused, peeked over the top of the white bag, seeking Kathryn's.

"You'll be all right." Kathryn smiled reassuringly and placed a hand on Ellie's back. "I'm here. You're safe."

After several inhalations, Ellie, pale and sweaty, put down the bag. "I'm okay."

"Good. Would you like me to run a warm bath for you?"

Ellie shook her head. "No. Just hold me awhile."

Kathryn turned off the light and slipped back into bed. She took Ellie in her arms and softly kissed her temple. "Comfortable?"

"Yes." Ellie squeezed her eyes tightly against her tears. She absorbed Kathryn's soft, nurturing strokes. "I don't want to lose you," she said.

"I'm right here, my love."

Another wave of tears flowed.

"Sweetheart, you've been traumatized by this whole event." Kathryn paused for a long moment, her hand resting on Ellie's pounding heart. "There's a healing technique I use for post-traumatic stress. Would you like to try it?"

"What is it?"

"It's called EFT—Emotional Freedom Technique. It involves tapping acupuncture points while describing the trauma and the emotions it evokes."

"Never heard of it. Does it work?"

"It's often miraculous."

"You think it'd help me?"

"We won't know until we try. We can stop at any point."

"Well . . ." Ellie's need for relief overrode her reservations. "Okay."

"Let's get in a better position. You sit on the sofa." Kathryn turned the light back on as she rose off the bed. "I'll sit in the desk chair facing you."

Ellie positioned herself on the cushions, her spine straight, her hands resting on her lap. "Ready. Now what?"

"Tell your story about the accident as you tap seven or eight times on specific spots. Let's do the set up by tapping on the karate chop part of your hand while saying something like, 'Even though I feel panicky and ashamed of myself about the accident, I love and accept myself deeply and completely.'" Kathryn demonstrated on herself and asked Ellie to follow her lead. "Next, comes the actual sequence starting with the top of your head."

Ellie mimicked Kathryn as she tapped on various points on her face and chest.

"Okay, good," Kathryn said. "I'll tap on myself along with you to keep you on track. Now, tell me what's upsetting you."

"You mean just talk?"

"And tap. Everything you can remember. All the details, every negative emotion. Tell your story all the way through. You'll repeat your story until you can tell it matter-of-factly and without emotion."

"That's it?"

"It is. It's simple, yet, as you'll see, it's very intense. I'll be helping you along, clarifying your emotions. If any of your feelings involve me, say them. I'm not judging."

And so, Ellie told her story of the accident. Again and again and again. Twelve times in all.

An hour later, Kathryn cuddled Ellie in bed, the nightstand light still on. "Some trauma may still be hiding out, sweetheart. If you feel panic or distress over the accident, go ahead and tap on your own. You know the sequence."

"Good thing because something has cracked inside me. Suddenly all sorts of fears are leaking out." Ellie burrowed in closer, her head on Kathryn's shoulder.

"Like what?"

"You've seen such an unflattering side of me, I'm afraid you won't love me. Oh, god, I suppose I should tap on it."

"Don't worry. I love you. More than ever."

"How can you?"

"Because you make it so easy." Here was a side of Ellie Kathryn had not seen, this insecurity and fear of abandonment. "We don't have to be clones of each other for me to love you. We can treasure our differences, our vulnerabilities." She pressed her fingers into Ellie's hair, massaging her scalp. "Remember when we first met?"

"Vividly."

"You were reading the paper and you said you didn't have the spiritual capacity to deal with the dreadful details of the news."

"Uh-huh."

"Well, as a biased observer, I'd say that in the past day, you've shown plenty of capacity to handle 'dreadful details.' And unexpected miracles."

"Hmmm."

"You know one of the things I love most about you? You can share your feelings. Do you know how wonderful it is to have a partner who can give voice to her inner life? To be brave enough to be vulnerable?"

"Pretty wonderful, I suppose."

Kathryn shifted and gazed at Ellie. "You know what I see when I look in your eyes?"

"No."

"Ellie, my love, I see home."

"I'm going to cry again."

"No, you're going to fall into a deep, deep sleep." Kathryn switched off the light.

As Ellie settled into slumber, Kathryn remained awake, scenes of the day flashing in her mind. She reflected on the Nebraskan prairie, the flat heart of America, and remembered the day so long ago it now seemed, of standing beside the globe in her study, tracing the route they would take. Ellie appearing on the other side, their four hands holding the world and all its hope.

Perhaps, Kathryn thought, she had been migrating for all her years, flying toward a new continent, alighting on its shores, relieved, into Ellie's embrace. Ellie who had been so brave all her life. Kathryn sensed the fissures in the land, the shifting plates at the edge, but Ellie was home ground, as rich and alive as Minnesota farmland. And today, her flood of tears had carved fertile new contours into the greening fields.

CHAPTER 48

*T*he technical support rep at the glass-fronted Lexus dealership offered Ellie a snazzy red coupe as a loaner car. Ellie zoomed west onto I-80. She was alive and free. Kathryn was at the hotel for another consultation with Ron Shaver.

Following her phone's GPS, Ellie drove directly to Pioneers Park Nature Center southwest of Lincoln at the edge of the tall grass prairie. She hoped the miles of trails there would be an antidote to the intensity of the previous day and the panic of the night. The air was fragrant with a host of blooming trees and flowers. Breathing seemed like a miracle.

Ellie stepped across a low bridge, her hiking boots clunking on the weathered wood, and gained the grass path through the trees. The magenta blossoms of redbuds and the white blooms of wild plums provided a vivid contrast to the maples and ash just leafing out. Gooseberries and wild geraniums edged the trail, and the morning dew, not fully evaporated in shady spots, darkened Ellie's boots. While her footfalls were quiet, her mind was not.

She remembered that Sunday afternoon, long ago it now seemed, when she revealed to Kathryn the reason for the trip. She had said that if she were caught and convicted, she'd teach English to her fellow prisoners. How naïve! How callow! When that very fate loomed, she had wanted to lie.

It was wrong. But she couldn't stop. How had she leapt so quickly to dishonesty?

Even Kathryn had understood her quick reversion to old behaviors. Living in a closet made lying an everyday necessity. Those were painful, lonely days when she couldn't share her life with her parents or her friends. Her dishonesty came from fear, a vestige of those early days.

Kathryn would say the fear come from a lack of trust. But Ellie did not always believe that things would work out.

And what of it? Did her fear—her momentary lapse in bravery and honesty—make any difference to the oaks and cottonwood trees? To the blue jay slicing its notes through the unfolding leaves? To the field of prairie grass rippling in the breeze? To Kathryn? It didn't seem to last night as she sobbed in Kathryn's arms.

The cry of a railroad whistle split the air, and behind it, the laughter of schoolchildren across the stream burbling its way to Salt Creek.

Could she embrace this shadow in herself? Well, wasn't that part of enlightenment? To be who you are, to trust who you are at your very core? All of it—the light and the dark?

And trust the same in others?

What Ellie could not accept in herself—the shadow, the imperfection— she could not accept in others. She was seeing now, with a heady clarity, that everyone was evolving and some—bigots and haters—just had a longer path to trod. She didn't need to despise them or judge them. She could say simply, they were on their own journey and find compassion for them as their fears gnawed at their souls like a thousand aphids.

Them. The bigots and the haters.

And me?

She didn't hate, she knew, but could she admit to her own bagful of prejudices? Could she love right-wingers? Could she disagree with their politics yet embrace their pinched hearts so often closed to compassion? Could she love her old student Roberta who had so traumatized her? And the activists who had shut down MichFest? The butches who turned their backs on lesbianism to become the transmen they believed themselves to be? The transwomen who claimed the term *lesbian*?

These were traumas for her, political and psychological. They aroused anger and resentment. She pictured Roberta's face twisted in fury and realized how that rage contorted them both. She did not want that energy. Not for her remaining days on earth.

Ellie spotted a log close to the stream and settled on the weathered surface. Last autumn's leaves lay clumped at her feet, moist and fecund, poised to nurture new foliage. She found herself intoning Dylan Thomas, the famous stanzas about raging against the dying of the light.

Ellie had taught that poem a hundred times. Once she had cheered it, as did her students—the young seem to love the passionate fight for life. But now, with decades stretched behind her, she found herself championing the dying father. Let the elders have their peace. Why rage against the natural order? Against the inevitable? Against reality?

A line from Rilke about death surfaced:

It stands before eternity and says only: Yes YES.

Now that perspective resonated. Say yes to what is. Mary had come to a tranquil acceptance of her death, and Ellie had, too. If she could say yes to death, why not to everything? Every experience had its place; everything was meant to be. Even the traumas she had experienced—she had to come to peace with them.

She heard then a voice in her head: *Tap on this.*

No, Ellie moaned. I don't want to process anymore!

Now is the time to heal this wound. The voice was firm, but compassionate.

But, she protested, this is so fucking typical! It's women who do all the emotional work while the men—and *former* men—prance and pontificate.

Overhead a robin throbbed its hopeful notes.

But wasn't her own emotional health, her own soul, more important than winning? And what was winning anyway, in the scheme of the universe? Ellie caught her breath. Could she lay down the shield and spear . . . yet maintain her feminist integrity? Could she state her truth and let go?

And so, Ellie began tapping on the fleshy side of her hand, saying, "Even though I'm furious with Roberta for humiliating me, I love and accept myself deeply and completely." She repeated this phrase several times, and then switched to tapping her energy points: "When Roberta

berated me, I felt ashamed and helpless. I resent him . . . her . . . dammit!
. . . *whatever!* . . . for intimidating me . . . ."

The tears came quickly.

After lunch Ellie and Kathryn drove to Bryan Medical Center. Sherry, whose husband had almost bled to death on the highway, had texted Kathryn asking for a visit.

"Thanks for coming," Sherry said, her small eyes blinking rapidly. "I wanted to thank you in person." She had cleaned up since Kathryn and Ellie had last seen her, her pudgy hands and arms washed of blood, her blond hair pulled off her face into a ponytail. She wore a clean, but faded tee-shirt that read: *America First.* "He had surgery last night. The doctors stitched him up pretty good. They said he would've bled to death without that tourniquet."

"I'm glad I was there to help," Kathryn said. "Sherry, how are you feeling? You were knocked about a bit."

"Just bruises. They're nothing."

Kathryn placed a palm on a dark, angry spot on Sherry's forearm. "They'll heal," she said as though her warm touch would make it so.

Sherry held her gaze. "I will. And so will Andy."

They sat around the corner from the elevators of the ICU in a small room with windows to the hallway. It lacked privacy, but the blue cushioned chairs were comfortable. The ventilation system hummed in the background.

Sherry chatted amiably about her daughter who was at Andy's bedside now and about their trip west. Thank heaven the accident had happened at the end of it!

"Would you like to see Andy?" Sherry asked. "They're gonna move him to a regular room soon."

"No, we'll just let him rest." Kathryn smiled as she rose from her chair. "But it's good to see you again and know the outcome looks positive. You and Andy have been in my prayers."

"You, too, Kathryn. You and Ellie have been Good Samaritans. Thank you for everything." She reached into her canvas bag. "I have a little present for you. It's not much, but it's something I make for church sales."

Oven mitts. White and gold with a verse stitched in ornate lettering: *And the Greatest of These is Love.*

"How thoughtful. I'll think of you every time I use them." Kathryn gave Sherry a hug, then stepped back and took her hand. "Take care. I hope Andy has a speedy recovery."

As Ellie watched this exchange, tears threatened to seep out. A gift from across the divide.

"Oven mitts?" Ellie whispered as she and Kathryn waited at the elevator.

"Yes, and heartfelt, wasn't it? I hated taking anything from her—they seem poor—but gifts are expressions of gratitude, and I always accept them in that spirit."

Kathryn touched Ellie's arm as they entered the elevator.

As the doors closed, Ellie's phone pinged. A text from Lexus. Her car was ready.

——∞——

Ellie dropped off Kathryn at the hotel and drove to the dealership.

"All clear," the agent said. His name plate said Matt Hayden. He was in his mid-thirties, clean-shaven, with bushy brown hair. "You were lucky—there wasn't much damage. We re-aligned the wheels and took care of the little dent in the front."

"Oh," Ellie said. "I didn't want that done." *For eighty dollars I could live with the dent.*

"Yes, I know." He handed her the invoice. "We didn't charge you. The work is on us."

"What?" Ellie looked at the bill. There wasn't a charge. "Really?"

"A state trooper stopped in this morning and mentioned you had a high deductible. You and your . . . ah . . . friend did a good thing stopping to help at the accident. He said you saved at least one life."

Ellie sensed the silence in the expansive room, as other agents paused to listen in. Easy-listening music played in the background. The air smelled of money and leather upholstery.

"That was Kathryn. She's a nurse. We just did what we could."

"This is our way of thanking you for being a good citizen."

"Gee, that's nice of you." Ellie squeezed back tears.

"Let's go get your car," Matt said. He put an arm around her shoulders, a comforting touch, and steered her through the door to the bay holding her repaired and washed Lexus. He pointed to the front bumper. "Good as new!"

"Thanks, Matt. I really appreciate it."

"Our pleasure." He gave her a frank look. "It must have been horrible."

"It was." She fought the sob waiting to escape her throat.

"Well, have a safe journey home, Ellie . . . and if you pass through Lincoln again, stop by and say 'hi.' We'll be in our new building west of town this fall—complete with a coffee bar and barista."

"Coffee bar? For real?"

"For real. Now, good luck to you."

Ellie got into the driver's seat and drove off, tears streaming down her face. She sat for a while in the parking lot of the Best Western, her breath shallow, her mind grasping like fingers at the cliff's edge.

What was happening?

Here she was in Nebraska, on the edge of the Bible Belt. Everyone she had met in the last twenty-four hours—even a tough state trooper—had been kind to her, a stranger, a woman, a lesbian.

The world *was* changing. The asteroid had hit.

It melted something in her. She could not name what she had lost, but she cried for it. And for whatever new world she was gaining.

CHAPTER 49

The lock to the room whirred and Ellie opened the door. Kathryn was sitting on the sofa, phone in hand, listening, still as a yogi.

"Just a minute," she said, "Ellie just came in." She put the phone on mute and took in Ellie's red eyes and blotchy face. "What happened?"

"I'll tell you later," Ellie said. "Who's on the phone?"

"Ron."

"Do you want me to go?"

Kathryn nodded. "Or you could put on your headphones and listen to some music. We're doing a quick follow up."

Ellie nodded and picked up her tech bag. "I'll assemble everything in the bathroom," she said retreating there. She heard Kathryn say, "Okay, Ron. Sorry for the interruption. You were saying . . . ."

Ellie settled on the bed closest to the bathroom and listened to Cris Williamson's *The Changer and the Changed* while catching up on email. She wasn't aware Kathryn had finished the call until she felt her weight on the bed. The earbuds came out.

"Call done?"

"Uh-huh." Kathryn put a warm hand on Ellie's leg. "What happened? You were upset when you came in."

Ellie told her about the generosity of the Lexus agent, and the tears started anew.

"Why, that's wonderful, Ellie. Why the tears?"

"I don't know. I'm sentimental . . . ."

"You are."

". . . and touched when people do something nice for me. It feels good to be appreciated."

"And accepted."

Ellie nodded, unable to speak.

"You are sweet and good. You deserve of all the wonderful things this world has to offer."

"Including you?"

"Including me." Kathryn's eyes smiled.

"I did some more tapping. Out in the woods."

"Really?" Kathryn scooted next to her and reached for her hand. "Can you tell me about it?"

"Sure," Ellie said. And she did.

—⊶∞—

Kathryn spent the next morning with Ron Shaver, their final face-to-face meeting. Meanwhile, the University of Nebraska Museum drew Ellie once again. She had been so flushed with hormones during her last visit weeks ago with Kathryn that she knew she had not done the museum justice.

But something more was drawing her to the displays of worlds gone by.

She wandered through the mammoth exhibit again, this time reading the plaques. She whistled when she read that of the more than 200 known species of elephants, all were extinct but two: the African and the Indian.

Ellie explored other galleries, walking attentively, on the lookout for something. A touchstone, perhaps, to ground her to her own changing world. She drifted upstairs to the dinosaurs.

The primordial world with huge monsters tromping on a lush, steamy earth had always thrilled Ellie. But now, as she examined the dinosaur bones and reconstructed skeletons, what struck her was impermanence. Entire species thriving in North America for eons had disappeared, and the very continent on which they strode had shifted its shape like a lava lamp.

Ellie sat at the back of the exhibit, the wooden bench firm, but doomed to a landfill. From the hallway came laughter and sharp plinks as children played with balancing blocks at a learning station.

Her tribe was on the way to extinction. After its glorious burst in the Seventies and Eighties, the Lesbian Nation was fading into obscurity. Her generation had been pioneers, lesbian feminists owning their identity—in the streets, at work, in politics—when it was dangerous. They had started women's presses, bookstores, and farms. Opened rape crisis centers and put on music festivals that drew thousands of women to safe, creative spaces every summer. They had been outliers, fingers curled in upheld fists.

Now those fingers bore gold bands. Outlaws and radicals had morphed into butterflies chased by wedding planners, their nets held aloft.

Queer, non-binary, and *gender fluid* were settling atop the Lesbian Era, burying this precious stratum for historians of later centuries to unearth. The Disappearing Lesbian as one academic called it.

Ellie shifted on the bench. Was she a dinosaur? And not only as a lesbian? So much of what she had been was past. Her academic career, her decades with Mary, her athleticism now whittled down to pickleball. She was a retired teacher who spent her mornings in a coffee shop and made annual runs to California for high potency cannabis oil.

But she'd lived her life with courage, hadn't she? She'd been one of the pioneers building lesbian institutions to support her people. She and Mary had even registered for domestic partnership when some warned it would be a list used for discrimination . . . or extermination.

All that counted for something, didn't it?

A movement startled Ellie.

"Mind if I join you?" Kathryn settled next to her.

"Sure. How did you get here?"

"Uber."

"Smarty. I'm not in a very good mood."

"Tell me."

"Oh, I'm sitting here feeling sorry for myself."

Kathryn cupped Ellie's cheek in her hand and brushed away a tear.

"We struggled, we old lesbians, when things were hard. I don't begrudge the kids, though I wish they could recognize that we blazed the trail they trot down so easily."

"You'd like some appreciation for what you went through?"

"I don't know what I want. I feel so lost. So doomed. Like one of these dinosaurs. We had such lofty expectations. We thought we could bring down the patriarchy in our lifetime."

Kathryn smiled gently. "Now that's what I call optimism."

"Life seems too complex. All the apps. All the genders. I can't even keep track of the number of planets."

"We're all like these creatures," Kathryn said, waving a hand at the Stegosaurus skeleton. "Our time is fleeting. Even my grandchildren . . ." She paused, a sudden catch in her throat. ". . . even their time comes and passes. We'll all be extinct as individuals, and eventually, as a species."

"Even the Earth," Ellie said.

Kathryn nodded. "What's that saying? 'The sun also dies?'"

Ellie laughed softly. "I think you've conflated Ernest Hemingway with Eckhart Tolle. You mean 'Even the sun will die.'"

"Yes," Kathryn said, smiling. "And think how wonderful, how miraculous that this tiny rock spinning in space has been gifted with life for billions of years—from tiny amoebas to blue whales. Aren't we lucky to have experienced it?"

"Yes." Ellie sighed deeply. "Yes, we are."

"And aren't we privileged to have lived in the era we did? We're the Woodstock generation. The anti-war and Earth Day generation. We marched for civil rights and rode the Second Wave of feminism. And you, Ellie Belmont, you got to feel the heartbeat of an Amazon Nation—no other generation will have your experience."

Ellie nodded.

"And trust me, more waves of feminism are coming. Perhaps a new and different Amazon Nation will arise."

Ellie brightened. "Maybe the *gender fluid* . . . or the *post-gender fluid*— will be the doulas."

"Exactly. We don't know what today's victories and setbacks are seeding for tomorrow. We only know that everything changes, and every generation has to define its own culture. I'm thankful for what we've had . . . and what we—you and I—have now." Kathryn took a deep breath and sighed. "The earth will open under us sometimes, Ellie. When that happens, we can explore and find our way back to the surface together. Just as we did after the accident."

They kissed then, their lips warm and giving.

"You know, of course," Kathryn whispered, "the dinosaurs never really went extinct."

"You're right!" Ellie's eyes sparkled. "Birds!"

"Huge pelicans and tiny sparrows. They're not what they once were, but then neither are we. Who's to say that something even better might emerge as humans evolve."

They lingered then on the bench, alert as two owls perched in the Tree of Life, their talons entwined, contemplating matters of life and death as museum goers drifted past like ash on future winds.

CHAPTER 50

*T*he journey north on Interstate 35 was bittersweet. Ellie and Kathryn passed places they had seen on the way out, but now they were tired. Long, companionable silences filled the car. When the radio played love songs, they held hands or rested a palm on the other's thigh. In her contentment, Ellie didn't notice the exit to Waterloo, the very name that had once resonated so deeply.

"When am I going to meet some of your friends, Kathryn?"

"Soon. Judith is probably sitting in my driveway as we speak. She's anxious to meet you. As is my son—Sarah texted me this morning wondering about dinner this weekend."

"Oh, my. Our social life is ramping up. Kris and Sandy want us over for bridge on Friday night."

Just then the skyline of Minneapolis came into view. Kathryn squeezed the back of Ellie's neck. "My house is going to feel awfully lonely after being with you these past weeks."

"I know what you mean." She thought then of her and Mary's house and how they had worked to make it their nest. She was ready to let it go.

"Why don't you stay with me," Kathryn said.

"You mean, like, live together?"

"It could be a trial run."

"I love the idea," Ellie said, her innards suddenly aflutter. "I've been thinking about it myself."

"If it suits us, we could stay in my house for the near term while we decide what we want to do. Maybe buy a condo or rent an apartment. You can do what feels right with your place."

"How about a move into Highland Meadows?"

"Maybe down the road a bit, Ellie. I'm not ready just yet, especially now that I have you. But we'll have lots of options."

"We'll find a solution that works for both of us." Ellie took Kathryn's hand and kissed it. "It's sudden, but it makes sense, and I feel ready. How did you get to this point?"

"I don't know. Maybe it was sitting in that museum with all those bones around us. We'll be bones, too, before we know it. So, really, Ellie, what are we waiting for? We may have twenty years together. Or twenty months. Or twenty days. Our health and cognitive skills aren't going to be any better than they are at this minute."

"Why waste time when we know what we have is right?"

"Exactly. We've been given a beautiful gift, Ellie—each other."

Ellie gently squeezed the hand of her very own angel. Kathryn's patience and passion, her ineffable spirit-centered wisdom, filled Ellie with a sense of purpose she had laid aside with Mary's death. And that purpose, she realized, was to honor all the miracles that made up her life. And she would start by loving without reservation. A sense of well-being arched over her like the canopy of stars twinkling on the other side of the azure sky.

In the distance, Minneapolis skyscrapers shimmered in the sun like Oz City. Spring was in full bloom: yellow daffodils waltzed in the ditches to a warming breeze; corn and soybean fields, seeded with hope, stretched to the horizon.

Delicious summer awaited.

ACKNOWLEDGEMENTS

A gigantic thank you to my wife, Nancy Manahan (*Lesbian Nuns: Breaking Silence* and *On My Honor: Lesbians Reflect on Their Scouting Experience*), for her support and encouragement. Her laughter and tears in all the right places gave me confidence that the story was on the right track. Our joint line editing sessions on our lanai were creative highs.

Many thanks to the readers of the manuscript who provided feedback: Lois McGuinness, Tess Imholt, Carol Anne Douglas, Betty Jean Steinshouer, and Sandra Jo Palm. A special call out to Ruth Baetz, whose early readings, edits, and analysis were invaluable. And to Cheyenne Blue, brilliant editor and fact-checker, who lifted the novel to a higher level.

A bow of gratitude to Patricia Anderson, Susie Symons, and Kate Manahan for help with therapy content, Nancy Manahan for Non-Violent Communication practice, Cody Thomas of the Nebraska State Patrol for crash protocols, and Anonymous for RSO information.

Thank you to the Carefree Writer's Circle in North Fort Myers for their attentiveness and suggestions. I especially appreciate Sara Yager for her aid in self-publication, book formatting, and cover design.

Thank you to Alison Solomon and the Gulfport Library for inviting me to read at three annual Lesbian Read-Outs while the manuscript was in progress.

Finally, a salute to Patricia Highsmith and her priceless *Carol*, which inspired and informed this book.

AUTHOR'S NOTE

I started writing *A Light on Altered Land* after I was denied permission by the copyright holder to publish a sequel to Patricia Highsmith's *Carol*, published in 1952 as *The Price of Salt*. I put my manuscript of *Carol, Recovered* on the shelf (actually, my personal cloud), and I set out to write a book that pays homage to that seminal work of lesbian literature.

In writing this novel, I had four intentions.

First, I wanted to write a book about psychologically healthy characters with integrity. I was tired of reading about dysfunctional people and relationships, stories in which characters constantly lie and conceal, and stories peppered with violence. I wanted to spend time with characters whom I would be honored to have as friends.

Second, I wanted to deal with the great wound of the loss of the Michigan Womyn's Music Festival. The tens of thousands of women who experienced the joy and freedom of that Amazon week in the woods of The Great Lakes State have a collective grief that has not been addressed enough in lesbian fiction.

Third, I wanted to talk about cannabis and its potential for relieving pain and other symptoms of chronic illnesses. I especially wanted to get the word out about Rick Simpson Oil (RSO) and its benefits. RSO and other cannabis products may not be the answer for every malady, but they do work for many. Given that RSO is still illegal in many states, I have no further comment other than it is a shame our laws are so restrictive.

Fourth, I wanted to show aging in a culture that does not respect its elders. Ellie and Kathryn confront ageism when they encounter it as well as acknowledge their own internalized ageism. We're never too old for romance and passion!

DISCUSSION QUESTIONS

1. What is the significance of the title?

2. How do Ellie and Kathryn model Non-Violent Communication, or other positive ways of interacting?

3. What would you do in Ellie's place driving a car when an accident happens? What values would make you keep on driving? What values would prompt you to stay and help?

4. What is your reaction to Ellie's use of tapping (Emotional Freedom Technique) to relieve trauma? What other techniques could reduce/heal trauma?

5. What is the significance of birds and dinosaurs in the book?

6. How do you respond to the demise of the Michigan Womyn's Music Festival, the loss of women's bookstores and publications, and the erasure of other lesbian spaces?

7. Ellie views transgender activism through the lens of radical feminism. Do you agree with that perspective? Why or why not?

8. At the end, does Ellie compromise her feminist values for inner peace?

9. Ellie relates an experience with a Mexican shaman in which she felt a deep connection to preceding generations of grandmothers. Have you felt similar connections? In what context?

10. How plausible is it that a heterosexual woman like Kathryn would fall in love so quickly and easily with a lesbian like Ellie?

11. What are your experiences with ageism?

12. Ellie has a very close relationship with her ex, Kris. How does this compare with your own relationship with former partners?

13. What do you think of the way Kathryn deals with her daughter (Jenn) and granddaughters (Gena and Maddie/Magel)?

14. What is your view on medical marijuana and CBD?

15. What do you think are the long-term prospects for Ellie and Kathryn's relationship?

16. How does Patricia Highsmith's novel *Carol* (originally *The Price of Salt*) inform this work?